She Ain't the One

Also by Carl Weber

Up to No Good
Something on the Side
The First Lady
So You Call Yourself a Man
The Preacher's Son
Player Haters
Lookin' for Luv
Married Men
Baby Momma Drama

Also by Mary B. Morrison

Unconditionally Single
Maneater (with Noire)
Who's Loving You
Sweeter than Honey
When Somebody Loves You Back
Nothing Has Ever Felt Like This
Somebody's Gotta Be on Top
He's Just a Friend
Never Again Once More
Soul Mates Dissipate
Who's Making Love
Justice Just Us Just Me

Published by Kensington Publishing Corp.

CARL WEBER

She Ain't the One

MARY B. MORRISON

Kensington Publishing Corp.
http://www.kensingtonbooks.com

DAFINA BOOKS are published by

Kensington Publishing Corp.
119 West 40th Street
New York, NY 10018

All Kensington titles, Imprints, and Distributed Lines are available at special quantity discounts for bulk purchases for sales promotions, premiums, fund-raising, and educational or institutional use. Special book excerpts or customized printings can also be created to fit specific needs. For details, write or phone the office of the Kensington special sales manager: Kensington Publishing Corp., 119 West 40th Street, New York, NY 10018, attn: Special Sales Department, Phone: 1-800-221-2647.

Dafina and the Dafina logo Reg. U.S. Pat. & TM Off.

ISBN-13: 978-0-7582-0723-4
ISBN-10: 0-7582-0723-9

First hardcover printing: October 2006
First trade paperback printing: October 2007
First mass market printing: February 2009

10 9 8 7 6 5 4 3 2

Printed in the United States of America

CHAPTER 1

Jay

I stepped out of my new BMW 650i convertible and handed the keys to the valet at Zanzibar Nightclub. I could tell he was impressed by my new car. I was impressed too. You see, I wasn't a rich guy who could buy things like this all the time. In truth, I was just a civil servant, but the BMW was a present to myself, a present to celebrate my new life and my divorce from my wife—I mean ex-wife—Kenya.

It had taken me some time to get to this point in my life, but I finally felt free for the first time in years. Free to find the woman I would spend the rest of my life with, or die trying.

Kenya and I had been married for the past ten years, the last three of which we'd been separated. I know it's pretty pitiful, but I wasn't even in love with her when I married her. She was pregnant, and I thought I was doing the right thing. When in truth I was doing nothing more than killing myself slowly. It was something I swore I'd never do again. If I ever got married again, I was going to be in love.

To date there was only one woman that I'd ever been in love with, and her name was Tracy. We'd had an affair three years ago, and things were going great until she found out about my marriage. She was the reason I'd moved to D.C. in the first place. I was hoping to rekindle the flame of our past relationship and recapture the one thing I was missing in life—love. The only problem was, I'd been in D.C. almost three months and had no idea how or where to find her. I wasn't even sure she was still living in the D.C. area.

After getting my parking ticket from the valet, I glanced at the entrance of Zanzibar. There had to be at least a hundred people waiting in line to get in. And from what I heard from my new coworkers about the waterfront clubs in D.C., that meant at least an hour's wait. I wasn't worried about that, though, because not only was I on the guest list, I had a VIP pass waiting for me at the door, thanks to fine-ass Monica, the head bartender.

I'd met Monica about two months ago, after sharing a plane ride from New York to D.C. That wasn't the only ride we shared. We also shared a cab ride back to her place, and about a half hour later, I rode that ass to sleep. I know I sound full of myself and perhaps a little arrogant, but I put it on her so good, she'd been blowing my phone up ever since. I'd been trying my best to avoid seeing her again, giving her one lame-ass excuse after another, but for some reason she wasn't getting the hint. Funny thing is, I probably would have hooked up with her right away if it wasn't for the fact that she was one of the worst pieces of ass I'd ever had. Can you say, *stiff as a board?* I swear to God the girl did not move one muscle the entire time during sex. If she was any indication of what the sex was like in D.C., I was going to have to rethink my relocation to the nation's capital.

I know what you're thinking—If Monica was so bad in bed and I was trying so hard to avoid her, why the hell was I meeting her at the club? Well, the truth is, she called me from a blocked number and caught me off guard. She offered to put me on the guest list at the club and give me a pass to the VIP lounge. I figured, what the hell . . . why not give her another shot? It couldn't get any worse than the first time. Besides, my divorce had just become final, and I was in the mood to do some celebrating.

When I walked up to the front of the line, it had to be about a five-to-one ratio of women to men waiting to get in. I could feel the women staring at me, and I felt like a movie star. I even heard one woman whispering, "Who is he?" to her friend.

Her friend answered, "I don't remember his name, but I think he was the guy who played in that movie with Monique, what's his name, Jimmy Jean-Louis."

"Oh my God! That's him," the first woman replied. "Damn, I got to give him some of this pussy."

I glanced at the woman and gave her a wink. She was fine as hell and could get a lot more than a one-night stand if she played her cards right. *It looks like Monica'll be going home alone tonight.*

You see, I kinda fancied myself as a player. Not trying to brag or anything, but I was a good-looking guy, five feet eleven with baby-smooth chocolate skin and, for lack of a better phrase, "good hair." I guess I gotta thank my mama for that. She was from Trinidad, and everybody knows that Trinis got good hair. Well, to make a long story short, I'd never had a problem with women falling all over me; it was guys I had a problem with, and as usual, they were hating.

One brother who was standing in line by the door actually had the nerve to say, "Who the fuck is that?" to the bouncer right after I told him my name and he gave me an orange wristband to get into the VIP area and let me into the club.

Once I got into the club, I made my way over to the main bar to find Monica. It was crowded, but I spotted her pouring drinks on the other end of the bar as she danced awkwardly to the music. I immediately busted out laughing. Now I knew why she was so bad in bed—the girl had absolutely no rhythm whatsoever. Just watching her dance reminded me how bad the sex was; I was about to fade back into the crowd when she spotted me.

There was no question that she was on me hard because, the second she saw me, she stopped what she was doing and headed toward me, grinning from ear to ear. I had to give her some credit, though. She may have been terrible in bed, but she sure was a pleasure to the eyes. I could see the jealousy in half the guys sitting at the bar as she approached me. If they knew what I knew, they wouldn't have been jealous at all; they probably would have bought me a drink in sympathy—'cause every guy knows there's nothing worse than a bad piece of ass.

"What you drinking, handsome?" Monica leaned over the bar.

I couldn't tell if she wanted a kiss or just wanted me to see her cleavage. Whichever one it was, I wasn't interested. "Hennessey," I replied as I took a step back.

She poured me a double and pointed to the VIP area. "I get off around two, so have a good time till then. Just remember who you're going home with."

"How could I forget?" I gave her a weak smile and walked away from the bar. *By the time she gets off from work, I'll be long gone and hopefully with a new playmate.*

I walked around the club for a while and danced with a few women before heading to the VIP area. I even ran into the girl from the door, Nikki, and we made tentative plans to meet up at the door around quarter to two, to hit a diner after we left the club. That way, if I didn't meet anybody more promising by then, I could get the hell out of the club with somebody to bed and not have to worry about Monica and her nonfucking ass.

I roamed the club for a while and actually found Zanzibar to be nice. The VIP lounge was higher than the club and gave me a nice view of the dance floor and the bar, allowing me to keep tabs on Monica. I settled into a chair in the corner by a rail that separated the club from the VIPs, so I could see almost everything going on and no one could see me.

One of my favorite things to do before I made a move on any women at a club was people-watch. Believe it or not, you could tell a lot about people just by watching them. Most of the brothers in the VIP were tall and big, so I suspected most of them were either football players with the Redskins or basketball players for the Wizards. Most of the women looked like video dancers or strippers, and all of them had GOLD DIGGER flashing across their heads, as far as I was concerned.

All of them but one, that is, and she seemed to be in her own world. Except when one of those pushy athletes tried to buy her a drink or asked her to dance. I'd never seen so many brothers get shot down by the same woman in my entire life. It was actually pretty humorous, along with being pathetic.

Whoever she was, she was one classy-looking female.

She wasn't flashy fine, but fine in a sophisticated kind of way, and because of that, she stuck out from the crowd. Her body was slim, and although she was sitting down, her strong arms and legs told me she was an athlete, a swimmer or maybe even an aerobics instructor.

I watched her for a good thirty minutes, and to be honest, I wasn't sure if she was white or black, she was so light. Truth is, whatever race she was really didn't matter to me; what mattered was how I was going to get her to talk to me so I could take her home.

My opening finally came about quarter to one, when a guy about my size, with a weird Charlie Brown–shaped head, approached her. I'd seen him ask her to dance a few times before, but I guess this time he wasn't taking no for an answer because he actually grabbed her wrist.

She tried to play it off, pulling her arm from his grasp, but I could tell she was scared. I stood up and walked over to where she was sitting. By the time I got there, Charlie Brown Head looked like he was going to slap her.

"Ahhh, hell no! Didn't I tell you not to talk to anyone?" I pointed my finger in the woman's face, then pointed to where I was sitting. "You didn't even see me sitting over there, did you? You just couldn't resist making a fool out of me, could you? I can't leave your ass alone for two seconds, can I?"

She looked confused, like she was about to say something to tip off old boy.

I raised my voice even louder to shut her up. "I told you about flirting with these motherfuckers. Wait till I get your ass home. That's why I didn't wanna come here in the first place."

I turned my attention to Charlie Brown, who was looking a little confused himself. I wasn't sure if he wanted to fight or back off; I wasn't about to give him a choice. It wasn't like I was scared. Hell, I had a black belt in karate, but I never fought with or over women.

"Do you know her? 'Cause if you don't, let me introduce myself—I'm her husband, and we got three kids. So unless you're her long-lost brother, I think you should find someone else's marriage to ruin." I stood my ground, and the brother took a step back.

There was something about the word *husband* that always seemed to make a man reconsider his actions when it came to a pretty woman. Most brothers didn't care if a woman had a husband, as long as he was not around to interfere, but the minute the old man showed up, all bets were off. Which obviously was the case with Charlie Brown. He didn't say anything; he just stepped off and walked away.

I stared at him until he was out of sight, then turned to the sister. And she was a sister, which I could tell now that I was closer to the nape of her neck and her full lips.

"Sorry about the macho man routine, but you looked like you could use a little help. My name's Jay. Jay Crawford." I waited for her reply, and I knew I was in there when she started to grin.

CHAPTER 2

Ashlee

I grinned to keep from crying, to keep from laughing, to keep from screaming hysterically in Jay's face. I didn't want this good-looking man to think I was crazy, but the reason I'd flown all the way from Dallas to D.C. and ended up at Zanzibar by myself was to escape my relationship blues. I could've easily gone down the street to the Channel Inn, but the concierge at my hotel said the crowd was too old. Or I could've walked a block down to H20, but there was a long line of what appeared to be college-aged students waiting to get in.

My objective when I left Dallas was to go to a city where no one knew me. I needed to spend some time alone trying to figure out where things went wrong between me and my ex. I wasn't looking for a new man; I was perfectly content grieving over my breakup with Darius, until Jay made me laugh. Maybe I could use Jay to forget about Darius, like Darius used his new fiancée to forget about me.

The saying "always a bridesmaid, never a bride"

for me was more like "always the ex, never the wife." A bitter lump of jealousy lodged in my throat as I imagined Darius and his bride-to-be, happy together.

Girl, lighten up and live a little, I thought, avoiding eye contact with Jay. *Darius is not the only man in the world for you and you've got two hundred pounds of chocolate proof standing right in front of you smiling . . . at you. Come on, forget about Darius, you deserve to be happy too.*

I was too choked up to say anything to Jay so I shifted my attention to his glorious body and frisked him with my eyes.

Jay stood tall, not stiff. With confidence he planted his foot on the stainless steel rim at the bottom of the bar stool. A hint of arrogance accented the arch in his back as he leaned closer to me. His arrogance was attractive, but I could tell Jay wasn't a player or a gigolo like the other men in the VIP section who'd approached me. Jay was just what I needed—comical, caring, and sexy as hell.

When he interlocked his hands atop the table, I almost fell off my stool. I couldn't help but notice this Mandingo had thick succulent fingers. His middle fingers were longer than his ring fingers, which meant his dick was longer than six inches. After riding Darius's nine inches, I hated when a man's middle finger was shorter because that meant regardless of the size of his hands, his dick was five and a half inches at best.

Thinking of best, I bet those hands could make me come hard without touching my clit. Mmm, mmm . . . look at the size of those feet. I can't wait to see his toes. Sure hope his second toe is longer than the big toe!

He nodded, showing me his pearly white teeth. He looked like he could've whupped up on every man in the club without breaking a sweat or unraveling his dark, curly locks.

"Hey, again, look . . . sorry. Maybe I shouldn't have interrupted, but I—"

Gently covering his knuckles, I said, "No need to apologize, lovely; I'm glad you got rid of him," then whispered, "I'm Ash-lee." Slowly smiling, I dipped my tongue into the crevice of my lips, gliding the tip along my upper lip to the opposite side. The Bobbi Brown red lip moisture that I swabbed on my inner lips made my mouth irresistible. Many men lusted but never tasted my cherry flavor. I loved the fact that this product didn't get on my teeth. I gave Jay a half smile and a wink before caressing my own hands.

Glancing around, I saw that people were starting to leave, which meant I had about fifteen minutes to make up my mind. I could make a new friend or go back to my hotel room alone.

Girl, stop trippin'. No one in D.C. knows you, not even Jay. Invite him to that big-ass suite you have at the Hyatt. For once in your life, think like a man, Ashlee. Men know how to have no-attachment fun and sex—have some fun and hell, if you feel like it, ride that dick too.

But if I asked him to come to my room at three in the morning, he'd want to fuck.

Precisely. What's the problem? His hands? His feet? That's not it. Then what's the problem?

Sex with another man would completely ruin all chances of getting back with Darius. Jay wasn't worth the risk. Or was he? I glanced at his feet again. But if I fucked Jay on the first—damn, I can't even call this a date—the first night, what would he think of me?

Who gives a damn? Stop dwelling on the negatives; think of the positives. Look at those dark chocolate lips, girl. You've got about twenty minutes before last call. Literally!

Making a move, I laughed, leaning my breasts toward this mouthwatering, tall man who'd saved me, or should I say saved that watermelon-head who walked away? I was about to cuss that idiot out if he hadn't peeled his raggedy fingernails away from my precious silky skin. God knew I had enough Darius-inflicted scars already. Emotionally. Physically. *What made that jerk think he had the right to invade my space and feel me up?* Oh, I was about to lay hands on that—I hated when a man disrespected me, and loved when a man protected me the way Jay did.

Focus, Ashlee, focus. You are not alone; you have some-one sitting across from you, okay?

"Um, um, um. Thanks for keeping me from slapping that man," I said angrily, then checked myself, meshing laughter with a contrived smile.

My handsome protector smiled, winked, then silently gazed at me, making me hot for sex . . . with my ex.

You got it bad, girl.

I pictured Darius making love to Fancy. Fancy seemed so perfect: her shape, her breasts, her multi-million-dollar real estate firm. *Bitch.* Wish I could say she was chasing after Darius for his NBA contract money, but that was a lie.

For some odd reason, Jay reminded me of Darius. I loved Darius so much that, even with laughter bellowing from my stomach at this very moment, my heart ached. I whispered Darius's name into the cob-webs of my confused mind. as Jay awaited a response.

I turned my long torso away from Jay, hoping he'd move on to one of the VIP groupies waiting to do anything for or with any man in the VIP section. A few of them were even staring at Jay as he stood in front of me, obviously waiting for him to leave so that they could pounce on him like a cat. (Ladycat—that was Darius's nickname for Fancy.)

Interestingly, those hussies prancing around us with way too much cleavage bursting out of their tops and pubic hairs peering from underneath their skirts didn't seem to impress him. Maybe Jay was a better catch than I realized.

As he scratched behind his ear, a perplexed grin replaced my rescuer's laughter, making his deep dimples fade from his cheeks. His beautiful brown eyes lowered from my eyes to my arm, lingering on the pinkish imprint that asshole's paw left behind, then back up to my eyes.

Seductively he asked, "Are you okay?" He shoved the bar stool farther underneath the high circular table, giving me a clear view of the large imprint of his dick freely hanging inside his slacks.

Damn. I'm much better now. Thanks.

I heard his question but didn't respond, second-guessing if his charm was natural or his way of trying to sway me into his bedroom, spread my legs, and then make a deposit with no return. More than likely, he just wanted sex. A one-night stand. A good time for himself. Certainly, he didn't care about me. If he did, he would've noticed I could've used a hug. I was sure that, in his mind, he'd already grazed his luscious tongue over my perky pink nipples, sucking them into a firm erection. My ruby-red lipstick was probably wrapping around his dick, trailing from his bulging head down to his nuts, until he'd come all over my face in a pleasurable roar while running his fingers through my long hair.

I don't know what I'll do if this man uses me up too. I stared through the window at the boats docked outside on the waterfront. The motionless vessels, synchronizing with my slender body, indicated the water was calm. So was I—on the outside. I was confused on the inside. I desperately wanted him, yet I didn't want to feel dirty afterward if I gave myself to him. Yeah, whoever this fine man was, patiently smiling at me, if he knew what I knew, he would leave now. Right now.

"Are you okay?" he asked again.

Not looking at him I whispered, "I'm fine." *And, God, please don't let him say, "You sure are," because I swear, if I hear that lame-ass line one more time, I'ma slap him so hard, the song playing in the background is gonna skip a beat or two.*

"Good." His mouthwatering smile commanded my attention, surprisingly making my panties moist.

Why he stood next to me exuding sexual implications, when he could've easily had any one of the so-called women in the room, I didn't know. Honestly, I did know but hoped I was wrong. I just couldn't take being a man's playmate again. I had a brain, and thanks to my doggish ex, my intelligence was attached to a broken heart—a lethal combination for establishing a new love affair.

Imagining Jay's thick lips kissing my clit, I repositioned my hips on the stool. Damn, he sounded good. I hadn't made love in almost a year; no man had made me want to. Foolishly I had had sex with Darius whenever he wanted because I didn't want to believe he didn't love me no more. Darius had gone from making love to me, to straight-up fucking me like I was a whore he'd picked up for a one-night stand.

Interrupting my thoughts, Jay continued, "You look like a smart lady. Do you mind if I ask you a quick question before I leave?"

Before you leave? Where are you going? He's supposed to be interested in me.

"Sure. Ask me anything." I gazed at his hands. Slowly my eyes trailed up his arm, over his biceps, shoulder, neck, to his dimples, and paused. How could I have missed those dazzling dimples? Gradually, I lifted my eyelids, invitingly peering into his eyes. Suppressing my rapid breathing, quietly I inhaled, imagining Jay finger-fucking the shit out of me right now on top of the table in the midst of hundreds of people. Maybe if he fucked me like he didn't know me, didn't want to get to know me, and couldn't care less if he saw me again, I wouldn't have any expectations of him. Expectations were the detour to the demise of my happiness.

Moaning a slow "Mmmmm," Jay was a welcome distraction from the previous sorry-ass men with their annoying-ass lines.

What's a beautiful woman like you doing sitting by yourself? Where's your man? Your husband let you come out alone? Those men knew good 'n well they were happy I was alone and couldn't care less if I had a man or husband. Besides, they were interrupting me depressing myself by dwelling on all the things Darius and I had been through.

Jay smiled. "Do you think a man can be friends with his ex?"

"Huhhhh?" *Thanks for interrupting my thoughts and making my pussy hot again.* I lowered my head as silence hovered over us. I couldn't escape the memories. My history with Darius defined me. Denied me from being free. Darius's mom married my dad, and I was naive enough to let him convince me that our parents' marriage didn't make us related. He reassured me it was okay for us to become lovers because even though we'd lived together as kids we weren't biologically related and there was no way that our kids would come out deformed. Darius always loved a challenge. The longer I said no, the more attention he'd given me. When I submitted to his desires, I thought if I made Darius happy, he would make me happy, and we'd be together forever.

"Was it something I said?" Jay asked, lightly touching my hand.

My pussy quivered. Reclaiming my hand, I answered his first question, "Not if you're still in love. Exes can never be friends; not true friends anyway."

I'd been foolish enough to accept a job working for Darius at his Los Angeles company, Somebody Gotta Be On Top. Sure as hell wasn't me—unless we were having sex. That no-good bastard used me up, then proposed to some . . . some . . . whateva. I should've kicked his ass or demolished his house, or made him lose that NBA contract, but all I did was listen to my know-it-all lawyer daddy and move back home from Los Angeles to Dallas. Living in a different city from Darius didn't make me love him any less. I loved him more.

"Yeah, I guess you're right." Jay flipped open his cell phone and looked at the time. "One more question and then I'm out—do you think a man is obligated to be patient and teach a woman who's horrible in bed how to please him?"

This time my pussy chilled out, now that I knew he was more concerned about which woman he might be taking home with him than trying to be my bedmate for the night. Couldn't blame him.

Exhaling, I replied, "No. Life is short. And although handsome, you're a little too grown to be teaching a woman what to do in bed. A real woman would already know. Find someone else to give your heart to, or whatever it is you're giving; there's plenty of lonely women looking for a good dick to sex properly." I could've penciled myself in as number *one*.

He smiled at me like I'd never been smiled at before. "Easier said than done—unless you happen to know a lonely woman that fits the description?"

I started grinning again. *This man had better leave*

*me the hell alone, or he's going to pay dearly for all my pain
and suffering.*

I knew what my problems were—I was beautiful,
wealthy, and too damn polite. My throbbing pussy easily fell in love with a good dick and then, by default, I
fell in with the man attached to the dick. After every
breakup, I hated men but loved sex. I especially dis-
liked the guys that used me, then threw me away like
recyclable trash.

Handsome raised his finger in the air. "Waitress,
give this lady whatever she's drinking on me before
she misses last call." His eye winked at her. His dimple smiled at me. There was that sexy-ass smile again.

*Let him lick your pussy and make you feel better, if only
for a moment. Then I'd risk falling in love with him . . .
but at least you'll temporarily forget about your pain.*

I wanted him to stay; he needed to leave. Was he
just not interested, or was it another woman? Deep
down inside I wanted him to stay; no, I didn't want to
be the one who asked him, I wanted him to ask me to
go home with him. But he didn't.

"A dirty Grey Goose 'tini," I said to the waitress.
She stood staring at Handsome as he handed her a
twenty-dollar bill, like she wanted to get dirty with
him right there in front of my face. *Slut! You're the reason why men treat us like sex objects.*

"Keep the change." He eyed her ass as she walked
away. He continued, "I'd love to talk to you some
more, but I really have to go. Here's my card. My cell
number's on the back . . . just in case you wanna get
together some time." He placed it on the table in
front of me and turned his body away, leaving me to
chase behind him.

As I glanced down at the Department of Justice
logo, my eyes froze. I didn't want him to see my de-

jected expression. "Thanks, Jay," I said, giving no indication I'd contact him later. "Have a nice night."

Before the waitress returned with my drink, I tore Jay's card in half, placed it on the table, and then started to walk away. Halfway to the door, I felt a tap on my shoulder. Crossing one foot over the other, I pivoted slowly.

"Excuse me, miss." The waitress stood in front of me, my drink resting on her tray. "Here's your dirty 'tini."

I removed the drink. "Thanks," I said faintly.

The waitress looked around. "So where's the cutie? I know you didn't let him get away." She seemed a little bit too happy to be sincere.

I didn't bother responding. Returning to the table, I leaned on the stool, sipped my martini, and ate two of the three olives. Swallowing the third olive almost whole, I noticed a woman drooling in Jay's face as she fingered his curly, thick hair, kissed his juicy lips, and then strolled toward the door.

Yeah, she definitely had "free pussy" swaggering in her hips for him, and by the way he nodded while staring at her ass, he was definitely fucking her tonight. *It should have been me.* Her pussy wasn't better than mine, so why should she have all the fun?

Oh, now you want to get mad. If you weren't so damn passive, he could've been yours.

Since I hadn't given Jay the option of calling me, I tossed back the remaining Grey Goose, picked up the torn card, and placed it inside my purse. "You may have him tonight, bitch, but tomorrow he's all mine."

CHAPTER 3

Jay

I could hear her starting to stir as I zipped up my pants and reached for my shirt across the back of the chair. If I was lucky, she'd stay asleep for the five minutes I needed to button my shirt, slip on my shoes, and head out the door. Unfortunately, luck wasn't on my side.

Two seconds later, she lifted her head and began questioning me like she was one of the cops on *Law and Order.* "Where are you going?"

I turned toward her just as I finished buttoning my shirt. Her lips were poked out like those of a spoiled child who wasn't getting her way.

She sat up slightly, and the sheet fell to her lap, exposing her flawless breasts and tempting dark brown, silver-dollar nipples.

My eyes drank up their beauty, but I continued to get dressed. If she was anyone else, I would have been removing my shirt, stepping out of my pants, and jumping into the bed headfirst to finish what we'd started late last night. However, she wasn't someone else; she was Monica, the head bartender at the club.

Once again she'd proven why she was, by far, the worst piece of ass I'd ever had. Why I was stupid enough to come back to her place last night for a second time, I don't know, but I'll tell you this much—she didn't have to worry about me being this stupid again.

"Jay, I asked you a question—where are you going?"

"I'm about to go home," I replied in a rather vanilla tone.

"Home?"

I could hear the shock in her voice as she glanced at the clock radio on the nightstand.

"But it's only eight o'clock."

I gave her a cross-eyed look. "And . . ." I slipped my feet in my shoes.

"It's Saturday; you don't have to work. I—I thought we were going to spend the day together."

I froze for a second, then smirked as I shook my head. "I don't know where you got that from. I never told you I'd spend the day with you."

"I know, but I figured after last night you might wanna spend some time with me. Go to IHOP or something like that."

I bent over to give her a kiss, hoping to get out of her apartment without incident. "Look, Monica, I'm sorry, but I got shit to do today, okay?" I was trying not to have an attitude, but it was getting harder because I absolutely hated when someone wasted my time. And last night was a true waste of my time.

"All right, but how about one for the road?" She kissed me, then pulled back the sheet, exposing the rest of her naked body.

I couldn't help laughing.

"What's so funny?"

"You. You're what's so funny. Do you really think offering me sex is gonna get me to stay?"

She gave me this confident smirk, then nodded like she had me wrapped around her fingers. "I don't *think*, Jay—I *know*. Now, get your ass over here so Mama Monica can put this pussy on you like you've never had it before." She gestured with her index finger for me to come closer, but I didn't budge. She really thought she was the bomb; that wench actually thought her shit was gold. "C'mere, Jay. Stop playing hard to get and come here; you know you want this."

I couldn't hold back any longer. I started to laugh again. It was time to tell her what every brotha before me should have told her long before now. "Look, I don't know what kind of brothas you've messed with in the past, but believe me, you weren't all that, aw'ight." I scrunched up my face at the memory and shook my head. "Matter of fact, you were actually pretty pathetic. You ever thought about moving when you're having sex?"

Her jaw dropped, and her eyes bulged. I'd just crushed her ego flat as a pancake, and I could see shock, then hurt, and finally anger run across her face.

"You so full o' shit, you know that? If I was so fucking bad, why'd you come over here tonight?"

"You don't really wanna know the answer to that."

"Yes, I do."

"Aw'ight, I'll tell you." I took a few steps toward the door, just in case she flipped. "The reason I came home with you last night is that I wanted to get laid and I didn't have any better offers."

"Oh, so you got what you wanted, and now you gonna front like it wasn't good to you."

"Got what I wanted? Don't flatter yourself, Monica—I didn't even come."

"Fuck you! Get out of my house!" Out of nowhere the clock radio went flying across the room, and I had to duck to avoid it. "You trying to tell me you didn't come."

"That's exactly what I'm saying. And if you don't believe me, check the condom." I glanced over my shoulder as I walked out the door. She didn't move, but I was sure once I was gone she was going to check the garbage can to see if I was lying or not.

In a way I felt sorry for her. I knew how I felt when I thought a woman didn't come, but I couldn't imagine what it was like for a woman to find out she couldn't make a man come.

Fifteen minutes later my cell phone rang as I was rolling down Fourteenth Street, headed to the Beltway and my apartment in Alexandria, Virginia. I let my voice mail pick it up because Monica had already called twice and cussed my ass out. The thought that maybe I should have kept my mouth shut about her lack of skills and just avoid her until she got the hint came to mind. Oh well, it was too late now; besides, somebody had to burst that bubble of hers. The girl was absolutely clueless.

The phone rang again. This time I was going to let her know that I knew just as many four-letter words as she did. I pushed the TALK button and yelled, "Will you stop fucking calling!"

There was silence for a few seconds. Then I was surprised by a voice that wasn't angry, didn't scream, and, more importantly, wasn't Monica's. "If you didn't want me to call, why you give me your number?"

"Huh? Who is this?"

"Obviously, it's not the person you thought it was, Jay," the woman on the other end teased.

I glanced at the caller ID on the phone, and it read TEXAS.

"Okay, you had your little fun; stop playing games. Who is this?"

"I guess you give your number to so many women, you can't keep track of them. You don't have a clue who this is, do you?"

Damn it. I hated when women played these games, especially when they were right. I didn't know anyone with a 713 area code. Then again, she could've used a calling card. "Look, I'm not having the best of days, so whoever this is, can you please just tell me who you are?"

"It's Ashlee, Jay."

"Ashlee? Ashlee who?"

The woman sighed; I think I was starting to frustrate her. "Ashlee Anderson. We met last night at the club. You rescued me from the guy with the big head, remember?"

A lightbulb went off in my head. "Oh, that Ashlee. Well, why didn't you say so?" A smile crept up on my face. "How you doing, Ashlee?"

I was glad she called, though, because I'd all but given up on her after she spotted me leaving the club last night with Monica. Ashlee was one classy-ass lady and, in all honesty, the only woman I'd met that deserved my time since I'd moved to D.C.

"I'm doing all right, but I'm a little bored. I was wondering if you could tell me some of the fun things to do in D.C."

"I can show you better than I can tell you. Why don't I pick you up this afternoon and show you around? I haven't lived here long, so we can do the 'tourist thing' together, you know. Go to the Washington Monument, the White House, the Smithsonian, and that kinda stuff. What do you think?"

There was silence on her end, like she was contemplating my offer. "I don't know, Jay. I was really planning on spending some time alone; I've got a lot of things to think about."

"Come on, Ashlee. I'll even throw in dinner. How about Legal Seafood? I know you like seafood, don't you?"

"Of course I do; I *love* fish but I don't eat shellfish."

"Well, all right. Then it's a date."

"Okay, but I don't want you to get the wrong impression—this is not a date; I am not looking for a man, and I am nobody's one-night stand."

Yeah, right! So you just called me out of the blue because you're not interested. This is going to be easier than I thought.

"If you say it's not a date, it's not a date. Now, where can I pick you up?"

"I'm staying at the Grand Hyatt on H Street near the Convention Center. Do you know where that is?"

"I'll find it. How about I pick you up around two?"

"Sure. I'll meet you in the lobby. Bye, Jay."

"Ashlee, wait. What's your cell number . . . just in case?"

"713—"

"Cool. Later, Ashlee." I clicked off the phone, grinning from ear to ear as I saved Ashlee's digits in my cell. I hadn't been this excited about a date or whatever you wanna call it in years. Ashlee did something to me that no woman had done to me in a long time—she excited me in every way. I could hardly wait to run my fingers through her long, pretty hair.

CHAPTER 4

Ashlee

Sunrays burst through the sheer drapes, warming the purple baby-doll nightie that barely covered my naked ass. I rolled over and spread my legs, allowing the sunshine to kiss my kitty, warming me from the outside in. I sure could've used some dick last night instead of going to sleep horny as hell. Tilting my pelvis toward the stimulating rays, I couldn't believe this Jay guy, but at the same time, I couldn't get him off my mind.

Fantasizing about Jay, I teased my pubic hairs. Sprawled atop the king-sized comforter, I double-checked to make sure I'd hung up my cell phone before tossing it on the pillow. Didn't want Jay to accidentally overhear me talking about him. Throwing my head backward, I laughed out loud. "Playa-playa . . . is he for real or what?"

Enjoying myself, I spread my lips wide and rotated my hips clockwise. At first I was thrilled about going out with Jay, but now I wasn't so sure. He might just be something or someone to do to take my mind off my issues until I leave tomorrow. At least that was what I was telling myself.

Neither my parents nor my ex knew where I was, and since I didn't know anyone in D.C. and didn't have anything better to do, I decided I could spend time alone tonight after Jay dropped me off in the lobby. Worst-case scenario—I'd have someone to think about as I masturbated myself to sleep.

I'd given Jay way too much credit. Jay was definitely a slickster, yelling, "Will you stop fucking calling?" in my damn ear before he even said hello. Clearly, he'd pissed some woman off, or she'd pissed him off. Hell, he'd pissed me off too, asking, "Ashlee who?" like he could ever forget me.

Jay acted as though I'd been the one running game on him in the club, with his casual effort to remember who I was. Or maybe he was so accustomed to handing out business cards that he'd lost track—if he'd ever kept track—of the women he gave his number to. But whoever he'd upset this early, he'd probably messed up her entire day.

That's how women were—easy. Easy to upset. Both easy and eager to please. *Desperate* might be a better adjective. It was probably that woman I saw flirting with him at the club twirling her finger in his hair. If it was her, I was sure she wasn't feeling all giddy and shit right about now. *I'm sure he'd flip her to one of his boys to fuck next.* I knew the routine all too well. I'd been "that woman" before.

That's how men were—users. Like the president: "Whatever you do, don't destroy the oil." At the club last night, Jay was probably saying to himself, "Whatever you do, just let me hit that pussy and then I'm out." Men. Orgasmic opportunists. As long as they got what they'd come for, a woman's desires rarely mattered.

I closed my fluttering eyelids and whispered, "Jay. Jay. What was his last na—"

Jay's thick lips suctioned my nipples into perfectly erect bulbs. I knew what I wanted from Mr. . . . Mr. Jay. Grabbing his head, I pushed until his lips pressed against mine like warm sunshine. Each time he licked, I rotated up and into his mouth. My juicy pussy pulsated. I wanted badly to come in Jay's face. "I can't hold back any longer. I'm ready. I'm come—"

Beep. Beep.

"—ing."

Damn it! I'd awakened to my cell phone chiming in my ear, indicating someone had sent a message. "Oh my gosh! What time is it?" I'd slept two hours.

Sitting on the edge of the bed, I felt moisture between my thighs, so I ran my hand over my vagina. I was soaking wet, and my clit was still throbbing. "Aw, damn!" I'd come in my sleep, dreaming about Jay.

Quickly, I went into the bathroom, turned on the water, more hot than cold, and then chucked my nightie into the laundry bag hanging behind the door.

Returning to the bed, I grabbed my cell phone, pressed a few buttons, then laughed at the picture Jay had sent me. He was so silly and so damn good-looking. I'd saved his smiley, perfect-teeth pic in my phone to match his number, so every time he called I could see his chocolate dimples. Then I assigned him a special ring tone. I took a picture of myself with my phone, then sent it to Jay.

I was happy as hell, knowing I could have that big dick swaggering inside me if I wanted. Retrieving my purse from the nightstand, I fumbled through more stuff than I used, removed the golden bottle with my name printed on the label, and shook two antidepressant tablets into my hand. I opened the five-dollar bottle of Evian water, tossed the pills to the back of my throat, and gulped half the liter.

I eased into the tub, the hot water suppressing my "bad-relationship" memories. Jay wasn't Darius. I focused on being happy, imagining Jay making love to me. I nestled my fingers over my pussy and massaged my clit. My body stiffened, so I let go, reassuring myself I could have the real thing tonight. I inhaled slow, deep, and long, allowing my lungs and stomach to expand. Exhaling, I felt the meds beginning to relax my muscles. Stress escaped my body.

"I will have a good time this afternoon," I repeated ten times. My shrink had said if I repeated anything ten times consecutively, negative or positive, I'd believe it. "I will only speak positive words. I won't fall in love with Jay's dick."

Maybe I could fall in love with Jay instead. I dried myself off. I slipped into my ultra-low-rise boot-cut denims and a long-sleeve midriff cutoff top that tied my naked breasts together, exposing great cleavage. With my flat abs on display, I headed to the elevator to meet my new man. On the ride down from the twelfth floor, I convinced myself I wasn't a bad person and what had happened to my son truly wasn't my fault. Just like Darius, I deserved to be happy too. And happy I was, when the elevator doors opened. The first person I saw in the lobby was Jay, standing proud.

Jay swaggered in my direction. "Hey, Ashlee. Damn, girl, you look good," he said, slipping his arms around my waist.

Despite everything I'd told myself about not readily trusting men, I melted in Jay's strong embrace. He felt good. Made me feel safe. Desirable. Womanly. In time, he'd make me feel loved.

"Thanks. You don't look so bad yourself." I stepped back and softly caressed his dimple.

"You look hot. I'm going to be the envy of every man everywhere we go," he said, opening the passenger door to his BMW.

I don't know what it was. There I was, sitting next to a complete stranger who excited the hell out of me. I didn't know his mother's name, his father's name, if he had kids, or a wife, or a woman, a man, or both, or whether or not he was a serial killer, serial dater, if he had any STDs, or his middle name. "So where to?" I asked, settling into his sports car. "Nice car; I love the color red."

Jay's grin resembled a child's. I shut my eyes, then opened them quickly. *Don't go there, Ashlee. Stay focused. Happy, remember?*

"You know us boys and our big toys. I just got divorced, so I figured I'd buy a little somethin'-somethin' for myself." He reached into the backseat and handed me the most stunning clear box of long-stemmed white roses. "A little something for you."

I wanted to ask him if he had kids but I couldn't. . . . Great, Jay was on the rebound too. Fortunately for me, men remarried faster than women, so I too could have a fiancé, if I played my cards right. Then Darius would beg me back, like he'd pleaded with Fancy to call off her engagement to that other guy. That's it— I'd give Darius a reason to come after me. Worst-case scenario—I'd marry Jay.

Opening the box, I sniffed the flowers, smiled, then bit my bottom lip. "Aaah, Jay, did you get these out of the lobby? I saw some just like these in a vase by the check-in desk."

He looked into my eyes to see if I was serious. When I grinned, he grinned back at me. "Oh, so you got jokes. I guess the box they came in and the card were in the lobby too, huh?"

"I'm just kidding. Relax," I said, seizing the opportunity to softly touch his thigh.

Damn! Was that his dick all the way down there? The card read *Closer to my dream.* I reassured him, "I'm your reality. They're gorgeous. Thanks." I closed my eyes and took one long inhale of the petals. I moaned, imagining they were a bridal bouquet and Jay was my groom, sweeping me away on our honeymoon. I placed the roses on the seat behind me. "So what was going on this morning? What woman was you cursing out and why?"

Did he buy the roses for her, then decide to give them to me? Ashlee, why can't you enjoy the man and the moment and stop analyzing every damn thing?

"Aw, hell no! You know better than to question me, woman!" Jay sped along the B/W Parkway. "Don't make me stop this car!"

Cracking up, I held my stomach. "You are so adorably dangerous; I like a man who's fearless like me."

My thoughts drifted, while Jay test-drove his toy at almost 120 miles per hour, smoothly swerving and dodging cars in both lanes. I enjoyed the fifteen-should've-been-thirty-minute ride from Washington to Baltimore. The colorful leaves—orange, purple, yellow, red—were a blur. I felt like there was nothing I couldn't do with Jay, including have sex with him tonight.

My period was due in two days, and my sex drive revved higher than his engine, making me tightly press my thighs together. Thankfully I had on jeans; otherwise Jay's leather passenger seat would've been juicy from that hot leather seat rubbing up against my panties . . . I exhaled.

After opening my car door, Jay held my hand all

the way from the parking garage to the Inner Harbor. "Uh-uh, woman, don't you dare touch a door when you're with me." Jay waited for me to enter the mall.

Legal Seafood was crowded, so Jay suggested the ESPN Sports Zone. I appreciated a take-charge type of man. I looped my arm underneath Jay's, hugging his biceps. He was all mine.

Strolling inside the Zone, I playfully said, "I bet you can't beat me rock climbing."

"Who said that?" Jay glanced around, pretending he couldn't see me, so I poked him in his side. He looked down. "Oh, you? Down there. In those heels?" He gestured toward my feet.

"Don't let the stilettos fool you; I do some of my best work in high heels."

"Like that?"

"No, like this"—I held out my pinky finger—"bet?"

"What you got to lose?"

"Nothing"—*except you. And that would make me sad. Very sad.*

A quizzical look flashed across his face. "Everybody's got somethin' to lose. This is my lucky shirt." Jay seductively unbuttoned his shirt, exposing his chest as if he were Taye Diggs in *How Stella Got Her Groove Back.*

Damn, Jay was definitely finer than Taye. My heart raced. "Not winners." *I'm never losing anything again, especially Jay.* I kicked my slip-on heels in the air, one at a time.

Jay caught them, flexed, gazed into my eyes, and then confidently replied, "Then let's do the damn thing, woman. Winner claims his or her prize."

Was he talking about rock climbing or climbing me? It was too late to back down, so I mounted the wall adjacent to his muscular body, pretending I was straddling him while trying not to touch him; else I'd forfeit before we started.

The operator pressed a button, and the mechanical wall gradually rotated downward. Jay was cool, his movement fluid. Each time his foot raised higher, his dick hung lower.

My left foot slipped off a rock so big I could've damn near sat on it.

He smiled. "Looks like you should've kept on those heels."

"Forget you, Jay." I regretted calling out his name, when I noticed the vultures buzzing around to prey upon my man. Reaching up, I gripped the first rock in sight, then yelled to the operator, "Speed it up!"

Jay grinned, easing his way up the wall, as if the operator hadn't increased the speed at all, while I scrambled.

Suddenly, I realized I hadn't worked out in almost a month. Unfortunately, my meds didn't give me a boost.

I'd just found my pace when Jay yelled, "Faster!"

By now a crowd had gathered behind us, I'm sure, to literally watch Jay's sexy ass make love to the wall.

I've got something for these sideshow hussies. Climbing sideways, I wrapped my leg around Jay's waist and crawled onto his back. My arms were now choking his neck.

Jay kept climbing. "You are so precious. I guess this means I'm your daddy."

Playfully I bit him in his back. Jay moaned a most provocative moan, and that shit turned me on so much my pussy puckered.

Surrendering, Jay let go and stumbled to the mat. He looped his arm around my waist, rotating my body in front of him, and I wrapped my legs snug about his waist. "Damn, woman, bite me again."

Breathing in his face, my lips almost touching his, I asked, "So did I win?"

"Only if you bite me like that later." The softness of his lips came to mine. "Shit! Let's go," he said. Jay lowered me to the floor.

I paused when my pussy grazed his dick. Instantaneously, my hips jammed into his dick before sliding down.

"I like that shit." Jay eyed my ass as I gathered my shoes.

Smiling up at Jay, I didn't ask where we were going, hoping our date—I mean outing—was over and my hotel room was his final destination. Within a blink of my eyes, my man disappeared from view when a woman's ass slid right in front of my face.

"Jay, right?" She didn't wait for his response. Pleasantly, she continued, "You look just like Jimmy Jean-Louis. We met last night . . . at Zanzibar . . . Nikki."

I knew I shouldn't have called out his name. Besides, how many hints was this Nikki woman going to give before Jay opened his mouth? I'd heard the women in Baltimore were bolder and less tactful than the women in D.C., but damn, this trick totally disrespected me. Keeping my mouth shut, I stood in their space, trying to recall if I'd seen her at the club. She didn't look familiar, but after this episode, I'd never forget her face.

Wrapping his arm around my waist, Jay shook his head, speechless, and hunched his shoulders at this Nikki woman.

"Hi, I'm Nikki," she said, this time extending her hand toward me.

Ignoring *Nikki*, I leaned into Jay, snuggled my arm behind his back, placed my hand on his stomach, and seductively asked, "You ready, baby?"

As he turned away from Nikki, Jay's eyebrows lifted and then his eyes widened, as if he was saying, *Sorry, Nik.*

Well, I didn't feel sorry for her at all. Nor was I going to compete for what was already mine. If Jay wanted her, she would've been his date.

As we walked away, the woman waiting for Nikki said loud enough for us to hear, "I can't believe you let him play you like that."

Racing around Jay, Nikki handed him his business card and flipped it over to his cell phone number written on the back. "I won't be needing this."

Do not get mad, Ashlee. If you show her that she's pissed you off, she'll get the satisfaction, and you'll end up hating yourself.

Ignoring Nikki for the last time, we continued our stroll. Why couldn't she just let it go, leave him alone? Obviously, Jay wasn't interested. He was being polite, and she'd definitely made her point. I intended to continue having an enjoyable evening with my new man.

Jay held my hand as we walked along the pier. He stopped in front of the paddleboats. "Wanna ride?"

I stared at the yellow boat. *Hell yeah, but not that thing.* This man knew what he was doing to me, but I wasn't going to give it up to him that easy. "But the sun is going down," I protested, "and we haven't eaten yet." I teased my stomach, closer to my pussy than my navel.

"I know." He led me inside the boat. "I'll feed you . . . eat you too. Later. Now have a seat." Jay sat behind me and straddled his thighs around mine.

"This is not how you're supposed to ride a paddle-boat. Besides, who's going to paddle?"

"Who's your daddy? I won, remember."

"Well, if I'm paddling, we'll float the entire time." And we did.

Jay leaned my head against his chest, untied my hair, and massaged my scalp. My eyes rolled to the back of my head. The tingling sensation crept along my skin, when Jay snuggled his dick in the groove of my spine.

"Ashlee, you're wonderful. I meant what I wrote on your card. Now that I've met you, I am closer to my dream."

"I don't live here, Jay."

"I'm not surprised. Isn't this how it always happens? Well, I wish you lived here."

"I love Dallas," I lied. If I never went back, that would be okay with me, but eventually I had to attend another court hearing.

"Well, I could love you." Jay's words traveled into the fading sunset. He continued to knead my shoulders, occasionally tracing his fingertip to my cleavage.

I had to have him. Untying my top, I cupped his palms over my breasts.

Jay squeezed my nipples between his thumbs and pointing fingers and caressed my breasts. He gently pressed his lips inside my ear, whispering, "You are so beautiful." Instantly, I came.

When the moonlight replaced the sunset, I'd drifted for so long I hadn't realized we were back at my hotel.

"I enjoyed you, Ashlee. Hopefully I can take you out again before you leave."

There goes that word *leave* again. *No. No one's leaving.* "You're welcome to come up to my room, that is, if you don't have other plans."

Smiling, Jay handed the valet his keys. He had to know how sexy he was, but he was more attractive 'cause he acted clueless. I couldn't stand men who spent more time in the mirror than me.

When I unlocked the door, Jay came in and stood in the living area. "Shit! It's freezing in here, woman!"

Quickly, I shut and latched the door. "Sorry, you

know how housekeeping always adjusts the thermostat. Make yourself comfortable. I'll warm you up later, but for now I'll fix you a drink."

First, I dumped the artificial flowers in the trash, filled the vase with slightly cool water, and placed my precious arrangement on the coffee table in front of him. Continuously moving, I retrieved a bottle of red wine from the liquor cabinet. "Is this okay?" I held up a bottle of Merlot.

"Yeah, that's real good," he answered between chattering teeth while eyeing my breasts.

A quick glance and I noticed my nipples had popped through my top like gumdrops. I attempted to fill Jay's glass halfway, or so I thought.

"Shit, woman! What are you doing?"

"Oh my. I'm so sorry. I—I was watching, um . . ."

He smiled. "It's okay. It's only—"

"Your lucky shirt. Let me get that off you. You can shower. I'll have housekeeping send your shirt to the one-hour cleaners." Damn, Jay's skin was smoother than it looked. Indeed, Jay was going to benefit from my mistake.

"Sure, I'll take a shower, but only if you join me." He adjusted his erection.

Oh, I wanted to see his dick. Ride him right. "Start without me; I'll be in later. Let me take care of your shirt first."

From the look on his face, I think he was shocked but pleased. I hung Jay's shirt outside the door in a laundry bag and called housekeeping. Then I waited long enough for him to get wet and slippery.

Before stepping into the bathroom, I popped two more pills with the remaining bottled water. For the first time in a long time, I was sharing my shower with a man.

For a moment, Jay's eyes lingered on my scarred

thighs. Then he lightly touched the scar on my back as he hugged me. "My God! What happened?"

Silence lingered as I fought back tears, recalling the horrible memories of Darius. "I'd rather not—"

"Ssshhh. No need to explain." Jay quietly placed his fingers under my chin and tilted my head backward. His juicy lips covered mine as his tongue invaded my mouth.

"Umm. Umm." I sucked his tongue; he sucked mine. I submitted, melting into his wet flesh. "Umm . . . um . . . um." My body jerked when Jay glided his fingers over my nipples. I took several long deep breaths. I was finally ready to let go of Darius forever.

"I want you, Ashlee," Jay whispered faintly.

Right before he hugged me, my pussy trembled. Then he held me as the warm water pulsated against our bodies. Jay felt heavenly.

We dried one another off; then his naked body caressed mine as we eased under the sheets.

"Here"—Jay patted his chest—"lay your head next to my heart."

I tucked my head underneath his armpit onto his divine chest, exhaled, and then closed my eyes. *Why couldn't every day be this perfect?* "This seems like a fanta—"

"Naw, it's real, baby. Wake up. Don't fall asleep on him." Jay wrapped my hand around his dick.

I jerked again, this time from the waist up. "Ooh, he's humongous!"

"You think?" Jay smiled proudly. "So do you like?"

"Mmm-hmm, I like. I like a lot."

Someone knocked on the door. A voice echoed, "Room service."

"I left the shirt *outside* the door!"

"Calm down. Stay here; I'll check it out." Jay hurried to the door. He returned to the bedroom, rolling a cart filled with covered plates.

Leaning against the headboard, I frowned, then smiled. "When did you have time to do this?" *Ashlee, you have got to be more aware of your surroundings.*

"Aha!" Jay revealed a platter of chocolate-dipped strawberries, a bottle of champagne, and freshly squeezed orange juice. He pulled the bedspread over my leg and placed the tray in my lap. "Look, I hate playing games, Ashlee—I like you, and I'm the type of man that can show you better than I can tell you. Trust me."

"Well then, show me." I couldn't believe what I'd said. That was the first time I'd asked someone other than Darius in God knows how long.

Pausing, he shook his head. "You have no idea what you're asking me to do to you."

"Yes, I do, so don't make me ask twice."

Jay placed the tray back on the stand. Suctioning off the chocolate, he massaged my toes with strawberries, then licked the redness from between my toes as he massaged the arches in my feet. He wasn't in a hurry, nor was I. Cool ice cubes traced my ankles. I'd never realized my ankles were so sensitive, until Jay's tongue absorbed the wetness.

"Ummm," I moaned, twitching at the tickling yet arousing sensation.

Jay kissed my scarred thighs. "Turn over."

I did as instructed and waited. The coolness of whipped cream smothered my ass and seeped between the crevices of my vagina.

Jay's hands rotated, parting my cheeks. Every time my cheeks opened, his long, thick fingers teased my clit.

I rotated my hips.

His finger stroked my shaft as more whipped cream greeted me.

My pussy swelled, gushing juices that flooded the sheets. "Damn! I'm making it obvious I haven't had a man make love to me in . . . forever." I made a motion to turn over.

"I like your juicy pussy. Relax. I'm getting it ready so I can fuck you like you've never been fucked before." When he whispered, "Ashlee" he slipped his long finger deep inside. "Damn! Your pussy is *tight*. You got my dick hard as hell, woman." Jay continued sliding his finger inside me.

"Oh my God! Oh my God. Jay, what are you doin' to me?" I wanted Jay so bad.

The pain was pleasurable. Thank God that was his finger and not that gigantic dick. I was on the verge of coming . . . on his finger.

Jay paced his rhythm, plunging a little deeper every few seconds, until he found my spot. Then he stopped.

My hips clamped down on his hand as he held his finger against my G-spot and maintained constant pressure. Damn, biting the sheets, I moaned, "Uh-huh. Uh-huh. Uh-huh! Uh-huh! Uh-huuuh! Oh, ba-*beeee*." Instinctively, my body took over grinding his finger. I fucked Jay's finger long and hard like it was the real thing.

Jay didn't move until I'd worn myself out. Patiently, he removed his finger; then he sniffed, licked, and sucked my juices. "Sweet." He kissed my breasts. "You ready for all of this?"

I grabbed his dick again—well . . . almost. It had grown, and my fingers weren't long enough to wrap all the way around him. "My God, what do you feed this thing?"

"C'mere and I'll show you," he said, nudging my lips closer to his head.

I didn't want to seem selfish, the way I'd originally thought Jay was. Boy, was I wrong! With the little energy remaining, I leaked a stream of saliva onto his shaft, stroking as best as I could, but honestly I was drained. Felt like I was suspended in air; I'd never felt this good.

When Jay's bulging head dipped below my waist, then popped inside my pussy, I braced my hands on his shoulders. "Wait, where's your condom?"

"I ain't got one."

"Then I can't do this." I tried to push him off me.

"I won't come in you; I'll pull it out, I promise."

I shook my head. "No. I've already gotten pregnant once on the 'I'm just gonna put the head in' promise. No condom, no sex. Sorry."

"Damn! How could I forget? What about you?"

"Haven't needed those in over a year," I lied.

"Damn! For real?" Jay's chest inflated. "Okay, what if I go to the gift shop and come right back?"

"Closed."

"Fuck!" He dialed the gift shop direct to confirm.

"Let's cuddle tonight, and pick up where we left off tomorrow." I slipped under the covers.

Jay exhaled, then crawled in beside me, obviously frustrated. He asked, "So, how many kids?"

"None," I said, rolling over.

"Abortion?"

"No."

"Miscarriage?"

"Nope."

"But—"

"Long story." I kissed him. "Good night."

CHAPTER 5

Jay

I walked out of Ashlee's hotel suite and slammed my hand against the wall. "Fuck!" I was so upset with myself. How in the hell could I have gone out of the house without bringing some condoms? I could have sworn I had one in my wallet, but then again, I wasted it the other night on that bad-sex-having-can't-make-a-brother-come-hope-I-never-see-her-again Monica. Damn! And after the way I had Ashlee humping and creaming all over my finger with that tight-ass pussy of hers, I just knew I was about to tear that shit up. Damn, I know that shit was gonna be good. I was tempted to plead with her to just trust me and let me go "raw dog" it. Then again I was glad I didn't—no need to die over some pussy. Besides, there's always tonight and she wanted it as much as me, if not more.

I pressed the DOWN button for the elevator and waited for its arrival. Just thinking about the whole foreplay incident and leaving without getting any added more fuel to the fire. I slammed my fist against the wall for the second time, and the elevator door

opened simultaneously. There was a white guy standing inside the elevator, looking wide-eyed and apparently startled. I must have scared the shit out of him
when I slammed my hand against the wall before stepping inside the elevator, because he looked shaken.

I mumbled a quick "What's up?" but could do
nothing to mask the pissed-off expression on my face.

The man eased back toward the corner, never taking his eyes off me.

I almost laughed at the short, stocky man, but if I
were him, I might've been scared of me too. I glanced
at my watch and realized it was damn near five
o'clock in the morning. I bet his short ass just left
from getting him some. And just looking at him, he
wasn't even a real playa. *Damn, Jay, how the fuck could
you forget to bring some condoms?*

The valet brought my BMW to the front door in
little to no time. I didn't mean to burn rubber as I
left the hotel, but I guess my anger had gotten the
better of me. I chose to ride toward home in silence,
but without the blaring radio, or someone to talk to,
my mind quickly replayed my last moments with Ashlee. Her naked body kept flashing into my mind.

It had been a while since I'd enjoyed a shower
scene with any woman. I was ready to be inside Ashlee right then and there, but for the first time in a
long while, I felt like taking things slow. She seemed
like the kind of woman a man should take his time
with. I could tell Ashlee was somewhat embarrassed
by the scars on her thighs, so I avoided staring at
them as much as I could, and I disregarded my mind
telling me to further question how she got them. Instead, I aimed to show her that she was still beautiful
to me by kissing and licking her thighs the way I do
my favorite dessert, vanilla ice cream.

All women loved my large-size hands, so I gave

Ashlee the same treat all women get—the finger fuck—just before getting the real deal. I never expected her to feel as tight as she did once I slid my finger inside her, so that came as a welcome surprise to me. My dick got even harder, growing at least another inch thicker, as I thought of having her tight pussy clamming me with every stroke. I loved the silkiness of Ashlee's wetness creeping up my hand as I finger-fucked her. Her moans were sexy as hell, and I could've very easily gotten off at the same time she climaxed, if I was masturbating. Her pussy contracted over and over again, gripping my finger as if it was a dick inside her. Her fluid was thick and plentiful, just the right amount of wetness for a man my size to enter a tight pussy with a condom without causing pain.

But entering Ashlee quickly became a fantasy as we both were rudely awakened by the discovery that neither of us possessed a condom. I should give myself an F on the playa's score card for this one.

Aaawww, fuck! Driving and reminiscing caused a brotha's shit to tighten up. God, do I hate having blue balls! Far, far too much pressure on a man. A woman can get horny, be on the verge of having sex, but then not get any and still keep her cool. But a man—almost getting some doesn't work. Nothing can keep us from getting blue balls except being able to relieve the buildup. The only thing on my mind was to find a way to let loose. It didn't matter what time of morning. I just needed some sexual healing, and quick! I knew who I could call—fine-ass Janice. I used to mess with her when we both lived in New York. She'd moved down to D.C. about a year ago. Only reason I hadn't called her since I moved was that Janice could get a little ghetto and always seemed to have some type of drama. But she'd also take it any way I tossed it at her and never make a complaint of how hard I tapped it either. Plus, the one thing I could count on was for her to throw that ass back when I was hittin' it, and unlike Monica keep it with rhythm too. Now I was horny as hell, and desperate times call for desperate measures, so I was willing to deal with her drama. The only problem with Janice was the possibility she just might have company if I didn't call her the day before. Janice wouldn't dare spend the weekend alone. She didn't have to. Janice is a freak-a-lic and proud to be one. She possesses far too much talent in bed than to lie alone and masturbate.

I had enough with reflecting. My balls hurt, and it was time to set forth things in motion. *I'll never know what I could get unless I make that call. Here goes nothing.*

"Hello," her sweet voice answered on the first ring.

"Hello yourself," I responded.

"Jay? Is that you?" Janice asked.

"The one and only. Yeah, baby, it's me. How are you doing?"

"Damn. It's been a long time, Jay. What you doing callin' me at five o'clock in the morning? I could be lying next to someone, you know?"

"Yeah, I know. And I know I didn't wake you, because you answered on the first ring. I also know you don't have company, because if you did, I would've heard the computer on your answering machine instead of your sweet voice. What you doing up at five on a Sunday morning? A fine chocolate thang like you should be getting her beauty rest." I thought Janice would laugh, but she didn't.

"I've been waiting on someone to call me. Looks like I got stood up. We both know that's a first." Janice's tone was rather solemn. This was my opportunity to pull the playa's card and make it work for me.

"Whoa, Janice, I'm sorry to hear that. Whoever this man is, he apparently doesn't understand who you are and what you're capable of. As a matter of fact, I'm ready to take a drive over there to see you now. What you think? Can I take his place? Can I be your breakfast in bed?"

"Only if you still pack the right sausage and if the meat is lean. You know how I eat hearty every time you bring me the plate."

"Oh yeah. Boy, do I ever know what you mean! I ain't met a woman who could swallow the sausage like you."

"Is that right, Daddy?"

"That's right," I answered in a deep seducing tone.

"Then you need to act like it and bring yo' ass on over here. I've got an itching inside my throat that I know only *your* dick can scratch. How long will it take you to get over here?"

"You ain't said nothin' but a word. I'm making a U-turn now. Get up and go unlock the door, then lie back in bed wearing nothing but your birthday suit. I'll be there in ten minutes with your morning nourishment."

"Mmm, I can't wait," Janice responded, purring like a kitten.

Janice's voice drove me wild. I began to speed because my balls were so tight I could feel them shrinking. I was less than five minutes away from Janice's place when I glanced over in the passenger seat and noticed one of the gold earrings Ashlee wore on our date. It must've fallen off without her knowing it. After stopping at a red light, I picked up the earring and glared at it. Without warning I began to feel a sense of guilt for wanting to go have sex with Janice knowing I was going to fuck Ashlee tonight. Where this feeling came from, I don't know. I've always been a playa—even when I was married—so it was extremely odd for me to be having a conscience about cheating on a woman I never actually made a commitment with.

I pulled up in front of Janice's house, but I wasn't

in a hurry to get out of the car. I sat dazed, thinking of the quality time I had spent with Ashlee and how much I really liked her. The earring remained clutched in the palm of my hand. I loosened my fingers and caught a glimpse of the shiny gold, which seemed to glitter even in the dark. I pictured Ashlee with both earrings on, and a flash of her smile came to mind. Then I realized I couldn't do it. Janice was about to be stood up for the second time in one day because I couldn't make myself get out of the car to be with her. My daze soon became short-lived as the throbbing between my legs damn near had me crippled. I cranked up and drove home, trying to keep a level head, the whole time praying I hadn't made one of the biggest mistakes of my life.

A hot shower and a nap did wonders for me this day. Some people think the key to getting over blue balls is a cold shower, but the difference is that hot water loosens your skin much quicker and a lot better. The second I woke up I reached for the phone to give Ashlee a call. I couldn't believe how much I started to miss being near her. She sounded a little groggy, but nevertheless, I was glad to hear her voice.

"Hey, Ashlee, this is Jay. I'm glad to know you're still in," I stated just after she picked up.

"What do you mean? Of course I'm still in. You just left fifteen minutes ago, remember?"

"Ashlee, it's now a quarter to nine. I left your suite just before five this morning. I think you're the one having a little trouble remembering." I laughed.

"Huh? Oh . . . I'm sorry, Jay. I guess you put me back to sleep before you left. Damn, I really need to be getting up anyway. Speak to me. What's on your mind, handsome?"

"Aahh, I like it when you call 'em like you see 'em," I teased.

"Always. I have to keep it real."

"Well, Ashlee, I just wanted to give you a call to let you know how much I really enjoyed spending time with you yesterday. I know we were both disappointed that we didn't get to take things on the physical level further than it went, but I believe that good things come to those who wait."

"Really? So am I correct to assume you feel we should wait?"

"Whoa, slow down there. Don't go putting words in my mouth that aren't there." I laughed. "I'm just saying that I like you. I see other times for getting closer in our future. I know you really wanted seafood last night and it didn't quite work out that way, so let me make it up to you. Come to my place for dinner. I'll cook up my specialty chicken and pasta. How does that sound?"

"You, cooking? I don't know. Sounds kind of dangerous to me." We both laughed. She continued. "Are you serious? You'd like to cook for me?"

"Sure would. What have you got to lose?" I asked just before quickly interrupting her response. "Uh . . . don't answer that." We laughed. "Scratch what I just said. Seriously, I'd be honored to cook a meal for you, Ms. Ashlee Anderson, and do anything else you might want me to do too."

I could sense a smile in her voice. "Well, since you put it so nicely, I suppose I could put a little trust in you. I'll also remember to bring a bottle of Pepto-Bismol, just in case of an emergency."

We laughed and talked a bit more before I hung up to go grocery shopping. Ms. Ashlee Anderson was in for a treat. Oh, and I made certain to put condoms and vanilla ice cream on the shopping list.

CHAPTER 6

Ashlee

Sighing heavily, I gave up on searching the hotel room for my earring. I'd looked everywhere I thought my gold hoop could've been. Oh well, I stretched across the sofa in my white boy shorts and turned on the television. I smiled reminiscing about how Jay had made me come last night. I didn't think I could have an orgasm like that with anyone other than Darius. And maybe Jay didn't get his last night, but tonight I was gonna make it up to him in more ways than one. I was going to make him come like fireworks on the Fourth of July. God, I felt like a schoolgirl again. Was I falling in love? No, not love, but I was definitely in like with Mr. Jay Crawford.

I'd only been in love once, but the feelings being in love brought were at times overwhelming. When I was in love, I soared high on a high so high I never wanted to come down. There was a dance in my step—damn near skip, hop—and my heart jumped with joy at the mere thought of him. There was a smile underneath my smile. A loyalty that men envied because no matter how hard they tried to penetrate that sacred barrier, I refused them, each one, every time, staying faithful to my man. Unfortunately, the man I loved was no longer in love with me; otherwise, I'd be married to him by now. I wanted so badly to be somebody's, but not just anybody's, wife.

I motioned with my lips, "Move on, girl. You've got it bad," then thought about Jay. I could fall hard for Jay. I could love him. And I know he wouldn't let me hurt myself, because I felt secure with his touch. His voice. The way he exhaled my name . . . Ash-lee, into the air. Jay was sensitive too. I liked masculine men with a little sensitivity. Not only did Jay call me; he actually offered to cook on our second date. Now, Jay is a real man. Part of the real reason I decided to see Jay was to keep myself from obsessing over Darius. I glanced at my cell phone on the coffee table.

Don't do it.

Whenever I wasn't talking to Darius, which was all the time nowadays, the smallest thing would trigger my memory, causing me to think about him, especially when I had idle time.

Don't do it.

Slowly, my head rotated side to side. Then faster, and even faster, wobbling my cheeks until I'd become dizzy. I grabbed my ears and screamed, "Stop it, Ashlee! Just stop it right now! Darius is out of your life! He doesn't love you anymore! He's going to marry Fancy!

"Over his dead body," I whispered.

Why'd I say that? I didn't mean that. Seeing Darius happy with anyone else other than me drove me crazy. Maybe I could be happy with Jay? I thought so. Why not? The knots in my stomach intensified my confusion.

My knees dropped to the carpet between the sofa

and the coffee table. My palms slid from my ears to my cheeks. Cupping my face, I collapsed into a ball. Tears streamed between my fingers, drenching my knees, then wetting the carpet as I moped about the love I'd lost.

"Get your shit together!"

Bracing myself, one hand on the sofa, the other on the coffee table, I stood in the middle of the floor sniffling. "Stop it, Ashlee," I whispered but wasn't convinced. "It really wasn't your fault." I slid my forearm under my nose, then swiped the snot on the back of my boy shorts, barely missing wiping my ass.

Why me? Why did he have to use me?

I deserved for Darius to treat me better, but clearly I realized that I shouldn't measure Jay to Darius, I thought, momentarily closing my eyes. As I inhaled long and slow, the rosy fragrance helped calm my nerves. Jay was selfless enough to treat me the way I wanted a man to treat me. With respect. Respect was always a good place to start. I smiled, picturing Jay in the kitchen wearing an apron. I laughed. Naw, Jay would never wear a silly apron.

Lowering the thermostat to sixty-five, I turned on the CD player and started running water for a shower. I'd kept Jay's scent on me long enough. Retrieving the golden bottle from my purse, I downed two tablets with water and stepped into the shower. The meds did make me feel better. It was the side effects that freaked me out. Memory loss. Severe mood swings. Blackouts.

Lathering my body, I repeated ten times, "Let Jay love you more than you love him."

I dried off, saturated my body with peach-scented body oil mixed with Nivea Skin Firming lotion, then slipped into a red-hot teddy, low-rise lace see-through matching slacks, and stepped into my sexiest clear-heeled open-toe stilettos. All for Jay, since he liked the color red. Gathering my hair into a ponytail, I lined my lips, slid a stroke of cherry shimmering gloss at the bottom, then meshed my lips together. I wanted Jay to focus on picturing my lips on his dick. Men were so visual and easy to please. I knew all the right things to do to get one. Finding and keeping the right one was my problem.

I packed my belongings in my suitcases, doubled-checked the bathroom, bedroom, and living room, to make certain I wasn't leaving anything. One last attempt to find my gold hoop earring, but unfortunately I didn't.

On my way out the door, I smiled. Skipped. "I'm going to see my new man," I cheered on the empty elevator, admiring myself in the mirror. Arriving at the checkout desk, I slid the room key to the receptionist. "Ashlee Anderson. Checking out. Oh, and if housekeeping finds a gold hoop earring, please make sure it's returned to this address," I said, placing my driver's license in front of the receptionist.

"Certainly, Mrs. Anderson," she said, motioning to the bellman to take my bags.

Heading toward the valet desk, I didn't bother correcting her on the Mrs. part. I stopped at the valet and asked, "May I have my ride?" handing the ticket to the attendant.

The okay-looking man responded to my breasts, "Certainly."

Waiting for him to return, I hummed, "Can't nobody love me better than you," while tapping my foot, then continued my groove. "The way you wrap your arms around me . . ." By the time my car rolled up, I was dancing.

Opening my door, the valet placed my luggage in the trunk, then said, "Drive safely, Ms. Anderson," as he slowly closed my door.

Seductively, I replied, "Thanks, love," anxiously driving away to get to Jay's house. A woman never tips a man under any circumstances. And a real man never takes money from a woman. Observing the street signs, I was in the southeast quad of D.C., so I pulled over and telephoned Jay.

"Hey—"

"Hi, handsome. I think I'm confused. What's your address again?"

"I live in . . . Ash-lee, I can come . . ." Jay paused, then said, "And get you, if you'd like."

"Naw, I'ma get you tonight. Just give me directions."

"For starters, I live in Alexandria, not D.C.—"

"Alex who?"

"Near the Pentagon Mall."

"Aw, I don't know why I assumed you lived in chocolate city," I said, nodding. "I got you. I'm on my way."

I hated the fact that D.C. had four quadrants with the exact same addresses and the only difference was the combination of north, south, east, and west. Once I found the freeway, I made it to Jay's house within twenty minutes. As I was raising my hand to ring the bell, Jay opened his front door.

"Hey, lady. Damn!" He stepped closer, sniffing up my neck. "Peaches! You know, I love fruit. You smell edible, woman," he said, leading me into his place.

Immaculate for a bachelor, I thought, glancing around the living room. "You just cleaned up, didn't you? I bet if I opened the closet, all of your stuff would fall out."

His body embraced mine, and then he tackled me to the Persian rug. Jay lay on top of me silently staring, then said, "You are so damn sexy. I want you to enjoy dinner because I can't wait for my dessert." His lips gently surrounded mine.

Vanishing into his embrace, I asked, "Can we skip dinner?" I wrapped my arms around Jay and held him, not wanting to let go.

"I'm not giving it up that easy, woman. Have a seat at the dinner table." Jay raced into the kitchen, then returned with two glasses of champagne.

Using my better judgment, I set the champagne aside.

The table was preset with fresh white roses, place mats, silverware, and china. When Jay uncovered the dishes, grilled salmon, red potatoes, and broccoli sat before us. "Wow, I'm impressed. You prepared this?"

Piercing into my eyes, he lifted his eyebrows as his head lowered.

"Okay, okay," I said, smiling while sampling the salmon. "Um, this is really good," I mumbled, then asked, "Didn't you say you just got divorced? Why'd she let you go?"

Jay choked on air. "Not tonight. Tonight is only about us. Besides, I don't like reliving the exes with the nextes. You sistas take everything personally."

Nodding, I said, "You're right," thinking how Darius used to be more than my lover; he was my friend since I was ten years old. And every time I talked about Darius, men instantly knew I was hopelessly in love. And I honestly didn't want to discuss Darius, so I didn't know why I asked Jay about his exes in the first place. We ate, joked, and laughed for almost an hour.

"What's for dessert?" I asked, removing the plates from the table so I had an excuse to see his kitchen. Whoa, to my surprise all the dishes were washed. The stove was clean too. Jay was definitely a keeper.

"Dessert is in the bedroom," Jay said, escorting me out of the kitchen.

Entering Jay's bedroom, I glanced around. Two burning vanilla-scented candles. An iridescent lightbulb in one lamp, red in the other. I had to smile again as I unbuttoned one of his buttons, then kissed Jay's chest. Unfastened another and licked his nipple. A third button unlatched and I teased his navel. Quickly Jay removed his shirt, pants, socks, underwear, and jumped into the bed underneath the red satin sheet. He clamped his hands behind his head, admiring my body.

"Damn, what's the ru—"

"Hush. Now slowly take off your pants, and then model your lace teddy for me."

I did as Jay asked, easing out of my slacks, bending over so he could see my ass. Then I pranced from one side of the bed to the other.

"Now unleash your ponytail and swing your hair."

I did. Not too fast. Not too slow, whirling my hair into a seductive mess.

"Now unsnap your crotch. Then crawl on top of me. I want to look at you."

When I pulled back the sheets, Jay's dick sprang forward. I still couldn't believe the size of that thing.

"This is all for you, Ashlee."

This what? I thought. *You and your dick or just the backed-up come in your balls?* "When did you have time to put on a condom?"

"That's not what you really want to know, Ashlee. Is it?"

I straddled Jay's stomach. Leaning forward, I caressed his head and kissed his lips. Jay placed his hands on my hips, raising me into the air, then lowered me onto his bulging head.

Using my knees, I braced and then paced myself, inching down his shaft. The penetration was slightly painful, so breathing deeply I took my time, but I hadn't had any real sex in forever, so I was determined to take in as much as I could.

"Damn, your pussy is so tight. I love this shit. No, don't squeeze. She's tight enough. You gon' fuck around and make me come."

Rocking back and forth, I moaned, "Oh, Jay. You feel so good," repeatedly. "But she's not squeezing you. I haven't been with a man in over a year. Oh, Jay, you feel sooo good."

"Ashlee, be quiet. You gon' fuck around and make me, damn, come with me, Ashlee. I gotta get this first nut out of the way so I can . . . come with me!" Jay groaned. His eyes rolled to the top of his head.

"Not yet, Daddy. A few more minutes," I pleaded, rocking on my spot, trying to come with Jay. Jay didn't disappoint. After he got his first nut, minutes turned into hours and once again my ass was worn out. This time my pussy was sore from all the friction of six different positions, but I didn't give a damn. My man did me right. Jay had come twice and me, well, I'd lost count. Afterward, Jay dozed off as we cuddled for an hour.

CHAPTER 7

Jay

The annoying sound of my alarm wailed like a banshee, startling both Ashlee and me. I threw a pillow at it, sighing in relief when the screeching sound somehow came to a halt. Although she appeared to be half asleep, Ashlee slid closer to me, burying her face in my chest and throwing her leg over my hip in an attempt to pin me to the bed. It was obvious she didn't want me to move, and believe me, the feeling was mutual. I was truly at peace, happy for the first time since I came to D.C. Unfortunately I had an eight o'-clock meeting with my new boss, so whether I wanted to or not I had to get up. I stroked Ashlee's hair, then kissed her forehead. I couldn't help running my hand down her side, then over her smooth bare ass. It was amazing that she looked just as sexy in the morning as she did when we finally went to sleep sometime around midnight last night. I caressed her ass again and she purred like a cat, exciting the hell out of me. The thought of making love to her one more time before I left for work weighed heavily on my mind. The only problem was it would have to be a quickie and I wasn't sure if someone as classy as Ashlee would be a quickie kind of girl.

"Jay, I can't begin to tell you how happy you've made me," she purred again, breaking our silence.

I looked down at her face and she stared at me with those big beautiful eyes. She kissed my lips, gently sliding her tongue into my mouth as she pulled me closer. Obviously a quickie was not going to be a problem. I reached for a condom, then slid on top of her. Ashlee abruptly broke our kiss with a frown.

"What's wrong?"

"I was about to ask you the same thing. What's the rush?"

Ah, maybe a quickie wasn't such a good idea, I told myself as I said, "I've gotta leave for work in about thirty minutes."

"Baby, I hate the idea of rushing to make love." She looked so sad as she said it.

"Hey, no problem. We'll just wait till I get home. Give me something to look forward to while I'm at work. And, girl, you sure got something to look forward to." I slapped her ass playfully, then smiled, making her blush, but it didn't take long for her frown to take over her face again. "Now what's wrong, you don't like that idea?"

"No, it sounds real good. The only problem is I won't be here when you get home from work. I'm going to be heading back to Dallas this afternoon," she answered soberly.

"What? So soon? I mean, why didn't you tell me this last night?" A bit stunned, I pulled myself a few inches away from her. I wasn't sure whether to be angry or sad. She'd really caught me off guard. I couldn't believe my ears.

Ashlee looked a little taken aback as she sat up to

face me. "Why? Would it have made a difference if I did? We'd still be right here where we are now, wouldn't we? Or would you have said no to this and kicked me out?"

"Yeah. I mean . . . well . . . um . . . no." I was dumb-founded and it took a few seconds to get my shit back together. "What I was trying to say was I feel like we haven't spent enough time together. I mean . . . I really enjoyed last night, but I wanna get to know you too. It's not just about the sex, Ashlee. And that doesn't happen very often with me."

She smiled, probably surprised by my honesty. "I feel the same way, Jay, but I need to get back—"

I cut her off. "I understand that, but does it have to be today? You can stay another day if you want to. I am worth it. Aren't I?"

She kissed me again. "I'm sorry, Jay, but I have a nonrefundable ticket and an appointment I can't miss. But this doesn't mean I won't be back. I like you, Jay, more than you may even think."

I couldn't believe how fast my heart was beating. What the hell was wrong with me? I was crushed. My stomach was starting to hurt. I felt like we were break-ing up after a long-term relationship. Ashlee pulled my arm around her as she nestled her head on my chest. The room fell silent. Even though I knew she had to go, I kept trying to think of things that would help change her mind. I was definitely into Ashlee, but it was time to start distancing myself from her be-fore things went too far and I couldn't turn back.

"Jay . . ." Ashlee looked as if she was fishing for the right words to settle my uneasiness. Then out of nowhere she gave me this devilish grin as if a light-bulb had just gone off in her head. "Why don't you just take the day off? My plane doesn't leave till four this afternoon. We can sleep in and make love the entire afternoon. I'll even make you breakfast in bed. What do you say?" She kept on grinning.

I wanted to say yes, bad. Matter of fact, I was about to say yes, but eventually reality set in. If I didn't show up to work today I might as well not show up tomorrow or the day after that. "I can't. I have a meeting at eight this morning that I can't miss."

Ashlee moved my arm, then removed her leg from my hip with a pout. "I guess I'm the one who's not worth it."

She stared at me sadly for a bit, then lowered her head onto the pillow. She'd just spanked me with my own words. I had no clue how to respond to that, so I kissed her forehead, then headed for the shower. Once I reached the bathroom door, I turned back toward Ashlee as she slid down to pull the covers over her shoulders. She looked like an angel as she closed her eyes and went back to sleep.

While I was in the shower, my mind was consumed with thoughts of Ashlee. I wondered what type of life we could have together. After being with her last night, I knew I wanted more. I needed more from her. As the hot water caressed my head and ran down my face, I pictured Ashlee's naked body in front of me. From her succulent breasts to her luscious pussy, I longed for her. From her sweet-smelling scent to her soft, glowing skin, I craved her. My dick got hard as I reminisced on how she straddled me and made me shoot a bullet as I came so fast. As I continued to recall my night with Ashlee, the water began turning cold, snapping me back into reality.

When I finished my shower and got dressed, Ashlee was sound asleep, so I sat on the bed next to her and gently shook her. "Hey, beautiful, I'm on my way out."

Ashlee sat up quickly in a panic. "Oh, I'm sorry. I'm getting up."

I pressed Ashlee's shoulders, forcing her to lie back down. "Nuh. You don't have to leave now. Sleep as long as you like, then let yourself out. Just remember to lock the door on your way out."

"Are you sure, Jay? I can just get up now if—"

"Shhh. No, Ashlee. You're fine. What time does your flight leave again?"

"Quarter to four."

"Would you like me to give you a wake-up call?"

"That'll be nice because I need to return the rental car."

"Aw'ight, then, I'll call you after lunch. Now get some sleep."

She smiled and my heart melted. I still couldn't believe our time together was being cut so short. She sat up in bed and gave me a warm embrace. We touched our lips together, but that was it for a good-bye kiss. I think we both felt a long passionate kiss would only make us more despondent. I wanted to stay wrapped in her arms forever, but I knew I needed to go.

Once I got to work, I couldn't focus. I felt like I was losing someone very special, and there was nothing I could do about it. I called her to make certain she was awake. Hearing her sweet voice left me pining for her. The whole day was a loss because I didn't accomplish a thing, and to make matters worse my boss postponed our meeting. All I could think about was speaking to Ashlee again. After returning from lunch, I called her to make sure she had arrived in Dallas safely. I got her voice mail on the first ring.

"Hi. You've reached the number you've dialed, so leave a detailed message for the person behind the voice you've reached," the recording said.

Ashlee's voice could make a man come all over himself. I decided to leave a message. "Hey, sexy. Just checking to make sure you made it back safely. Give me a call as *soon* as you get this message. If you get it once you land, that's the *soon* I'm talking about. In case you can't tell, I'm missing you already. Get back at me. Peace."

I looked at my watch and realized Dallas is on Central Standard Time and Ashlee's plane might not have landed yet. Anxiety had me getting way ahead of myself.

I tried to reach Ashlee again just before leaving work. Her voice mail still picked up on the first ring. I began to worry because she should have made it back home. I left her another message, then contemplated calling the airport to see what flights had been delayed. I quickly dismissed that thought once I remembered I didn't know what airline Ashlee had flown out on. I couldn't clear my mind, so I wrapped up for the day.

I tried to call Ashlee on the drive home, but once again I was greeted by her voice mail. I felt sick that I hadn't spoken with her since she left. I popped in a mixed rap CD, trying to steer my thoughts in another direction. I turned up the volume and jammed all the way home through the thick rush-hour traffic. I made it to my place around six-thirty.

After I'd shut off the ignition, a sudden silence reminded me that Ashlee was gone. The empty spot where her rental car was parked when I left was further confirmation she wasn't there. I got out of the car and headed to my door. I got ready to stick the key in, but I didn't have to because the door was ajar. *Damn. You trust people to lock up and secure your place as they leave, but this is what happens instead,* I thought. I sighed and headed in the house.

I noticed something was different. The lights were off, and there were several candles lit all over the place. Various aromas were flowing freely, teasing my nose and altering my mood into something mellow. I closed the door and set my keys down. Just then, Ashlee appeared from the kitchen, dressed in a black and white French maid's uniform. She had on a pair of pasties and a bow tie on the upper part of her body. I was pleasantly surprised for more than one reason: I was happy to see her there, and she made great eye candy standing seductively in that French maid's uniform. Her hair was pulled up, and she wore the clear-heeled open-toe stilettos I'd seen her in the night before. I couldn't help drooling as I spoke.

"Ashlee, what are you doing here? Your car isn't out there. What happened?"

"I returned it, then caught a cab back to your place," she said, staring at me.

I panicked. "So you left my crib unlocked?"

"No, silly. You're different than most people . . . you leave a key hanging in the kitchen, labeled *spare key*." She smiled.

I slapped my forehead, then shook my finger at her. "Ah, but you still left the door ajar just now."

"Oops. My bad," she said. We both laughed. Ashlee started toward me, and I swear I never witnessed anyone glide the way she did. "I thought about what you said. I couldn't leave just yet," she responded, taking my tie off.

"And what did I say?"

She kissed my lips, then my neck. "You said you felt we haven't spent enough time together, and that you wanted to get to know me."

"True. We haven't," I responded, looking over her shoulder, sniffing. "And I don't know you." I sniffed again. "Mmm, do I smell food?"

Ashlee began unbuttoning my shirt. "Yes. I cooked oriental chicken over rice with steamed asparagus and buttered rolls," she said in short breaths between kissing and licking my nipples.

"Lady, you have on a French maid's uniform, but you cooked an oriental dish?"

"Yes, and one doesn't have anything to do with the other. Dinner is for your feasting appetite, and this costume is for your sexual appetite. I was hoping we could do dinner last. I'm kinda hungry for something else."

Ashlee squatted, then unbuckled my belt. I became so excited, I began dripping in my drawers before she could pull my dick out. "Wait a minute, Ashlee. Hold on. I need to get myself together here. I just got off work."

"So? And?" she asked, biting on my briefs.

I could feel Ashlee's warm breath through my underwear. She massaged my balls as she licked between my thighs. I sighed, "Oooohhh, shiiiittt." My knees buckled, and I could hardly stand there. "So, and I think I need to shower," I managed to say.

Ashlee got up and headed over to her purse on the coffee table. As I watched her walk away, I noticed her French maid's costume wasn't much of a uniform at all. Not only did she wear pasties, but she also had on a black thong. The apron only shielded her front side.

I couldn't see what Ashlee was doing at first, but then she turned and allured me over with a slow-motion finger. Once I got close to her, she told me to sit down on the couch. I sat and watched her open a condom and then pour a lubricant inside. I was confused.

"Why are you doing that?" I questioned.

"You'll see." Ashlee kept her eyes on the lubricant.

I asked her to turn around, and when she did, I saw her firm ass smiling at me. I smacked her bottom, then untied the apron string. She turned to face me, and I pulled her pussy into my face. I didn't bother to remove the thong because it really wasn't in my way. She tasted so damned good, I could've sucked her juices all night.

She slid the condom on me, then straddled me the way she had before. I gripped her hips and swirled her bottom in swift repeated motions. Either my dick was getting harder or the lubricant was doing something to the condom to make it warmer and tighter. She sat up straight with her eyes closed, moaning and pulling the pasties off her tits, as I forced her to take all of me. The many positions we did before must've loosened her up. She seemed to be enjoying every inch of my big, thick dick inside her.

She opened her eyes, then leaned forward to place one of her breasts in my mouth. "You hungry, Daddy?"

I nodded, then sucked each breast hard as she fed them to me one by one, and then both at the same time. I enjoyed every minute of being smothered by her full, firm breasts. The pasties had left something fruity-tasting around her nipples, leaving them savory sweet. She began to bounce her bottom in sync with the way I swirled her hips. When my moans became louder than hers did, I knew it was time for a new position or else I would come before I was ready.

"Hold on, baby," I said, just before standing, holding my hands under her ass.

I used her ass to make her rock back and forth on my dick in a rapid, nonstop session. She gripped my neck and screamed in my ear, "Aaaahhh. Don't stop, Jay. Please don't stop."

When I felt her pussy getting hotter, I knew she was almost there, and so was I. It was hard to hold her up when she reached her climax, but I didn't stop. She trembled until the very end, even as I released into the condom. By this time, she had one leg still wrapped around me and was standing on her toes with the other foot. I was too weak to hold her up, and she couldn't do anything to help herself either.

After the first round, we had worked up a serious appetite. We ate, then fucked some more. I'm sure she was just as sore as I was by the time we were done. We cuddled and drifted off to sleep.

I was awakened when I heard Ashlee fumbling around.

"What are you doing?" I asked.

"Oh, baby, I didn't mean to wake you. I just got out of the shower, and I'm packing."

"Packing? For what? It's ten o'clock. Where are you going?"

"To the airport. I changed my flight so I could catch the red-eye. I felt like I had left you hanging this morning, so I rearranged my flight to spend more time with you."

I was impressed. I sat up in bed. "Com'ere."

She walked over and sat on the bed with me. I reached under her chin and pulled her face to me, then kissed her. I gazed into her eyes and again wondered what I could say to make her stay.

"Jay, please don't."

"Don't what?"

"Make me feel guilty again. You're everything I could want in a man, and I've enjoyed every minute of my stay here, but it's time for me to go home."

"There's still so much I want to know about you."

"Okay, I have a few minutes. Let's spend a little time getting to know each other. You go first."

"Okay. I'm Jay Crawford. I'm divorced, and I'm a social worker." I smiled.

"All right. I'm Ashlee Anderson. I'm single and I'm in between careers."

"Wait. That's not telling me anything, Ash—"

The doorbell interrupted me. Ashlee jumped up. "Sorry, Jay. That's my limo to the airport."

I got out of bed and put on my robe to follow her to the door. "Ashlee, we haven't finished talking."

She opened the door to tell the driver she was on her way out. She turned and responded to me, "I know, sweetheart. I won't wake you tonight, but I promise to call you in the morning."

"I've got one better for you. How about I see you this weekend?"

"Jay, I can't—"

"I'll come to you. That is, if you don't mind a little company this weekend."

Ashlee flashed me that sweet smile. "I'd love it, Jay," she said, stepping to me.

"Have you ever been to Dallas?" she asked.

"Just to see the Cowboys," I replied.

"Well, now you have something even better to see."

"Amen to that," I whispered.

Ashlee made sure to plant the kiss on me that would leave me yearning for more. I stood in the door and watched until I couldn't see her limo anymore. Before going back to bed, I blew out all the candles and got on the Internet to book my flight.

Ashlee had done it to me again. She left me intoxicated with thoughts of her. She managed to take my heart all the way to Texas when she left, but that was okay. The weekend was only days away, and I would be in Dallas to reclaim what was mine—a sexy red woman by the name of Ashlee Anderson.

CHAPTER 8

Ashlee

J ay was the best thing that'd happened to me in a long, long time, but I was trying my damnedest not to get caught up. The energy surrounding my heart pressed against my chest, beckoning me to rip my boarding pass in half and haul ass in my red stilettos all the way back to Jay's place. As I ushered my ticket toward the opening, the machine snatched it and then spat out my stub. Boarding the red-eye flight, I took my seat in first class. I could really fall in love with Mr. Crawford.

Ashlee Crawford, no, hyphenated Anderson. I could get used to that.

My thoughts drifted as I reminisced about how eager and how easy Jay was to please and be pleased. We got along from the start. No awkward moments. Our comfort level was that of old friends happily re-uniting.

Propping the pillow against the window, I closed my eyes. I'd handled that Nikki girl pretty well but sure as hell hoped she didn't resurface in my man's life later. One of many things I'd learned the hard way from Darius was that a man could fuck a woman and then pretend he didn't know her at all.

As I thought about Jay, my lips curled almost into a U. Although Jay was a wonderful chef, I wanted to cook every day for him and welcome him home after a hard day's work in my French maid outfit, my birthday suit, or surprise him. As long as Jay never cheated on me, I knew exactly how to please him, tease him, and never let him get bored. I could work from home and raise our three babies. With Jay's features and my beauty, we'd have exotic-looking supermodel kids.

I wasn't attached to my life in Dallas, but I did have some unfinished business. Deplaning at Dallas/ Ft. Worth, I retrieved my car from long-term parking. I know I told Jay I'd call him in the morning, but the voice mail he'd left when he thought I'd left D.C. earlier, echoed "Hey, sexy . . . Give me a call as *soon* as you get this message. If you get it once you land, that's the *soon* I'm talking about," so I decided to give him a jingle.

When Jay sleepily answered, I positioned my lips on the receiver. In my sexiest voice, slowly I exhaled, "Hey, lovely. I thought about you all the way home. Don't want to wake you, I'm pulling into my garage."

"Thanks for calling, woman. I still smell your scent in my sheets."

"Really? Well, I can still taste your seeds."

He chuckled and I blushed.

"God, I can't wait to see you again. Are you really coming this weekend?"

"I'll be there. You just make sure you're there to pick me up."

"Don't worry," I whispered. "I'll be there."

"I have a surprise for you when I see you."

"Jay?"

"Yeah, Ash?"

"Don't spoil me if this is just temporary. I don't know what I'd do if you broke my heart." I was barely hangin' on to my sanity as it was. "I'll call you, later," I said, then quietly hung up when Jay didn't respond. It was time for me to get back to life, back to my reality.

Entering my home, I found everything nice and neat as I'd left it, except several glasses in the sink, which meant my dad had stopped by while I was away. I'm glad I got in late because with all my drama, I'm sure my nosy, stay-at-home neighbors were wondering where I'd disappeared to for days.

Looking around my living room, I noticed a slit in the mauve wallpaper where I'd thrown the knife like a dart. The same knife I'd contemplated committing suicide with weeks ago. I'd have the wall repaired before Jay arrived this weekend. I was so excited to have him visiting I couldn't sleep, so I filled my Jacuzzi with steamy water, poured a glass of red wine, then laughed thinking about Jay's lucky shirt.

Twisting the white cap off the yellow bottle, I flushed the remaining antidepressants down the toilet. "No more," I whispered. "It's time for me to get back to being normal. I didn't need medication before Darius and I don't have to take it now that he's gone."

Walking into my son's bedroom, I thought, how was I going to explain this to Jay? Little Darius's toys, crib, playpen, clothes, Spider-Man border clearly said I had a child. As I shook my baby's rattler, a lump formed in my throat, so I placed it back on his dresser.

"Let me get out of here," I said, closing the door. Maybe I could somehow lock his room, or this would be a chance to see if I could trust Jay. I could simply ask him not to open the door.

Tossing my clothes onto my extra-high bed, I stood naked in the middle of the floor.

Don't do it.

There was that haunting voice in my head. Would I ever be my old self again? Happy. Loving. Innocent. My innocence was taken away by Darius, but Jay had certainly made me feel more than lovely. Jay made me feel special.

Don't do it.

Desperately I wanted to call Darius and curse his ass out for having told me, "Maybe if you would've loved yourself more and me less we wouldn't have to have this conversation." He always had a way of making me feel our problems were my fault. Picking up my cell, I speed-dialed my dad.

Sleepily, he answered, "Hey, sweetheart, where are you? How come you haven't returned my calls?"

"I'm home, Daddy. I'm safe. Go back to bed, I'll call you after my appointment."

"That's right. I'll be over early to take you."

"I don't want you babysitting me. I'll be gone before you get here. Let yourself in. Love you, good night."

Actually it was already morning. The sunrays peeped through the skylight over my Jacuzzi. As I eased into the lukewarm water, fond thoughts of Jay brought a smile to my face. Where was I going to take him? I'd barely spent much time around Dallas since I'd relocated from Los Angeles about a year ago. I'd think of something, but for now I had to focus on my psychiatric appointment in a few hours. In addition to my losing custody of my son, my court-ordered sessions with the shrink were the real reason I had to return home.

Damn social worker deemed me an unfit mother. I'll show her. "I'll show her," I said aloud the second time as tears streamed down my face.

I wiped my eyes with wet palms covering my cheeks.

Sliding under the water, I stayed there until I could no longer hold my breath. How was my baby doing? I wanted to touch him, hold him, smell him, change his diaper, rock him in my arms. Little Darius was barely eight months old.

"Fuck!" I screamed, stepping out of the tub. "Why did his father have to win custody?" My baby was the only person who loved me unconditionally. Now he was growing up with him. With them.

I wouldn't hear his first words. Wouldn't see him take his first steps. Worst of all, he'd lie at another woman's breasts calling her mommy, not me.

My three-bedroom house was too quiet. Picking up my phone, I dialed the number 1 then pressed 0 but couldn't hit the TALK button.

Put down the phone, Ashlee. He doesn't need to hear your problems. But I needed to hear his soothing voice, so I tapped the green button.

"Hey," Jay answered on the first ring, "I see you're missing me too."

I tried to calm my voice, but it trembled as I said, "You have no idea how much I," choking out the next two words, "miss you."

"Ash, what's wrong?" Jay asked.

I heard the smile in his voice instantly shift to concern. "I'll be okay. Jay, can you please come a day earlier? I need my rescuer."

Without hesitation, Jay replied, "You don't have to ask twice. I'll be on the next thing smoking Friday morning."

"Thanks. Good morning," I said, watching the sun light up my bedroom. "E-mail me a copy of your itinerary."

"No problem." There was silence for a second and I was about to speak when Jay cut me off.

"Um, Ashlee . . . I don't now how to say this but I think I'm . . ." he stopped himself.

"You're what, Jay?"

"Nothing. I was just thinking out loud."

"So if it's nothing, then tell me what it was."

"Like I said, it was nothing. I'll talk to you later, okay?"

"Okay, baby. Bye."

"Bye, hon."

Amazingly within a few minutes, Jay had lifted my spirits. And I think he was about to say those magic words. I think he was about to tell me he loved me. Hanging up the phone, I cradled myself into the fetal position thinking every woman wasn't born for motherhood. How could anyone believe that being a single parent was instinctive behavior? If I had more support, I wouldn't have done stupid things like leaving my son in the car overnight chasing behind Darius, or leaving my baby alone in a running car to go back inside to get medication that I was mentally addicted to, or covering his tiny face with a blanket to drown out his incessant crying. Perhaps I should leave well enough alone, skip my appointment, grant Darius full legal and physical custody permanently, and start over with Jay.

With Jay by my side, I could find the strength to fight my battle. Any battle. Dozing off, I mumbled, "I love you, Jay Crawford."

"Get up," a voice whispered in my ear.

Resisting, I pulled the pink comforter over my head.

"Ashlee, get up, now. You have to go to your appointment."

Lowering the spread below my chin, I said, "Daddy, I thought I asked you not to come."

"That's exactly why I'm here. Now get dressed so we can go."

Quietly I brushed my damp hair into a ponytail, eased into a pair of blue jeans, sneakers, and a form-fitting T-shirt while my dad waited in the living room.

Not looking up from the paper, he said, "Go change into something casual but dressy."

There was no need to argue with an attorney. Obviously this court-appointed degree-holding psychic would judge me on some level by my appearance. Changing into a pair of brown slacks, a mocha-striped button-up shirt, and mocha medium-heel shoes, I awaited his approval.

Placing the paper on the coffee table, he stood, opened his arms, and said, "Come here."

Our words were exchanged through a long embrace. "I'm worried about you, sweetheart."

"Don't be," I said, knowing that I was worried about me too. "I'll be fine. I met a wonderful man in D.C. and I want you to meet him too."

En route to my appointment, Dad tried to sound happy for me. "That's great. Another man, huh? Tell me about him."

"He makes me feel good. I like him a lot. A whole lot. He'll be here this weekend."

"Well, any man that excites my little girl that much, I can't wait to meet." Daddy's words were exactly what I needed to hear, but the look he gave me was all skepticism.

CHAPTER 9

Jay

I parked my BMW in long-term parking at Reagan National Airport. Happy as shit that within hours I'd be in Dallas making love to Ashlee. Even though we spoke every night until two, at three o'clock in the morning I still missed her more and more each day. I'd had it bad for some women in the past, but only one had ever had my nose wider opened than Ashlee had mine now. Yeah, I really had it bad, but I think she had it pretty bad for me too, especially after the call we had earlier in the week. Her tone was sad, almost as if she needed me to be there, right then and there. When she asked that I fly to Dallas a day early, I could sense something wasn't right with her. Ashlee had left my house with a sense of urgency to get back home, but once she was there, her calls sounded as if home was the last place she wanted to be. Then again maybe she was just missing the hell out of me. I shook my daydream, then got back in line for screening.

My gate wasn't far once I got out of the screening

line, so I didn't have to rush. When I arrived I took a seat in the waiting area at my gate. Of course my thoughts were still focused on Ashlee, that is, until my phone rang. Glancing down at the caller ID, I smiled at the name that came up. It was Kyle, one of my three best friends of over thirty years.

I quickly connected the call with a grin. "What's up, dawg?"

"You got it," Kyle replied in his very New York accent. "Me and Wil are headed down to D.C. this weekend and we're staying at your place so don't make any plans."

I sighed my disappointment. "No can do, chief. I'm at the airport on my way to Dallas as we speak. My flight leaves in about thirty-five minutes."

"Dallas? What you going down there for? It's not like the Cowboys are playing at home this week. They're playing in D.C., aren't they?" Everyone close to me knew I was a fanatic about the Dallas Cowboys. It cost me almost three hundred dollars a month to get the NFL package on cable just so I could see all their games.

"Look, man, I'm sorry but I'm gonna have to catch the game on TV down there. You're not gonna believe this but I think I've found the one."

"Jeeeezus, where have I heard that before?" His voice was starting to sound a little agitated and condescending. "Look, Jay, you don't wanna get on that plane, trust me."

"Kyle, you have no idea what I have waiting for me in Dallas. No way I'm missing this plane. Unless you know for a fact it's falling out of the sky."

"No, I can't tell you that, but we did get you a sky-box for the Redskins–Cowboys game this weekend in D.C." A shot of adrenaline shot through my body. I'd actually tried to go online and buy two tickets to this

game when I moved to D.C., but I just couldn't jus-
tify paying more to see a regular season football game
than I pay for my rent and car note combined. Trying to get a ticket to a Redskins game in D.C. at regular price was like trying to hit the lottery, damn near
impossible.

"You serious?"

"Serious as a heart attack, bro. I know it's a few
months early, but happy birthday, Jay."

"How'd you guys get tickets?"

"Not tickets my friend, a skybox. Complete with
liquor, food, and the best seats in the house." I was
getting excited just listening to him. "So whoever she
is that you're going to meet in Dallas, you better tell
her you'll see her next weekend 'cause Wil had to
pull a lot of strings to make this happen."

I didn't know what to say. I was torn.

"Jay, you still there, buddy?"

"Yeah, I'm still here. But I can't go to the game,
man. You guys enjoy yourselves and stay at my apartment, aw'ight? Al's got a key to my place."

There was silence for about three seconds, and
then out of nowhere Kyle exploded. "Jay, what the
hell's going on? Are you in some kinda trouble?"

"No. I'm not in trouble," I quickly replied.

"So you mean to tell me that you're going to miss
a chance at going to a Cowboys, Redskins game just
to visit some skirt? The same football team you changed
your wedding date for because they were playing that
Saturday instead of Sunday?"

"You don't understand."

"Well, you've got thirty minutes before you get on
your plane. Make me understand."

"All I can say is I found her, Kyle. I finally found
the woman I'm going to spend the rest of my life
with and if I miss a football game, well then, so be it."

"Well then, I'm happy for you, bro. I know how bad you wanted to find Tracy."

"It's not Tracy."

"What do you mean it's not Tracy? I thought the entire reason you moved down to D.C. was that you needed to find your one true love, Tracy." Kyle's tone was now sarcastic. "I knew that Romeo and Juliet shit you tried to sell me on about Tracy was a load of crap."

"It wasn't crap, Kyle. I do love Tracy. I just couldn't find her and met somebody else."

"Jay, you're always meeting somebody else."

"Dawg, you don't understand, man. I done left my player ways behind me. I'm falling in love with this girl Ashlee."

"Make the right choice, dawg. We doing the sky-box up big. Hit me later. Peace." Kyle hung up after I didn't say anything.

He'd been against my moving to D.C. and leaving my two daughters behind in New York from the start. I sat back down and dialed Ashlee's number.

"Hey there, sexy," I said just after she answered.

You know, I wasn't even thinking when I said those things to Kyle, but now that I thought about them I really meant them. Don't get me wrong, I wasn't ready to get married or anything, but I wanted her to know that I cared and that this wasn't just a fling, that it had real possibilities. Truth is, I could see myself settling down with Ashlee. Hell, I'd even researched Dallas apartments and government job postings on the Net.

"Hey, handsome," she responded.

I could almost see her smile. Guilt hit me hard and I remembered something my old man once said. When a woman becomes more important than your friends, then you better marry her because she's your only true friend. Love was starting to hit me. "You on the plane yet?"

"No, but . . ."

"But what?"

I tried to get the words out but I couldn't do it. I could not tell her I wasn't coming to Dallas. Kyle was going to kill me, but I was just going to have to be dead because, once-in-a-lifetime experience or not, I was not going to hurt my Ashlee in any way.

"Baby, I'll be boarding my plane in about half an hour. You've been on my mind, and I couldn't resist hearing your voice before I got on the plane."

"You always know the right things to say, Jay. I'm glad you called. I've been thinking about us and what we'll do when you get here."

"You sound like that's a hard decision to make or something," I teased.

"No. I'm just not accustomed to going out here. I've been in Dallas for a year, but I never go out. I'm not familiar with the popular places to go."

"Sweetie, just let me sweat the small things. I've heard of a couple of nice places, but if we don't leave your house my entire visit, that's fine too. I just want to be with you again, Ashlee."

"Aw, that's sweet."

I could almost see her pretty smile behind her words. "That's only the half of it. I can't begin to tell you how much I've been missing you."

"You wanna try?" she asked.

"Well, first, let me ask you a question."

"Okay."

"Do you believe a man can love a woman even though he's spent more time on the phone with her than in person?"

"Yes. I believe it's possible, but I also believe a man

could be in lust at such an early stage of a relationship."

"Okay, but what if sex is no object for him? If he's good-looking, drives a BMW, and has a nice-paying job, he wouldn't have too many problems satisfying his lustful ways, right? Or, do you not agree?"

"I agree. So, what are you saying?"

"Ashlee, I'm saying what I feel for you is much more than lust. I fell out of lust the day you went out with me. On our first date, I learned there's more beneath the sexy frame I saw at Zanzibar."

"Oh, really?"

"Yeah. Do you remember what I said to you on the paddleboat?"

"We did a lot of talking that night, Jay. And you said a lot of things I'll always remember. "

"Well then, maybe you remember me telling you that I could love you. Do you remember that?"

"How could I forget? I thought it was one of the worst lines I'd ever heard."

"Yeah, well, it may have been a line then, but . . . well, Ashlee."

"Yes, Jay?"

"I, I, I love you," I finally spit it out as I waited, hoping, no, praying that I hadn't run her completely off.

"Wow . . . I don't know what to say," she replied.

There was silence on the line. Although she went silent, I swear I could hear a smile coming through the phone. I had no idea why I just said that, other than the fact that I'd probably just lost my mind, but I was glad I did. We just kind of held the phone, listening to each other breathe. I wondered if she could sense my smile coming through the phone or my heart slamming up against my chest like a mallet. I got butterflies when I heard the airline attendant announce that it was time for first class passengers to board.

"Ashlee, sweetie, I have to go. It's time for me to board the plane."

"All right. You get to me safely, Jay."

Uh-oh, she hadn't said it back. "Well, I'll certainly do my best."

"And, Jay."

"Yes."

"I love you too," she said just before hanging up the phone.

The butterflies in my stomach went wild and I knew I'd made the right decision.

CHAPTER 10

Ashlee

Pacing back and forth in Dallas/Ft. Worth's baggage claim area, I anxiously stared through the glass window at hundreds of faces exiting the plane. *No, that's not him*, I thought, continuously scanning. I exhaled, "That's not him either." Momentarily, I stepped away from the mass exodus to double-check the monitor. Jay's flight had arrived from Washington, D.C., fifteen minutes ago. "Shouldn't take him that long to get to me."

Impatiently, I moved closer to the glass wall, peering at the travelers on the other side exiting the arriving flight at gate A25, and waited. Butterflies fluttered inside my stomach. I was too excited to keep still, so I paced in front of the revolving door, periodically standing sideways to let everyone go by. "Where is he?" Opening my cell phone, I retrieved my incoming calls, scrolled down once, then dialed Jay's number.

Glancing at my caller ID, I saw that fifteen seconds

had gone by without any answer, so I spoke into my headset, "Hello?"

"Hey, beautiful," a seductive voice replied from behind me as a chocolate arm wrapped around my waist. "Can I take you home?"

Swiftly, I turned, dropping my phone into my purse. Jumping into Jay's arms, I smiled from the inside out, hugging his neck tight. "Jay, baby," was all I could say before he smothered my lips with kisses.

"Mmm, Ashlee, you just don't know . . . um, um . . . how much I missed you, girl."

Tears swelled, clouding my eyes until I blinked them onto my cheeks. "I'm messing up my mascara. I spent all day getting pretty for you, and now I'm making a mess of myself." Jay didn't know how good I felt with his arms around me. Shedding tears of joy, I wanted him to hold me forever and never let go, but I backed up to avoid getting makeup all over what might be his second favorite shirt.

"Don't you dare back away from me, woman," Jay commanded teasingly, pulling me closer to his chest.

"I don't want to mess up your shirt, baby."

"Forget this shirt. You don't know how much I've missed you." Jay's lips dried my tears, then smothered me with more kisses until my lipstick became his. I stepped back, this time to admire my man from head to toe: Almond-colored slacks, chestnut shoes, and a button-down long-sleeved shirt. A brown jacket was thrown over his forearm. For the first time, I noticed his black duffel bag lying beside his feet.

"Ashlee, you make me feel so good. Promise me you won't stop loving me."

"I promise to love you, Jay, but you have to make the same promise to me too."

"Woman, I could never stop lovin' you."

"I'm so glad you're here. You hungry?"

"Starved," Jay said, rubbing his stomach, then removing a bag of peanuts from his pocket. "Can you believe they think this is going to satisfy a brotha's appetite? They must be crazy. Get me to some real food."

"I have just the place in mind. Seafood, since we never made it to Legal. But I also cooked a little something to hold you until we get to the restaurant. Oh, and Club Fifth Avenue is another option if you want to hang out and have fun tonight. I've never been but heard they have karaoke, food, and speed dating, but you won't be needing that last part 'cause you're taken."

"Sounds aw'ight to me," Jay said, grabbing his other bag from the conveyor, "but can a brotha get to the crib and chill for a minute first?"

En route to my house, gusty winds and pouring raindrops the size of silver dollars appeared from nowhere. Turning on my windshield wipers, I glanced over in Jay's lap.

"Whatcha lookin' at, woman?"

Smiling I said, "My chocolate stick."

As he reclined his seat to give me a full view, Jay's dick arched underneath his zipper. "You know we thought about you all the way here."

"Did you now?"

I had to laugh, then said, "Me too . . . I mean I thought about you too. Both of you." I smiled, reaching for it, but the car swerved. It took me a second to get the car under control.

"Keep your eyes on the road and your hands on the wheel, woman. You can see him when we get to your house."

"Okay, we're almost there anyway."

When we got to the house, I opened the front door

and waited until Jay was inside. He slammed the door, pushed me up against the wall, and ripped open my blouse. Buttons bounced to the white carpet.

His tongue slid down my throat. In and out he delved repeatedly. He sucked my lips, then my tongue, then kissed my face as he whispered, "I need you, Ashlee."

Tears streamed down my face as I hungrily kissed him back. My trembling hands unfastened his shirt, lowering it over his shoulders, then down his back while I licked his nipples. Unbuckling his pants, I palmed Jay's hard-as-steel erection into my hand, gently stroking what I desperately wanted inside me. I never wanted to share my body with another man so badly. From this day on, my heart, soul, and pussy belonged to Jay. The hell with Darius.

"Take me, Jay. Take me right here, right now," I begged, desiring all of this man inside me. I stepped out of my panties, standing in front of him in only a ripped-open blouse and skirt. "Please, Jay, put it inside me," I urged, placing my hands on newly repaired mauve-colored wallpaper.

Lowering my arms, Jay turned me around, kissed my lips, then softly said, "I have to get to my bag. I don't have a condom on me."

"No!" I held on to him so he couldn't get away. "I don't care about a condom right now, baby. You're the only one I'm sleeping with and I know I'm the only one you're having sex with. I trust and need you to put him inside me. Now."

I grabbed Jay's dick, guiding it toward my soaking wet pussy. He resisted, and the physical roughness made me even more excited.

"Stop, Ashlee. I want you, too, but we don't need to be stupid. Neither one of us wants a baby."

The word "baby" snapped me back into reality.

Stepping backward, I released him so that he could retrieve his bag.

"Is this your bathroom?" he asked as he headed for little Darius's room. "I gotta pee before I do anything."

"No! Don't. That's my junk room," I lied. My heart raced as I slid between Jay and the door in a panic. I stuck out my hand like a traffic cop. Pointing to my bedroom, I said, "The bathroom's upstairs."

"Aw'ight, chill. You act like you got Tupac in there or something." Jay laughed, then said, "I'll meet you upstairs. Why don't you slip into something a little more comfortable?"

"Okay."

"You are so beautiful," he whispered, kissing my lips again. His kisses trailed along my cheek to my ear as he pressed his full, moist lips into my earlobe. "Umm," he moaned. My nipples tingled along with my pussy. I couldn't believe how wildly excited I was by this man and how stupid I'd almost been.

"You're silly, you know that!" I yelled, taking the opportunity to light the twelve cinnamon candles throughout my room before turning on John Coltrane's *Coltrane For Lovers* jazz CD to a volume barely audible. The first track, "My One and Only Love," was my favorite next to "After the Rain."

"Ashlee," Jay called out from the bathroom.

"Yes, baby."

"Can you come here for a moment?"

When I opened the door, all of the lights were off. Jay had lit all my candles and a few of his own. The Jacuzzi was filled with suds, covering his chest and partially exposing his firm chocolate nipples.

"Join me," he said, extending his hand.

"You're just full of surprises, aren't you?"

Jay's finger pointed, then curled as his eyelids lowered. Gently, he said, "Don't make me ask twice. Come to me."

Abandoning my clothes in the middle of the floor, I stepped into the tub and sat across from Jay.

"Relax," Jay said, taking my foot into his hands. Kneading the arch, he rotated his thumbs on the ball, then pressed into the joints between each of my toes. "So, tell me. What was bothering you?"

Instinctively, my body tensed.

"Oh, baby, that's not good. Relax. Look, Ashlee. I want you to know that you can trust and can talk to me about anything."

I closed my eyes and exhaled. "I will. I promise. But not right now," I said, massaging Jay's foot the same way he'd done mine. "I want us to have a great time together this weekend. Your being here is all I need."

Easing my toes up to his mouth, Jay sucked my pinky toe, patiently working his way over to the big one. Moaning with delight, I hummed, then said, "Aw, yes, Jay."

What was I going to do when my man had to leave me? He'd just arrived, and already I was suffering with separation anxiety. As I made a motion to move closer to Jay, he bit the side of my foot. "Stay on your side of the tub."

Was he crazy or what?

"Tell me something about yourself that I don't know," I said. "Wait, something significant, like it could make or break our relationship."

"Is that why you asked me to come a day early? Why don't we discuss what's going on with you?" Jay said, pressing his big toe inside my pussy. "You want me?"

Playfully kicking water in his direction, I said, "That's so unfair."

"You haven't witnessed unfair yet," he said, standing. "Come here."

I swear my heart stopped when I saw Jay's beautiful dick dripping with water and pointing at me. I sat there, staring in amazement. Without using his hands, Jay's dick moved up to his navel, then back down, pointing at me as he emphasized, "Didn't I say come here?"

When I stood, Jay's head pressed against my clit, then slid between my thighs. "I missed you," he said, sniffing my damp hair.

Stepping out of the Jacuzzi, our naked bodies embraced. Jay placed his hands under my armpits, lifted me into the air. Automatically, my legs hugged his waist as Jay braced my back against the wall. Squatting, he thrust upward.

I hoisted myself higher, panting while tapping his shoulder. "Condom, baby?"

Lowering me to the floor, Jay exhaled. Stooping to his knees, he slowly kissed my outer, then my inner lips before easing his tongue over my clit. "I had to taste her. I miss her," he said, sliding his middle finger inside me, teasing my G-spot.

"Stop, Jay, you gon' make me pee on myself. It feels good but I think my bladder is going to burst."

Something I said must've excited him because Jay started sucking all of me in and out of his mouth. My fingers gripped his curly locks as his finger fucked me deeper. My legs felt like overcooked spaghetti. The more I pushed Jay's head away, the more determined he'd become.

"Aaaaah, God, that feels soooo good. But, baby, baby, you gotta stop. 'Cause I really am going to pee on myself!" I shouted, and then it happened, I began to spray Jay like a cat. "Oh my God, Jay, what are you doing to me? Eeeeaaaahhhh!"

There is absolutely no way to explain how good I felt as I flooded myself onto Jay's face. My entire body slammed against the bathroom wall, knocking over the metal stand that once held my potpourri vase. For the first time in my life I experienced pure ecstasy, and although I knew I'd be embarrassed later for that moment I did not care.

"Relax," he calmly repeated. He had to hold me still because I was not in control of my body. "Relax, you didn't pee, Ashlee. You came. That's what they call a G-spot orgasm."

I still could barely breathe. "No way. I had a what? A G-spot orgasm?"

"Yes way, baby," Jay said, standing tall. "Haven't you ever heard of women spraying like men when they come?"

I nodded, though I was still unsure about what had just happened but truly glad it had. Darius had never made me come like that and I wasn't sure how many of those explosive orgasms I could handle from Jay. Well, I knew one thing. I was never going to let him go.

Stooping to my weak knees, I eased Jay's head in my mouth, sucking gently while stroking his shaft. I wanted to return the pleasure he'd given me, but I also wanted to get in my bed and bask in my most memorable moment of ecstasy, my first real orgasm.

"Yes, baby, suck my dick. Damn, your sweet lips feel so good."

Slowly Jay rocked back and forth. I could feel his muscles tighten with every stroke. His dick was strong. Hard. Big. And now that his shaft was in my mouth it seemed even bigger than I had remembered. Continuously, I stroked and sucked my man, using one hand to massage his balls.

"Umm," I moaned. "You taste so sweet."

Teasing my hair, Jay rubbed his fingertips into my scalp. Next thing I knew, Jay's hands gripped the sides of my head directly behind my ears as he fucked my mouth like it was my pussy.

I really wanted to please Jay, so I hung in there like a trooper with every stroke, massaging his dick faster and faster.

"Damn, Ashlee, you ready, baby? I'm about to come. I can't hold this shit any longer . . . damn, baby, damn you," Jay grunted, coming in my mouth. "Urruhhh!"

I felt the wave of semen flowing from his dick down my throat as I swallowed repeatedly. When he finished, Jay had to lift me from my knees because I had zero strength to stand on my own.

"Let's chill for a moment," Jay said, leading me to the bed. He looked whipped.

As he lay on his back, I snuggled my head under his arm, resting into his chest. Believe it or not I was still trembling from my, what was it? Oh yeah, G-spot orgasm. "I love you, Jay."

"I love you too, Ashlee."

CHAPTER 11

Jay

Can you say worn out? I was totally drained the morning after my arrival in Dallas, and despite hearing Ashlee move around the room, I was determined to sleep in. If she wanted to get up at the crack of dawn, that was on her, but if she expected a repeat performance of the night before, she was going to have to let a brother get some rest. I swear to God that woman tried her best to drain every last drop out of me. So, what I needed was some sleep in order to recharge my battery, and I was determined to get it, until I felt her sit on the bed next to me.

"Jay, Jay," Ashlee whispered, then began to gently plant kisses on the side of my neck, face, and ear. The entire time her hand was massaging my ass through the thin sheet. "Jay, get up. Come on, baby. I know you hear me."

She continued to kiss me until our lips finally met. She eased her tongue into my mouth and believe it or not, even after all the sex we had the night before, I started to become aroused right away. I remember thinking that maybe I'd created a nymphomaniac and by the time I left Dallas, they were going to be rolling my dick away in a wheelchair. When I finally managed to open my eyes, Ashlee was looking down at me, grinning. She was fully dressed in what looked like an expensive pink jogging suit, and her purse was strapped over her shoulder like she was about to leave.

"Hey, sexy, where're you going?"

"I'm not going anywhere. We're going out to—"

On that note, I closed my eyes and buried my head under the pillow, cutting her off. "You must be crazy. I'm going back to sleep. That's where I'm going. Wake me up when you get back."

"No, Jay. Stop it." She pulled the pillow off my head. "You've gotta get up, baby. We've got breakfast plans."

"Breakfast?" I glanced at the clock. It was only 8:00 a.m. "Lady, get back in bed. The only thing I want to eat is sitting right here next to me. Now c'mere." I reached up and pulled her on top of me, kissing her.

"I know, baby, and there's nothing I'd like more, but . . ." Ashlee pried herself from me, then stood up. "Jay Crawford, will you please get up? We've gotta get over to the Marriott. We've got a nine o'clock reservation. Besides, I've got a surprise waiting there for you."

"Baby, I'm not gonna lie. I'm really beat. Can't it wait until noon? Just two more hours and I'll go wherever you want."

"No, Jay, it really can't. We've got to go now." I couldn't figure out what the heck was going on, but I could hear the urgency in her voice. "Please, baby. This is important."

Against my better judgment I sat up for the first time, staring at her. "What are you up to?"

"Don't worry, baby. I'm not about to propose— yet." She handed me a towel and a washrag.

"Hmm," I sang. "Okay, okay. I'm getting up, but you owe me when we get back."

"Whatever you want," she promised. "Just hurry up, okay?"

It only took a total of fifteen minutes for me to shower and get dressed. The entire time, Ashlee kept rushing me like we were two hours late. I knew she was up to something, but nothing I had to worry about. The bright smile on her face and her singing to radio tunes helped me determine there were good intentions behind her surprise. She couldn't hide her excitement as she drove us to the Marriott.

Once we got inside, Ashlee told the hostess her name, and we were escorted to a table where a man was seated. The first thing that came to mind was, who the hell was he? I looked at Ashlee for a sign that the hostess had made a mistake, but the man, a tall salt-and-pepper brother, stood to hug her. Then they exchanged loving kisses on the cheeks. She turned to me.

"Daddy, this is Jay Crawford, the man I've been talk-ing so much about." Ashlee gripped my waist. "Jay, this is my father, Lawrence Anderson."

Can you say ambushed? Because that's how I felt, like Ashlee had just kicked me square in the balls when I turned my head. I hated meeting women's parents, especially their fathers, and by the looks of him, her pops wasn't exactly happy about meeting me either. For about five seconds, he just stood there eying me from head to toe.

"It's a pleasure to meet you sir," I somehow man-aged to say. I waited until his eyes met mine before extending my hand to him.

"Yeah, same here." He reached for my hand.

We quickly shook hands, and then we both reached to pull Ashlee's chair out at the same time. Her father paused and looked a bit shocked at first, but then he let the chair go and motioned for me to continue. Ashlee sat down as I gently pushed her closer to the table. I wasn't very hungry to begin with, but now the little appetite I'd had was lost. I only ordered juice and a bagel.

Ashlee's father frowned. "What are you, on a diet? They have a great buffet here, probably the best in town. It's a little expensive but you don't have to worry about the bill, I've got it. So, order anything you like."

"Sir, I'm not on a diet. I'm just not hungry this morning. I tried to tell Ashlee that when she woke me—" I stopped myself in midsentence. It probably wasn't the best idea to disclose the fact I'd slept in his daughter's bed. "I mean when she called to wake me up."

Ashlee patted my leg under the table as if to say "nice try."

"Yes, Daddy, he did tell me on the way over that he wasn't hungry. But I didn't want to let the two men I love most in the world miss the opportunity to meet." As awkward as the moment was I have to admit I loved the way she smiled. "I figured the two of you should chat a bit and get to know each other."

Her father smirked, then took a sip of coffee.

"So, Mr. Crawford—"

I cut him short. "Please, Mr. Anderson, call me Jay."

"All right, Jay . . ." He ran me through a series of twenty questions back to back to back.

I sweated a little more after each question, hoping the next one wouldn't be so personal. After he learned about my divorce and children, I figured he'd tell

Ashlee to give me my walking papers. Then the long-awaited easy question came. "So, do you like sports?"

I nodded and he continued.

"So, Jay, who's your favorite football team?" he asked.

"Well, believe it or not, although I'm from New York, I'm a die-hard Cowboys fan," I replied.

"Dallas Cowboys?" He raised an eyebrow.

"Are there any other Cowboys, sir?" I said.

"Not in Texas." He set his cup on the table, then sat back in his chair eying me suspiciously. "So, who's your favorite Cowboy?"

"All time or on the team now?"

"All time," he answered.

I grinned. "Far as I'm concerned, nobody's better than Mercury Morris. Man, could that brother fly!"

He nodded his head slowly. "I would have expected you to say Michael Irvin or Emmitt Smith."

"They're okay. I mean they won us three Super Bowls, but there's nothing like the original Cowboys that Tom Landry coached."

He started to grin, then turned to his daughter. "You know what, Ashlee? I think I see why you like him," he said, laughing. "Jay, you're my kind of man."

"Ah, thank you, sir."

Whew! I was relieved at his response. Ashlee seemed to be taking deep breaths also. She began to laugh and talk right along with us. We sat and enjoyed more small talk over breakfast, and I actually ended up going to the buffet twice before we prepared to leave. I shook her father's hand, and then she gave him a tight hug. She turned and smiled at me.

"Let's go, handsome," she said. She led the way as I followed her to the door. I reached in front of Ashlee to hold the door open, then stepped through, not realizing her father was on my heels until he grabbed my wrist and squeezed it.

Aw, shit! Here it comes. I knew this morning was too good to be true. Ashlee apparently didn't notice I wasn't behind her, because she kept walking.

"Sir, is there a problem?" I asked, looking down at his hand on my wrist.

I looked in his eyes as I awaited his response. "Take care of my little girl. You hear me? I'm putting my trust in you. I love her. And just because you're a Cowboy fan doesn't mean shit." His tone didn't sound angry, just that he was stating fact.

"Yes, sir, Mr. Anderson. I understand a hundred percent. You don't have to worry. I love her too."

He let go of my wrist, and I caught up to Ashlee just as she made it to the car.

"What do you wanna do now?" she asked, getting into the car.

We waved as her father's car passed us. I held the door, staring at her. "You know you owe me for making me sweat like that, right?"

"What? I had no idea you'd be so nervous." She laughed.

"Mm-hmm, yeah . . . whatever. Just remember you owe me."

"Well, why don't we just go back to my place so I can make it up to you? I'm sure you got a little more sweating in you to do, so why not spend it on me?"

I nodded and smiled. "Now, I like the sound of that," I said, closing her car door.

CHAPTER 12

Ashlee

Making love to Jay again felt so wonderful I had a reason to sing soprano again.

"You light up my life, you give me strength, to carry on, you light up my day, hum, hum, hum, hum." Removing the satin sheets from the bed, I continued singing, dancing, with the sheets until I became entangled, falling onto the mattress pad.

"Mrs. Ashlee Crawford," I said aloud repeatedly, absorbing the joy and happiness of being in love.

Happiness was an emotion I doubted would embrace me for a long time. But I was I wrong. Thanks to Jay, oh, how wrong I was.

Leaving my bed naked like my heart, I inhaled Jay's manly scent one last time before twirling the flat and fitted sheets into the washer.

The few errands I needed to run to the drugstore to pick up my prescription, to the salon for an overdue shampoo, blow-dry, and curl, to the bank to—phew, I'd better get going. Grabbing my purse, sliding the strap up my arm onto my shoulder, then easing behind the steering wheel, I tooted my horn at my nosy neighbors, as I rolled down my window and yelled, "Have a great day, ladies."

Parking next to the salon, I hadn't noticed the bridal shop. I was a believer in karma, and this was definitely a good sign so I entered. The spacious room shined with white gowns. I know it sounds corny but I felt like Alice in Wonderland.

A tall, slender woman greeted me, "May I help you?"

"Oh, yes. I'm just looking right now, thank you."

"So are you shopping for a friend or perhaps your sister? So who's the lucky guy?" she asked, following me.

What the hell did she mean a friend or perhaps my sister? This wench just pissed me off. I stopped dead in my tracks and whipped my head in her direction.

"I'm shopping for myself, if that's any of your business." Attitude was dripping from my voice.

She took a step back. "Oh, I'm sorry. I didn't mean to offend you. It's just that you're not wearing your engagement ring. It's bad luck not to wear your engagement ring." We both glanced at my left hand.

"Um, I, I, um, forgot it at home," I lied. "I was doing the dishes right before I left the house."

The woman smiled, probably afraid she'd lost her commission. "One day won't hurt. So when's the wedding?

I thought about Darius and Fancy's wedding the first week in June. So I blurted out, "The first week in June."

"June, that's right around the corner. We need to take some measurements and get you fitted." She pointed to the fitting area and I began to walk over there. After taking my measurements, she hung three gowns for my viewing. I gasped at the third one.

Strapless, with lots of beads, and lace, and the longest train I've ever seen.

"I'll try on that one," I said, admiring the Mermaid style.

"Take your time, honey. Your wedding is an occasion to last a lifetime. Try on these two first, then try the hand-stitched, genuine imported pearls, imported lace, and imported embroidery gown. This is a Vera Wang original, darling."

It was everything I'd ever dreamt of in a wedding dress. It was perfect. "I'll take the Vera Wang."

"I really don't want to sell you something you're unsure about, because once you buy the gown of your dreams, it's yours, honey. No return. No exchange. No refund," she exclaimed, pointing to the store's policy posted behind the register.

"Let me try it on," I insisted.

"Certainly, right this way. Uh," she said, blocking my hand. "I'll bring the gown to you."

Entering the huge changing room, I quickly removed my clothes, leaving on my white panties and bra.

Assisting me with the dress, she must have fastened fifty buttons. "Your hair could use some help, honey."

"Follow me. Step carefully," she said, motioning.

My cell phone rang so I rushed to check my caller ID, then answered, "Hi, baby."

"Hey, I had to hear your voice. My plane just landed so I'ma call you back to hear that sweet sexy voice."

"Jay."

"Yes."

"How much do you love me?"

Dropping the train, Lila squinted.

"A lot. A whole lot. Believe that."

"I love you too. Bye, baby," I said, kissing the receiver before hanging up. My chin dropped to my breasts when I saw myself. I've never looked more beautiful. Adrenaline pumped through my veins. "It's perfect. Everything is too good to be true."

"Are you sure you don't want to try on the others?"

I started shaking my head. "No way. I have the best man. He's my joy. Besides, wedding gowns are like men. When you find the right fit, stick with it."

"I'll try to remember that."

Removing my gown, I waited for Lila to place it in the perfect wrapping.

"That'll be twenty-one thousand dollars."

My eyes widened as I swallowed hard, damn near choking. Inhaling, then exhaling, I hesitantly handed her my American Express card. I didn't have a ring or a proposal. What I did have was the man of my dreams and I was never letting him get away.

"Honey, go get your hair all pretty," she said, leaving my credit card in my hand. "Emotional spending shouldn't change your emotions from good to bad. You want to say holy matrimony, not Holy! Matrimony! If you know what I mean. If you still want the gown afterward, it's yours."

Lila gave me a lot to think about while sitting in the stylist's chair. I'd never wanted anything so badly. After my appointment I bought the gown. Now all I had to do was get Jay to propose and put the past to rest, namely my ex, Darius.

Picking up the phone, I dialed Darius's home number, not caring if Fancy picked up.

Darius answered, "Well, if it isn't my son's sometime mom."

"Darius, I have some great news! I'm getting married. I met a great man and he loves me!" The excitement resonated in my voice. I could hardly breathe.

Darius said, "That's because he doesn't know how crazy your ass is."

I wanted Darius's approval, not his judgment. "I thought you'd be happy for me."

"You a straight trip, Ashlee. My fiancée is all stressed out raising your son. And—"

Interrupting I said, "Our son."

"I know he's mine! You know that too! But I'm on the road all the time, and while you're running around all stupid in love and shit, your son is driving my girl fuckin' nuts with all his crying! And I'm sure it's because he knows she ain't you!"

"But you were the one who filed for custody!" I started crying. "You got what you wanted! Now you see how hard it was for me trying to raise our son by myself. You thought being a parent was easy! Now you know! It ain't easy, Darius! I felt so abandoned by you that I almost killed myself. You wanted him! You got him! You keep him! And I don't give a damn. In fact, I hope Fancy loses her mind like I lost mine. Maybe then you'll see I wasn't so crazy after all!"

"Bitch, don't call me with that shit!"

"Bitch?"

"Yeah, bitch!"

I started laughing in Darius's ear.

"What's so funny? I bet you'll shut the hell up when I drop your son off on your doorstep."

Instantly I became silent, praying that Darius wasn't serious. The past few months I didn't have to wake up in the middle of the night. I didn't have to drag my baby on my hip everywhere I went because neither of my parents would babysit. Waking up every morning either with Jay or missing Jay or making love to Jay was how I imagined Darius and Fancy lived before they won custody of little Darius. "Look, I just called to share my happiness with you. I'm practically off medication, and I'm getting married.

"Well, you need to keep taking your meds because obviously you can't remember that you already told me about your little fiancé and . . . obviously you've forgotten that you, Ashlee Anderson, have a child! Don't call my damn house unless you're calling to come and get your son!"

Hanging up the phone, I admitted, Darius was right. With or without my child, I was a horrible mother. Truth was, our son was better off without me in his life.

CHAPTER 13

Jay

My return flight to D.C. was three hours and fifteen minutes, but it went by faster than I expected. There was constant, heavy turbulence, but it didn't even faze me as I relished pleasant thoughts of Ashlee and the way she made love to me over the weekend. I'd had my share of great lovers over the years, but if I had to rank Ashlee, I'd put her on the top of the list, right behind Tracy. Goddammit, why was I always comparing Ashlee to Tracy? Tracy was my past. Ashlee was my future.

As I stood in front of the baggage carousel daydreaming about Ashlee and the great weekend we'd had, I caught a glimpse of a woman walking past me who literally made me drop my bag and do a double take. She was holding the hand of a little boy and moving pretty fast, even with the boy in tow. I couldn't make out her face, but there was something about the way she walked, something about her sexy, bowlegged walk that gave me déjà vu. It reminded me of the reason I'd moved to D.C. in the first place. It reminded me of . . .

"Tracy!"

I hollered her name again, unable to control myself. My heart started beating like a jackhammer in my chest. I tried my best to will the woman to stop and turn toward me before she headed out the door. She didn't, and my heart sank low. I picked up my bag and was about to turn back to the carousel when the little boy tripped and fell. Lucky for him, his tiny backpack broke his fall, and the woman kneeled down to help him. That's when déjà vu became "oh my God!" and I honestly felt like my life was flashing before me. Without saying a word, I dropped my bag and began to haul ass toward the woman and the boy.

"Tracy," I called to her again when I was ten feet away.

She was talking to the boy and wiping the tears on his face as I approached. She looked up at me, and her face turned as pale as if she'd just seen a ghost. "Jay," she spat. "Jay, is that you?"

I nodded and she stood up. We stared at each other for what seemed like an eternity. I guess we were both reminiscing on what was probably the best six months of our lives . . . that is, until the boy called her Mommy. That's when I finally got the courage to speak.

"You let your hair grow out." I felt like slapping myself. I hadn't seen this woman in almost three years, she looked absolutely stunning, and the only thing I could come up with was that her hair grew out.

She touched her head self-consciously. "Yeah, I did it about a year ago."

"It looks good. I like it." I'm not going to lie. I wanted to kiss her. I'd wanted to kiss her for almost three years. Tracy was the reason I moved to D.C. in the first place, so that we could rekindle the flame of our past relationship. The only problem was that I'd been in D.C. almost three months and had no idea how or where to find her. I'd just about given up hope once I'd met Ashlee. For the first time since Tracy had walked by, Ashlee popped into my mind, but I quickly dismissed her as my body and mind were completely taken over by the woman who was once my sunshine.

"Thanks. So, what brings you to D.C.?" she asked, looking everywhere but in my eyes.

I wanted to say "You," but I didn't want to scare her off or give her the satisfaction. "I live here now."

"You do?" Surprise was all over her golden brown face as she looked over her shoulder. "What about your wife and kids?"

"I'm officially divorced and single." I glanced at the boy standing at her side, hugging her leg. "Tracy?"

She looked over her shoulder again.

"Yeah," she replied as if she knew what I was about to ask.

"Is this my son?"

She didn't respond, and again silence was shared between us. She looked down at the boy, then rubbed his head. Her silence was my answer.

I kneeled beside the boy. As I looked into his eyes, I could see a resemblance to me greater than that of my children with my ex-wife. He had my chocolate skin tone and my curly black hair, which had been trimmed, leaving him with low, faded waves. My heart skipped a beat as I looked into the eyes of a young life I helped create. I reached for his hand, but he wouldn't loosen his grip from Tracy's leg. I was disappointed, but I also knew that my absence in his life was the reason he didn't feel comfortable with me touching him.

I stood so I could talk to Tracy. It was time to get an understanding of why she'd been avoiding me.

"He's so handsome." I was choked up. "Why? Why did you keep him from me?"

"Jay . . . I . . . I wanted to," she said, seeming nervous. She looked into my eyes for the first time since she'd stood up from the floor. "I had to learn to follow my head instead of my heart."

"And what is that supposed to mean?"

"Jay, you know how much I loved you. I went against my parents' wishes to be with you. But once I thought about our situation, the fact that you were still married and everything, I realized I had to let you go."

"That might explain you, but what about Jason? I'm his father, Tracy, and you kept him from me too."

Her eyes started to well up with tears. "I know, and I'm sorry about that. I was just trying to do what I thought was right."

"What? Tracy, all I tried to do was love you. What are you saying?"

"I know you loved me, Jay, but you also loved the wife and kids you went home to. Occasionally having you with me wasn't enough."

"C'mon now, Tracy. You know if my children weren't there I would've left long before I met you. We've discussed that already. When you came into my life, I had finally found a sense of happiness. My heart was with you. I laid my head on my pillow nightly, wishing the woman lying next to me was you."

I reached to touch Tracy's shoulder, but she took a step back. She grabbed her son's backpack and tucked it under her arm before picking him up. She looked at me with tears in her eyes, sighed, then looked around. "Jay, I'm sorry. I know it was wrong to keep Jason from you, but I had to do what I had to do in order to move on with my life."

I reached for her hand, then waited for her to snatch

it away. She didn't. Instead, she cupped her hand into mine. "Jay, I have someone. And we have so much in common with our music. We both just came back from auditioning on *Pop Star* and we both moved on. One more tryout and I'm actually going to be on TV."

I felt more disappointment in my heart. A huge lump formed in my throat, making it hard for me to speak. I don't know why it never crossed my mind that she could be in a relationship, considering all the time that had passed. It hurt to think of another man loving her and touching her the way I used to. I let her hand go and rubbed my head to collect my thoughts. It took me a couple of minutes before I could say anything.

"Oh . . . well . . . um . . . that's cool. I'm, ah . . . happy for . . . you. 'Cause, see . . . um, see . . . I got me somebody too," I responded, a bit tongue-tied. "Yeah, me and Kenya finally got that divorce I kept telling you I was gonna get, and now I have a great woman to call my own. And I love her too."

Tracy nodded. "That's nice, Jay. I'm glad to hear that."

"Yeah . . . um, her name is Ashlee," I said, still fishing for something to say to mask my pain. "I just got back from seeing her in Dallas."

Tracy opened her mouth to say something, but before she could respond, a male voice rang out from more than fifty feet away. "Tracy," the man said, beckoning her.

She looked over her shoulder and gasped. "I'll be right there. Jason fell," she said. She turned back to me. "Jay, I have to go."

"Is he your husband?" I asked, nodding toward the well-dressed man.

"No, but he's very special in our lives," she said, looking at our son.

She turned to walk away, but I stopped her. "Wait a minute. You gonna leave just like that? What about a contact number? What about Jason? You may have moved on, but I'm not going to let you take my son away from me again."

The man called to Tracy again. "Tracy, what's the matter? C'mon. The limo is waiting for us," he yelled.

She turned to walk away from me. "Jay, don't worry about him. Jason's taken care of."

"It doesn't matter. He's my son, and I should be in his life. Tracy, please," I begged, placing my card into her hand. "The least you could do is let me see him."

She didn't say anything. She folded the card in her hand, then slid it into her pocket, nodding.

I watched as Tracy walked straight into the arms of another man while carrying our son on her hip. I could tell she was explaining something regarding me and our conversation because she pointed in my direction a few times as she spoke. He placed a kiss on her forehead, then stroked her chin. He took my son from her arms, and then he and Tracy turned to look at me before heading down the hall, hand in hand.

Once they were out of my sight, I felt tears fill my eyes. I fought hard not to let them fall. I began daydreaming about what Tracy and I used to have. I'd never loved a woman as much as I loved her, but her father couldn't understand that. Tracy was only nineteen and in college when we met. I was well into my thirties, married with children, but still looking for love. I found it when Tracy came into my life. Many things were wrong in my marriage, and I desperately wanted out. Although to some people I might have seemed like a dirty old man, my heart was clean and honest when it came to Tracy. I wanted to be everything she needed me to be, but during that time in my life, the cards just weren't dealt in our favor.

I hadn't counted on running into Tracy in the airport. It was a good thing my flight got in early or I might've missed her. Jason was even more adorable than I had imagined him to be. Tracy didn't assure me she would be in touch, so the only thing I could do was hope.

I got mad at myself for even letting Tracy affect me. *She actually did me a favor by shrugging me off,* I thought. *Now I know the only thing we can have between us is our son.* Sure, Tracy looked good and all, but I had a beautiful woman in Texas missing me. Tracy was my past but Ashlee was my future.

CHAPTER 14

Ashlee

Jay had easily become my best lover, my best friend; he'd quickly become my everything, which wasn't hard to do since I didn't have any other friends, hadn't worked in over a year, and was deemed an unfit mother when I'd lost custody of my infant son. Once I quit working for Darius, having money wasn't a concern, so I decided to take a break from the nine-to-five lifestyle. Thankfully I had Jay, my rescuer, to occupy most of my time or at least my thoughts.

Jay already had my father's acceptance. Now all I had to do was get my mom to approve of him.

"Mama, are you almost ready?" I yelled from the kitchen while roaming through old baby photos in an album I'd retrieved from my mother's family room.

"In a minute, Ashlee," she replied in a normal tone. "I don't know why you're so anxious to go with me on my business trip anyway. You need to get a life, sweetheart."

Ignoring my mother, I wanted to surprise her, prove to her that she was wrong. I did have a life. And despite her negative comments, I'd found a good man who loved me more than I loved myself.

"Oh my," I said, covering my mouth as I stared at the Easter family pictures from when I was five years old.

This was back when my mother, father, and I used to be a real family. Mom was dressed in a sleeveless pearl-pink tapered dress that showed off her stunning legs. Off-white lace gloves covered her hands and wrists. A short string of freshwater pearls neatly rested above her collarbone. Her hair was meticulously secured by a diamond clip, pulling her front hairs away from her pronounced cheekbones while allowing the remaining bundles of curls to flow behind her ears, over her shoulders, and halfway down her back. I always adored my mother, but not in a mother-daughter relationship kind of way. I envied my mother. I wanted to be my mother. Sexy. Elegant. Womanly. Confident. She did give me her name, Ashlee, only changing the *y* in her name to an *e* in mine. But that was about the most we had in common.

I smiled at the picture of my dad, who had worn an off-white suit that matched the color of my mother's gloves. The butterscotch hankie in his lapel matched his shoes and tie. I inherited my father's laid-back attitude. Even when things weren't to my liking, I seldom complained. The desire to always please my parents had overflowed into my relationships with men. I thought being cute and pretty made other people want to be around me.

Tears welled in my eyes, splattering on the pretty pearl-pink dress I wore in the photograph. The puffy lace stood high, covering my arms from my shoulders down to my elbows. The tapered top and wide bottom were separated with the widest cream-colored ribbon tied to the back in a big bow. Spiral curls danced all around my innocent face. My gloves and pearls matched my mom's.

Every Sunday morning at church, we were the proud family. Unfortunately, those few hours spent between eleven and one o'clock were the only consistent time that we were together. Once Daddy got home, he went straight into his study and worked beyond sunset, past dinner, and well after midnight. Maybe Daddy wanted a family but wasn't a family man. What if I wanted the same but wasn't cut out to be a mother?

"Mama! Are you ready?"

"Ashlee, didn't I teach you anything? Now, you know ladies don't yell. Let's go. Here, take my bag and put it in the car."

Quietly, I did as I was told. Placing the Gucci carry-on in the trunk, next to my black leather suitcase, I silently sought my mother's approval. As she drove her sparkling crimson Jaguar to DFW Airport, I shifted my eyes to the corners, admiring how flawless her makeup was. Naturally long lashes batted upward to perfectly arched brows, and downward to full, shimmering mocha lips. Mama's French manicure matched her toes. The crisp white halter top exposed a little cleavage, the short skirt stopped midthigh, and the tapered blazer accented her strong biceps. Mother looked more like my sister but acted like an acquaintance.

"Honey, who is this guy that you want me to meet? Tell me about him."

"Well . . ." I paused, saying a quick prayer that Mama would be impressed. "His name is Jay Crawford. He works for the Department of Justice. He lives in D.C., and he loves me. Daddy already met Jay, and he really likes him. They have a lot in common."

"Is that right?" Mother glanced over at me. "Then why didn't I meet Jay here as opposed to you insisting on traveling with me over two thousand miles to meet him? I hope you're not using me as an excuse for you to visit Jay," she said, parking in the short-term lot. "Does he know you're coming?"

My cell phone rang a happy tune. Quickly, I answered, "Hey, baby. I miss you."

"I miss you too," Jay said.

Standing at the first class ticket counter, my mother demanded, "Ashlee, can you get off the phone long enough for us to check in?"

Maybe if she hadn't been so demanding of my father, they'd still be married.

"Who's that?" Jay asked.

Ignoring Jay's question, I swiftly blurted out like I was disclosing the side effects for my medication, "I miss you, baby. I'll call you back in a few hours. Bye. Wait. What time do you get off from work?"

"I'm not at work today. Where are you?" Jay asked.

Scratching the nape of my neck, I felt my heart thumping against my left breast. What did he mean he wasn't at work? Why not? Where was he? I needed to move closer to Jay. Who was he with? Long-distance relationships made men cheat. What was he doing?

"Ashlee, get off the phone," Mother commanded.

Ending the call with a soft "bye," I retreated into my mental world, exploring all the possibilities of why Jay had taken the day off without telling me.

I got it!

Dialing Information, I requested the number for Legal Seafood on Seventh Street Northwest in D.C. "Yes, I'd like to make a three o'clock reservation for three people for today . . . okay . . . three thirty is fine. Thanks."

Now Mama can take me off her schedule early, and I can spend the evening and night at Jay's house.

Powering off my cell phone, seated on the plane

next to my mother, I asked the questions that I'd wondered about for years. "Mama, what's the real reason you divorced Daddy? And why haven't you remarried?" Mama was gorgeous, sexy, and could almost pass for being my twin. Except her attitude projected an extremely secure woman, while my attitude made me appear more confident than I was.

Placing a black silk mask over her eyes, my mother reclined her chair, then exhaled. "Ashlee, you are your father's child. Passive-aggressive. You think being nice will solve all your problems. But when that doesn't happen, you get angry at the other person, then you get mad with yourself, then you hate everyone and everything around you. I worry that one day you will seriously hurt yourself, someone else, or both. To answer your second question, I'm happy being single. I love dating younger men. I see who I want, when I want, I don't have to lie, and I don't have to explain my whereabouts to anybody."

Best if I didn't ask my mother anything else. Better if I relax and think about what she'd said. Opting not to take the antidepressant meds inside my purse, I closed my eyes, reclined my seat, and exhaled my frustrations into the air blowing in my face through the vent above my head.

I was elated to see the escort driver at Reagan National Airport holding up a sign with the last name Anderson. Handing him both roll-away bags, I walked around to the opposite side of the black Lincoln and got in the back when the driver opened my door. I could've opened the door myself, but Mother would've frowned upon that.

"So, finish telling me. How long have you been dating this Jay character?"

"Almost three months, Mother, and he's not a character. He's a very nice man."

"I'll be the judge of that. You didn't think Darius was a character, but at least you finally stopped chasing behind him, making a spectacle of yourself. So you should be glad there's a new man in your life. Just don't run him off too."

Oh my! I forgot to call Jay! Powering on my cell, I dialed his number, relieved he answered right away.

"Hey, baby. What's going with you? You hung up so fast. I tried callin' you back, but your phone was turned off."

"Jay, honey. Can you meet me at Legal Seafood?"

"What? Now? Here?"

I heard the hesitation in Jay's voice, but I couldn't accept no for an answer. "Please, I *need* to see you now. It's not like you're at work."

Jay laughed nervously, then said, "Woman, you are crazy. Are you always this unpredictable?"

"So, is that a yes?"

Mother stared at me, shaking her head while combing her hair.

"Yes. Only for you, that's a yes. I'm about fifteen minutes out, but I'm on my way."

"Thanks, baby."

Happily, I stared out my window along the twenty-minute ride to the restaurant. All I wanted to think about was Jay. Distracting me, I watched my mother remove her flawless foundation, then perfectly reapply her makeup in a moving car. Blowing me a kiss, she looked stunning. *Maybe I should have a makeover for Jay.*

"Pick us up at five," my mother said to the driver as he doubled-parked in front of Legal Seafood.

Confidently, I said, "I won't be needing a ride to your hotel. I'm leaving with Jay," although Jay had no idea I was going home with him.

"In that case, pick me up at four thirty," my mother instructed, extending her hand to the driver as she got out of the car. Mother's hairless legs glistened in the sunshine.

Entering the restaurant, I was pleasantly surprised to see Jay sitting on the bench in the waiting area. Instinctively leaping into his arms, I pressed my lips hard against his, welcoming Jay's tongue inside my hungry mouth.

Not wanting to let my man go, I smothered Jay's face with tons of pecks. I felt his strong arms wrap around my lower waist, pulling me closer. When he pressed his moist lips to my ear, I shivered.

Jay seductively whispered, "You don't know how glad I am to see you. You're coming home with me so I can have my special squirt dessert." My entire body tingled at the thought of how. Jay consistently made me come. Squeezing my vaginal muscles, I felt my body jerking hard in anticipation of having another G-spot orgasm. I was tempted to bypass lunch completely and let him whisk me home. That is, until my mother cleared her throat. For the moment, I'd completely forgotten about her.

Breaking Jay's embrace, I said, "Baby, I want you to meet my mother, Ashley-with-a-'y' Anderson."

My heart thumped into my breast as I watched Jay's dimples disappear. As he shook his head, his forehead wrinkled, almost connecting his eyebrows. Seemingly annoyed, Jay whispered in my ear, "Ashlee, you have got to stop doing this surprise shit. I'm a grown-ass man, not some little boy who goes along with everything you do."

Oh, but you will not only go along with everything I do, you, my love, will do everything I say, I thought, smiling innocently at Jay.

Looking at my mom, Jay said, "Hi, Mrs. Anderson. I'm—"

"Handsome. Indeed, you are decadent. Call me Ashley. And the pleasure is mutual."

My mother's smile was wide and bright enough to light up the entire restaurant as she eyed Jay like he was her favorite piece of meat. If she weren't my mother, I'd slap her in the mouth.

Jay grinned at my mother, extending a handshake, when suddenly my mother's hand twirled up to my man's lips, beckoning, then receiving a gentle kiss.

"Mmm, nice touch," my mother said, blowing my man away with those long-ass lashes. "You have very soft lips."

That was probably the same way Fancy had stolen Darius from me. Mother and I didn't spend that much time together, but if she didn't correct her flirtatious behavior she'd witness my, as she called it, passive-aggressive behavior turn violent. Why did everybody who came into my life push me to the fuckin' edge?

Thankfully, I was saved by the friendly hostess, who said, "This way, please."

I walked ahead of my mother, damn near walking backward to watch her ass until we sat at a window diagonally facing the Verizon Center across the street. Mother obviously made it a point to sit next to Jay but across from me.

Handing us menus, the hostess said, "Your waiter will be with you in a moment."

"So, Jay, Ashlee tells me you work for the Department of Justice."

Jay smiled, then said, "Yes, I'm a social worker."

There went that blinding smile across Mother's face again. Now that I saw her in action, I understood how she lured younger men.

"Really? I'm meeting with a Mr. Sheldon Thomas in your department tomorrow. Personal, not business."

She didn't tell me that. I tried my damnedest not to show how pissed off I was.

"Naw, really? Sheldon is my counterpart."

"Well, if you're not busy after my meeting, perhaps we can do a late lunch. Here's my card." Sliding her card between Jay's thick fingers, mother let her touch last way too long. "Nice touch," she said before speaking to me. "Ashlee, darling, are we ready to order?"

I learned more about my mother in those few minutes than I had in years. Finally, I understood what Mother's comment about my passive-aggressive behavior meant when I simply answered, "Yes, Mama." I was raging mad on the inside.

Slowly tracing the rim of the water glass with her pointing finger, Mother asked, "Oh, Jay, what do you recommend *I have*?"

Almost choking, Jay shook his head, then replied, "Umm, the crab cakes are a must."

"Fabulous. Order for us. So, tell me, Jay, how did you and Ashlee meet?"

Jay's eyes lit up, which made me feel better. "Didn't Ashlee tell you?"

"I wanna hear it from you," Mother insisted.

Jay glanced at me as if he wanted to be rescued.

"Don't look at her. She's not the one you're talking to. Now tell me, how did the two of you meet?"

He tried one last time to look at me, but Mother's finger stopped him.

"We met at a club. In the VIP section. Late one night."

My mother glanced over at me and I felt ashamed. All of what Jay said was true, but it was how he'd said it. So matter-of-fact.

Continuing, Jay said, "I was minding my own business. People watching, ya know."

"Yesss, I do know," Mother said, caressing Jay's dimple with her thumb. "I bet they were watching you too."

Looking at me, Jay smiled and said, "Then I saw an angel and later learned her named was Ashlee Anderson. Mrs. Anderson, I love your daughter."

Now it was my turn to smile. "And I love you, too, baby."

"And I'm going to be sick," my mother added as she leaned over the table to give Jay a kiss.

The waiter stood between us holding a pad. "Are you ready to order?"

That was rude. Couldn't the waiter see my lips were poked out? I missed if Mother actually kissed Jay and it was all this damn waiter's fault.

"Yes, the lady will have . . ." Jay said, gesturing toward my mom, "the world-famous crab cakes. I'll have the same. And, honey, what would you like?"

Squinting at Jay, I replied, "The same," because clearly he didn't care enough to ask beforehand. *Wait until I get him home. He's going to wish he'd ordered for me.*

"Ashlee, honey," Mother said, lowering her head while lifting her lashes. I could tell by her tone that she was about to embarrass me. "You're allergic to crab, remember?"

"Oh. Well then, I'll have the salmon," I said sternly to the waiter. Oh, I hated my mother sometimes.

Revisiting Jay's earlier comment, she said, "It's Ms., not Mrs., and call me Ashley." Touching his hand, Mother continued, "Jay, you handsome devil, may I ask a favor?"

"Sure, Mrs., Ms. . . . Ashley," Jay answered, looking unsure.

"That's good that you love my daughter but please be careful, that and take excellent care of Ashlee. My daughter is special and she has a tendency to forget things when she doesn't take her—"

"Mother," I hissed, between clenched teeth, "whose side are you on? I can handle *my* man just fine. Thank you very much."

Mother did a sexy hunch, then said, "In that case, I'm sure you've told *your* man all about your son. Whose father is your brother?"

Jay's hairline collapsed to his brows and nobody spoke for at least five seconds.

"You got a son? By your brother?" Jay questioned, clamping his hands above his dick. He leaned back in his chair, adjusting his slacks to give space to his crotch. Fortunately before Jay commented his phone rang and our food came.

I couldn't believe my mother was sneaking a peep at my man's dick as he pushed back his chair.

"Excuse me," Jay said, answering his phone. "Hello . . . Uh-huh? . . . No, I'm not busy . . . What? . . . Where are you? . . . Don't be crazy . . . Sure, I can be there in fifteen minutes . . . Of course I'm on my way . . . Thanks, I really appreciate this . . . Bye."

Before he was halfway out of his chair, I grabbed Jay's arm. "Baby, who was that? Where are you going?"

Shaking his head, Jay tossed his white linen napkin onto the table. "I gotta go. I'll call you later."

Although I felt like screaming, *Sit your ass down!* I said politely, "Jay, honey, I'll bring you your food."

Jay's cold eyes narrowed directly into mine, making every hair on my body rise to a chilling fright. I froze. His lips tightened with anger as he reiterated, "I said, I'll call you later. Obviously, we've got some things to talk about." Facing my mother, Jay respectfully said, "Have a good evening, *Ms.* Anderson."

Heartbroken by Jay, pissed off at my mom, I looked at my mother and said, "Now I get it. I'm a constant reminder of all the things you despise about my father. That's why you never once objected to me living with my father after the divorce. And that's why you disapproved of me dating Darius, 'cause Darius was a constant reminder of my dad's marriage to Darius's mom."

And that's why no matter what I did right, in my mother's eyes I would forever be my father's daughter, not hers.

Exhaling, Mother folded her arms and said, "You're right. Satisfied? Now here's where you get either passive or aggressive, exactly like your father. Go ahead, honey. Let me have it."

Questioning whether my mother was jealous of me, I swallowed hard, hating her for ruining my should-have-been perfect dinner and possibly destroying the best thing that'd ever happened to me—my relationship with Jay.

Leaning across the table, I dug my hand into a crab cake, smearing it on my mother's face.

Backing away, Mother yelled, "Are you crazy, Ashlee? See, this is what happens when you don't take your medication. I didn't mean for you to do this." Mother peeled away lumps of crabmeat from her eyelashes.

I hissed, "Mother, you'd better pray Jay doesn't break up with me tonight. 'Cause if he does I'll be knocking on your hotel door with more than a damn crab cake."

CHAPTER 15

Jay

I was on my way home when my phone rang for what seemed like the millionth time. Instead of ignoring it like I'd been doing since I left Legal Seafood this afternoon, I answered it because I knew this time it wasn't Ashlee blowing up my phone. I knew this because her ring tone was Lil' Kim and Fifty Cent's "You Got the Magic Stick" and the tone that was ringing was Fifty's "P.I.M.P.," the ring tone for my boy Kyle.

"What up, dawg?"

"Just checking up on you, player. What's going on?" Kyle asked.

"Man, life is beautiful. I just spent the afternoon with my son Jason and Tracy."

"Hold up, man. How'd you do that? I thought Tracy was MIA."

I could hear the surprise in Kyle's voice. "Damn, I didn't tell you? I ran into Tracy a couple of months ago in the airport. She was with some dude she called her boyfriend who's supposed to be helping her with her music. Old girl wouldn't even give me a number or anything. I had to damn near beg her to take my card."

"Man, now, that's cold."

"Who you tellin'? I'd pretty much written off seeing them, but today Tracy just calls me up and asked me if I wanna meet her and Jason in the park. Kyle, man, it was like watching a little me. The boy's a natural athlete, just like his old man."

"Man, I can't tell you how happy I am for you. So, what you gonna do with that girl Ashlee? I guess you gonna kick her to the curb now, huh?"

"Kick her to the curb? That's my girl, Kyle. I love Ashlee." I did still love her, even though I had plenty of questions after what her mother told me at lunch today.

"My bad, but you love Tracy too."

There was silence on the line for a minute while I thought about what he'd said. "True that. I'll always love Tracy. She's my son's mother, but she got a man. She made that very clear today, and you better believe I'm not crossing that line because I wanna continue to see my son. Besides, like I told you, I love Ashlee. I'm not going to do anything to hurt her."

"Hey, can I ask you a question?"

"Yeah, sure."

"Is this Jay Crawford? 'Cause the Jay Crawford I know is not this sensible." We both laughed.

"Yeah, well, I'm getting wiser with age."

"Good."

Kyle and I talked for a little while longer about my other kids, his kids, sports, and what was going on up North. We ended the call with the promise that he and his wife would come down for a visit in the next few weeks. The only thing we didn't talk about was the comment Ashlee's mother made right before I left the restaurant.

Truth is, I hated to leave in the middle of my first meeting with Ashlee's mom, but I felt that finally spending time with my son was an opportunity that shouldn't be missed. Otherwise, I would've stayed right there at the table, listening to Ashlee's mother spilling her guts on her daughter. *Three months into the relationship, and I never had a clue about Ashlee having a kid.* Her mother obviously thought I knew, because she spoke freely. I imagine Ashlee was ready to crawl under the table. "What's done in the dark soon comes to light," I said out loud with a smirk. Then again, who the hell was I to judge when I needed to find a way to tell Ashlee about my little secret—Jason?

I pulled up to my place and thought my eyes were playing tricks on me. I did a double take, and there stood Ashlee, leaning against my door with her arms folded. *I'm gonna catch it now,* I thought. *Then again, maybe not. She's got a lot of explaining to do, too. I still couldn't get it out of my head that she might have had a baby with her brother.* I got out of the car and walked up to her.

"How long you been—" I started.

"Shh," she interrupted, placing her finger on my lips. "Don't say anything. Just let me explain."

I nodded. "Aw'ight. Go ahead."

She had a sincere look in her eyes. "Jay, I wanna apologize for not telling you about my son. I wanted you to know, but I was embarrassed at not having custody of him . . . which is another story within itself—one I wasn't sure you'd understand," she said, pausing after every three or four words to kiss me.

"What I wanna know is, is your baby's father your brother?"

She stopped kissing me for a second, then answered, "No . . . well, yes . . . kinda."

My eyes lit up. "Kinda?" I was starting to feel a little nauseated.

"He's my stepbrother through marriage. We're not related by blood. My mother has a tendency to blow things out of proportion."

"Ooohhhh, I see. Well, I'm not gonna lie, she does a great job." It was all starting to make sense. From what I could tell, Ashlee's mama was a true-life drama queen.

"Jay, I love you, baby. Can you forgive me, please? I know I should have told you and I'm sorry."

Ashlee groped between my legs and kissed my neck. I wanted to scream, *Yeah, I forgive you. I got another kid too.* But I wanted to make her sweat a little first. Her sex during the times we weren't mad was the bomb. I could just about imagine she'd cause an explosion between the two of us as she desperately tried to make up. So, instead of answering her question, I allowed her to fondle and cling to me while I unlocked my door. I backed her into the living room, then peeled her arms away from me. At first she looked puzzled, but then she came at me and forced her tongue deep into my mouth. My dick damn near busted out of my pants.

I'd had enough of trying to play hard. I gripped her ass, then kissed her back. Before I knew it, she climbed up on me and wrapped her legs around my waist. Her skirt rose above her hips, revealing that she wasn't wearing underwear, and exposing the neatly shaven pussy I'd fallen in love with. She began grinding on me as we continued to savor each other's tongues. She drove me crazy when she began licking my ear.

"Let me feel you, Daddy," she panted. "Unzip your pants and fuck me now."

"Hold on, baby. I got you," I said, carrying her into the bedroom.

I placed her down on the bed, then went over to my dresser. "What are you doing?" she asked, jumping off the bed.

"Getting a condom."

"No, you don't understand. I want to *feel* you," she said, unbuttoning my shirt.

I was surprised at her request. "What? Are you on the pill?" I asked.

"Yes, baby. Ortho Novum, and I take 'em faithfully," she responded, tongue-fucking my ear.

I kept thinking we shouldn't take our relationship to the next stage, but Ashlee wasn't making it easy for me to decline her. Going to the level of having unprotected sex meant I needed to really trust her. I didn't want three baby mamas and four kids. At the moment, all I knew was that I loved Ashlee, and she had ways of making me weak. She began licking my chest, easing her way down to my nipples. When I dropped my pants to the floor, she fell on her knees almost simultaneously. Her tongue was wet and warm on my skin, as it had been in my mouth. I ran my fingers through her hair and guided her head toward my throbbing dick. Watching Ashlee softly kissing the head made precome seep onto her lips. As she backed away, the sticky fluid clung to her wet lips.

"You taste like chocolate, baby. Um, I love chocolate." Her beautiful brown eyes looked up at me as she proceeded to give me a blow job to die for. Normally I wouldn't want a woman eyeing me while giving me head, but Ashlee was different. No, Ashlee was special.

She pushed me down on the bed to continue her oral deed. When I was ready to return the favor, she shook her head, moaning, "No, baby. I want you to be serviced." She pushed me back down, then did the sexiest catwalk as she crawled on top and mounted me. My body repeatedly jerked from the impact of having her wet, pulsating pussy on my dick. As I closed my eyes, sweat dripped, then poured from Ashlee's body onto mine as her hips gyrated in slow motion. She whispered, "Don't move, my love. Let me pleasure you." I swear, it took everything in me not to bust my biggest nut ever inside her before we were both ready.

Ashlee let out sighs and moans that were louder than I'd ever heard from her. She rode me fast and furious, making it more difficult for me to hold back. I knew I had better flip things so I'd control what was going on. I turned her over. She spread her legs from one side of the bed to the other, making sure I had plenty of room to dive in. But when I decided to go nose first, she went crazy, barely able to keep her legs open. I didn't let up on her until she was begging for mercy.

My dick was so hard it had begun to throb. As she lay there gasping, I stuck it to her fast and furious like she'd done with me. I knew she wanted it rough because she began to grind just as hard as I was laying the pipe. When she started calling out my name, I knew she was close. Then I felt it. The gripping was so strong I couldn't hold back. The fact that she kept screaming, "Come with me, Daddy" didn't help either. I gave it all to her, then collapsed, barely able to breathe.

I managed to roll off Ashlee before smothering her with my deadweight. She was obviously worn out, because she was asleep within minutes of reaching our climax. After catching my breath, I turned over to watch Ashlee sleep. She looked strikingly beautiful. Her skin was smooth and even-toned. I laughed to myself when I thought about how she waited outside for me to get home, thinking I was mad at her. She went to extra lengths to prove she wanted to make up for her dishonesty. My conscience began to weigh on me about my own deceit, so I woke her up to talk.

"Ashlee," I called. "Ashlee, baby, wake up."

She grunted. "Why? What time is it?"

"It's not about the time, baby. I wanna talk to you about something. I need you to wake up."

"Ugh. Okay. I'm up. Talk."

"First, let me say I was surprised to see you standing outside my door this evening. I'm not sure how long you were out there, but if you were outside for two minutes, that's one minute longer than I would've endured."

"Oh, I wasn't going anywhere until I saw you and had a chance to make things right between us," she said.

"Thanks for being so dedicated. I also want you to know that from now on, you don't have to stand outside my door."

"I don't?" she asked in a comical tone. "Why not?"

"Because the key hanging in the kitchen labeled 'spare key' is yours. I want you to have it. That way I can show some dedication back to you."

"Sweetheart, I don't know what to say. I guess I should start by saying thank you," she said, then leaned in to kiss me, sticking her tongue out first.

"Wait, Ashlee. There's more we need to discuss."

She slid back down in bed. "Sure, baby. I'm listening."

"Ashlee, I was disappointed to hear you'd been keeping your son a secret from me."

She nodded. "Jay, I know. And I meant what I said about being sorry for hiding that part of my life from you. But I thought we were moving on. What can I do to make you forgive and forget?" she asked, reaching to grope my dick. "Can't you forgive me?"

"Yes, I can. But only if you can forgive me too," I stated with my tone fading.

Ashlee sat up in bed. "I don't get it. Forgive you for what?"

"Ashlee, there's something I should've told you," I said, pausing to take a deep breath. "I have a son too." I looked down to avoid the shock in her eyes. "His name is Jason, and he's three years old."

She was quiet for a minute. I wanted to look up at her reaction, but I was afraid I'd see disappointment. She shifted several times as if she was trying to figure out the best way to say what was on her mind. I sat silently, awaiting her response.

"This is so crazy. I can't believe this. Here we are . . . two people in love . . . together for three months . . . yet we've never felt comfortable enough to tell each other the truth before now." She paused and sighed. "Where is your son, Jay?"

"He lives with his mother here in D.C. She's a woman I was seeing at a rough time during my marriage. I actually fell in love with her, which took me by surprise because I wasn't even in love with my wife when I married her."

Ashlee sighed deeply. Then tears fell down her cheeks. Her voice broke as she spoke. "So now what? How do I know you're not in love with her now? Before I know it, she could convince you to go off and be with her for the sake of family. I don't wanna get hurt, Jay."

"You won't."

"How do I know you won't hurt me!" she asked in more of an exclamatory tone than a question.

I pulled Ashlee close to me, then softly kissed her lips. It pained me to see her cry. I wiped her face, then kissed her several more times. "She's moved on with her life, Ashlee. She has a man she says she loves dearly, and he's even helping her raise our son, which I'm not happy about. But I'm forced to deal with it. And besides the fact that she's moved on, so have I. I love you, Ashlee. I just told you that you can have a key. Doesn't that prove something?"

She continued to cry. "Jay, I wanna know I haven't lost you. You make me happy, and I don't know what I'd do without you."

"Ashlee, you haven't lost me. You found me, and I found you, remember? And I'm happy. No more secrets. I promise. I just need to hear the same from you."

She sniffed. "No more secrets. I promise."

"Good. Now dry those tears. I know it may be a little tough right now, but I only wanna see you smiling."

Ashlee put on the best smile she could muster, which wasn't very much, but I accepted it. I held her tight and began to gently stroke her back. After several minutes of silence had passed, she pulled away.

"I'm okay, Jay. Thanks for having that talk with me. I'm tired. I think I'm ready to go back to sleep now."

I kissed her forehead. "Okay, sexy," I responded.

She turned over. We lay motionless with our backs to each other. Though Ashlee was quiet, I knew she wasn't asleep. I could sense all was not right with her, and I felt helpless not knowing what to say or do to make things better. I could only hope our sudden revelations hadn't destroyed her ideas and future plans for us, but time would have to tell. I couldn't be sure of what Ashlee was feeling at the moment, and I was left with a thought of *what next?*

CHAPTER 16

Ashlee

After Jay confessed about Tracy and his son, I couldn't sleep. My stomach was in knots. I tossed and turned, trying to get comfortable, but I couldn't. I lay in the bed, with my back to Jay; my eyes were wide open. I stared into complete darkness praying my relationship with Jay wasn't over. Lifting the satin sheet, I eased from under Jay's heavy arm, sat on the edge of the bed, and prayed he'd stay asleep. When Jay didn't move, I quietly left his bedroom and stepped into the living room. Slowly twisting the knob, I pulled the bedroom door shut behind me, carefully releasing the handle.

Quietly I cried, wondering all sorts of things. Who was Tracy? What did she look like? Was she prettier than me? Younger? Older? Could Tracy fuck Jay better than I could? Could she make him happier than I could? Would Jay leave me for Tracy and Jason? How could I compete with Jason for Jay's heart? For Jay's time? I didn't want to share Jay with anyone, especially a three-year-old. I wasn't worried that Jason was

Jay's only son. What bothered me the most was, Tracy lived in D.C. and I lived in Dallas.

The outdoor lights beamed through the living room's vertical blinds, casting a dim light, as if the room were lit by candles. Desperate to uncover the truth behind Jay's confession, I searched for signs of another woman's presence.

I should go back to bed. I'm the woman in his house. He gave me a key. What more do I want? What am I going to do if I find something? I should trust him until he gives me a reason not to.

I scanned his coffee table, end table, sofa, and chairs, on top, and underneath. I shoved my hands between the cushions, digging for earrings, panties, or whatever I could find. I found nickels, dimes, quarters, and lint. I stood in front of the entertainment center's wide-screen television, glanced at the DVD and CD players, then peeped between his bookshelves. Nothing stood out. Sniffing the Persian rug, I had to know if a female's scent lingered. The only hint of a familiar freshness was Febreze.

As I suspiciously opened the door to his guest bedroom, the first thing I noticed was his laptop computer on a rectangular desk by the window. The screen was black. I skated my finger along the mouse pad, and the screen brightened to a colorful display. Jay was logged on to the Internet. A closer look revealed that Jay's e-mail account was fully accessible.

Leaning over the laptop, I couldn't resist clicking on the drop-down button to check the latest Web sites he'd visited. My eyes froze. Ten or more URLs were for apartment complexes in Dallas. A few more were for jewelry stores; specifically, engagement rings.

Why must my foolish heart keep searching for something wrong with this man? I didn't know why, but I turned on the light, then opened Jay's desk drawers. All of his bills were current. Opening the file cabinets, I scanned his divorce papers to Kenya, his birth certificates for two kids, not three. The one for Jason was missing. Next, I slid the mirrored closet door to the far left. The shoe boxes on the top shelf were out of reach, so I rolled the computer chair in front of the closet and shook each box. The rattle inside the black Nike box clearly wasn't a pair of size 13 shoes.

Swiftly taking the box into my trembling hands, I removed the lid. Inside were stacks of letters. As I read the addresses, I saw they were sent from Tracy Brown, postmarked three years back. The letter on top was never opened. Jay's name was crossed out and the words RETURN TO SENDER were boldly printed across the top.

Opening the letter, I found a check and a note:

Tracy,

I'm never going to stop loving you. I promise you one day we'll be together. Believe that. I'm really close to divorcing Kenya, and if you'll have me, I want to marry you. I want to spend my life with you. Nothing or no one makes me happier than you. I know your old man hates me. Can't say I blame him. Tracy, my one and only true love, here's another check for $500 for our son. Next month I get a raise, so I'll start sending $600. Mark my words, one day we will be a family.

Without a doubt truly yours,
Jay

Stuffing the check inside the envelope, I don't know what possessed me, but I sat on the bed and kept reading until I'd read every single love letter in the box. Crying, I thought there was no way Jay could possibly love me more than this woman Tracy. *I can't compete with her.* When the sunshine peeped through the window, I stood on the computer chair, sliding the black box into its original space.

"Ashlee, what are you doing?"

Damn near falling off the chair, I hadn't heard Jay enter the bedroom. I'd forgotten to close the door. How long had he been there?

"Oh, I . . . I was just, um, looking . . ."

"For?" Jay questioned, waiting for a response.

"Well, baby, if you must know, now that you've ruined my surprise, I was checking to see what size and types of shoes and clothes you like. That way when I shop for my man, I can buy you what you like."

Laughing, he said, "You are unpredictable. I've never had a woman who cared so much about me. Usually it's the other way around. I'm the one buying clothes and stuff. C'mere and give me one of those juicy kisses."

Jay pulled me in close. His lips covered mine. I stood there letting him embrace me, but now I had more questions than answers about Tracy . . . but not for long. Soon I would know everything there was to know about Ms. Tracy Brown.

Following Jay back into his bedroom, I was too stressed to have a G-spot orgasm, or any other kind.

"What's wrong, baby?" he asked, cupping my face into the arch of his palms.

"Nothing's wrong," I lied, knowing everything was wrong. I was so mad at Tracy for stealing my man's heart that I couldn't look Jay in the eye.

"I'ma hop in the shower so we can catch brunch at Georgia Brown's. I'm starved. Come scrub my back for me. I love the way you lightly scratch your nails into my flesh."

Now wasn't a good time for me to scratch Jay. His flawless body might become flawed like mine. "I'll be in in a minute."

Once I heard Jay happily singing Jamie Foxx's "Unpredictable" in the shower, I dialed the investigator at my father's attorney's firm, thankful he answered on a Sunday.

"Raymond, good morning. This is Ashlee Anderson. I apologize for calling so early—"

"Hey, little Ash. How's life treating ya?"

"I could be better. That's why I'm calling. I've only got a minute, so please listen carefully. I need you to find out everything you can about a Tracy Brown. All I know is she lives in D.C., she has a son named Jason Brown. The father is Jay Crawford, his address and phone numbers are . . . Jay has an ex-wife and two daughters . . ."

I told Raymond the little information that I knew, then said, "Oh, hold on a minute. One more thing." I hurried to Jay's cell phone, which was resting on his nightstand, fully charged, and searched his phone book. *That's odd. No name entry for Tracy, and too many 202 area codes to guess. Hmmm.*

"That's it for now, Raymond. I need to know whatever you find out right away. I'm engaged to marry Jay, and I need to know everything about everyone in Jay's life."

"Well, your father taught you well, little Ash. I'll send you an e-mail attachment with details."

"Including pics, Raymond. I need to see what this tramp, I mean woman, and her kid look like."

"Consider it done. I'll get somebody from our D.C. office on it right away. Should I bill your father?"

"No! Don't bill my dad. Send the bill to my house. Bye."

Jay walked into the room with a towel wrapped

around his waist. His chest glistened with baby oil. His smiled turned into a frown. "Who was that? And what are you doing with my cell phone in your hand?"

"That was my son's father, and since I was on my phone, I couldn't see the time."

Silently, Jay pointed at the digital clock on his nightstand.

"Baby, you know those clocks aren't always precise. I trust cell phones," I said, placing Jay's cell phone back on its charger.

"Well, I trust you, baby. C'mere." Wrapping me into his slippery body, Jay asked, "By the way, I've been meaning to ask you about your brother-slash–baby daddy. What's your son's father's name?"

Silence. Dead silence surrounded us. My heart raced with anxiety. I didn't want Jay to know the truth. What made him ask that question?

"I want to enjoy my last day with you before I go home. Can't we talk about this another time?"

"Baby, I asked you a simple question. I've told you about Tracy and my son. Don't you think I deserve to know about your son and his father? Since we're going to be together, no more secrets."

Eventually he'd find out from my mom or the *National Inquirer*. I mumbled, "Darius."

Hunching his shoulders, Jay pushed me away, staring into my eyes. His look wasn't as cold as the day he left me and my mom at Legal Seafood, but he obviously wasn't letting up until I told him more.

"Darius Jones-Williams." There, I finally told Jay the truth.

His eyebrows lifted. "The NBA player? He's your brother? Your ex?"

"Trust me, *player* is the operative word. Sit down for a moment so I can explain." Partially folding one leg on the bed and placing my other foot on the floor, I faced the man that helped me to get over my ex.

"Well," Jay said, sitting on the edge of the bed, facing me, "I'm all ears."

"My mom hates Darius because my dad met Darius's mom when I was six and married Darius's mom when I was ten years old. My mom didn't want to raise me because I reminded her of my dad, so Darius and I grew up together like sister and brother, but he said it was okay to have sex because we weren't biologically related."

"He who?"

"Darius."

"That's the sickest thing I've ever heard," Jay lamented.

Exhaling, I said, "Long story very short, I have a soon-to-be one-year-old son by Darius, who's being raised by Darius's wife, Fancy."

Holding my hand, Jay asked, "Why isn't your son with you? Doesn't the court automatically award custody to the mother?"

Here's where the truth ended and the lies began. There was no way I could tell Jay I'd lost custody of my son because I'd endangered little Darius's life on several occasions by almost suffocating him, by leaving him in a rental car overnight while I shared a hotel room with Darius, and the day Child Protective Services took my baby away, I'd left him in a running vehicle while I went back inside to answer Darius's phone call.

"You know how it is with these big-time athletes. Whatever they want, they get. After Fancy miscarried, Darius filed for custody of our son and they won."

Truth was, my conscience was eating me alive. I should be behind bars for the horrible things I'd done to Fancy and my son. I didn't mean to hurt them. Tears welled up in my eyes. I buried my face in the pillow because I couldn't face Jay. I especially couldn't tell Jay that after my son was born, I lied to Darius and told him our son had died of HIV complications. I thought if Darius believed both of us had HIV, he'd only be with me. I also couldn't tell Jay that I'm suicidal. I think my problem is . . . I can fall in love, but I don't how to fall out of love without hurting myself or someone else.

Jay's strong hand traveled up and down my spine, massaging my back. "Baby, I'm so sorry. I know how much it hurts not to be able to see your own son. I hadn't seen Jason in years."

I cried harder because the difference between Jay and me was that he wanted to see his son. I didn't want to see mine. Little Darius was a constant reminder of his father, and if I couldn't have both of them, I was better off not seeing either of them. I even refused to watch any of the Atlanta games on television just to avoid seeing Darius play basketball with Fancy seated courtside, holding my son.

Hopefully, after last night's lovemaking session without a condom, I was pregnant with Jay's baby. That was it. Jay wanted us to have our own child! He was so clever. Otherwise, why would he have agreed for us not to use a condom? Oh, that's right, I lied and said I was on the pill. Oh well. Too late to sweat the small stuff.

"Baby, I'm here for you. Whatever you need, you'll never have to ask me twice," Jay said, pulling me up off the pillow.

His arms pulled me close to his chest. I felt loved, safe, but I was still insecure about that Tracy chick.

"Jay?"

"Yes, Ashlee."

"Promise me you'll never leave me, no matter what."

CHAPTER 17

Jay

It was Sunday night. I just finished watching *The Sopranos* and taking a shower before jumping into the bed. The sheets were cold, and I wished Ashlee was underneath the covers waiting for me. I stared at the ceiling, thinking of how perfect our weekend together had been, even though she was driving me crazy since she went back to Dallas with her constant calling and questioning me about Tracy. It was definitely time to start thinking more seriously about moving down to Dallas so she wouldn't be so insecure. I was sure she knew I loved her, but the distance and her jealousy of Tracy were becoming a huge obstacle in our relationship. Stupid thing was, I hadn't even seen Tracy but two times, once at the airport and the time we met at the park. Hell, I still didn't even have her number. The more I thought about Ashlee, the more I had the urge to pick up the phone and call her. So that's exactly what I did.

"Hey, you," she answered. "I knew you'd call."

"Hmm . . . is that right? You've got me figured, huh?" I smiled.

"Yep." We both laughed at that, and then Ashlee said, "So, Mr. Crawford, how was your day?"

"It was good, kinda busy. I painted the guest room," I replied, running through the day's activities in my head. "Oh, and believe it or not I actually went to church. What about you? How was your day?"

"It was good. I didn't go to church, but I did a lot of thinking, a lot of contemplating."

"Contemplating, contemplating what?"

"Killing your baby's mama." She said it so nonchalantly I almost took her seriously.

"Excuse me!"

She laughed. "Calm down, Jay. I was just kidding. You're the one who always says I don't have a sense of humor."

"Yeah, but that's not funny," I scolded.

"I know, Jay, I'm sorry. Really, I was just joking. I would never do anything like that," she said, then quickly changed the subject. "Jay, do you know I love you?"

"Yes, baby. Do you know I love you too?"

"Yes, but I love you more."

"No, boo, I love *you* more."

We went back and forth, debating who loved who the most. It was kind of fun, made me feel like a kid again. My train of thought was interrupted by a *beep*. Ashlee continued to sing more I-love-you's until I stopped her.

"Hold on a minute, Ashlee. Somebody's on the other line."

"Who's calling you at this time of night—" I heard her say just before I clicked over.

"Hello," I answered.

"Jay?" a soft feminine voice asked. The hairs on

the back of my neck stood up. I recognized Tracy's voice right away.

"Yeah. This is Jay."

"Jay, it's Tracy."

I took a deep breath, trying to stay calm as I smiled at the phone. Despite the fact that I loved Ashlee, deep down I still had a thing for Tracy. I guess I always would.

"What's up?" I was too shocked to say more to her. Although it was good to hear her voice, I never expected her to actually call, especially not so soon. I sat up in bed, anxious to hear why she had decided to call.

"Jay, I need you," she said in a desperate tone. I sat up in the bed immediately.

"What's wrong?"

"Jason and I need you to rush us to the emergency room. My parents are out of town. I didn't know who else to call. Will you help us?" she asked, spitting her words quicker than I'd ever heard anyone speak.

I panicked when I heard her say *Jason* and *emergency room*. Suddenly, I could hear him crying in the background. I jumped out of bed and grabbed a pair of pants. "Sure. What happened? Where are you? Are you okay?"

"I'm okay, but I think Jason might be hurt bad. Please . . . just come as quick as you can. I'm scared."

I went to the dresser to write her information on a piece of mail. "Give me the address to where you are, Tracy."

She gave me the address to a Giant food store. I got dressed in between listening and writing the directions to her house, so by the time I hung up the phone, I was only missing my shoes. They were sitting at the foot of the bed. I got a pair of socks out of the drawer and sat on the bed to put on my shoes.

My phone began to ring. *Oh, shit,* I thought, looking at the caller ID. I'd completely forgotten about Ashlee.

"Hello," I answered.

"Jay, what happened? I know you didn't hang up on me." She was in disbelief.

"Oh, baby, I'm sorry. Listen, a friend of mine from work is stranded, and I'm the only one who can help him out, so if you don't mind, I'll call you tomorrow." I hated to lie to Ashlee, but I didn't wanna hear her mouth.

"A friend? What's your friend's name?" Ashlee's tone was very accusatory. I had to think quickly.

"Ah, ah, Jason," I blurted out. I quickly realized my mistake and tried my best to cover it up. "I mean . . . ah . . . Jeffery." Well, if she wasn't suspicious before, she damn sure was now.

There was silence before she spoke. "You think Tracy . . . I mean *Jeffery* would mind if I talk to you until you reach him? I had hoped we could chat a bit more tonight." There was no doubt in my mind she was testing me.

I made sure to be careful with my reply. "Well, I'm sure he wouldn't mind, but I still need to call you back. I can't get dressed and talk to you on the phone at the same time."

"Hmm. Okay. Then I'll look to hear back from you soon." I was just about to hang up when she said, "Jay, you know I'd cut your dick off if I ever caught you cheating on me, don't you?"

Instinctively I placed my hand on my Johnson to make sure it was intact. "I guess it's a good thing I never cheated on you," I told her as I hung up the phone.

I was out the door in a flash and in my car. I had no intention of calling Ashlee back. I loved her, but who needs her kinda drama when it comes to your kids? No matter how fast I drove, it seemed as if I couldn't get to him quick enough.

When I found the Giant supermarket, I parked and got out of the car. Tracy was standing in the lighted entrance, carrying Jason. I jumped out of the car and opened the passenger door to let them in, then jumped back in the car. I didn't say anything, but what I really wanted to know was why I was picking her up in front of a supermarket instead of her house.

"What happened, Tracy?" I asked as I drove away.

She had to speak loudly over Jason's crying. "He was supposed to be in bed asleep, but instead he was jumping up and down on the bed in the dark—something I've told him over and over again not to do. As I passed by his room, I could hear his laughter and the springs bouncing, so I opened the door and turned on the lights. That's when he bounced down on his butt, then onto the floor."

"Where is he hurting?" I asked.

"His arm, I think it's broken. He won't let me touch it."

I looked over at Jason as he cried pitifully. I silently wished there was something I could say or do to take his pain away. I reached over and rubbed his head. "Don't worry, little man. I'll have you at the doctor's soon. You'll be feeling better in no time," I said.

After I'd sat in the waiting room for three hours, Tracy finally came to get me. "He has a hairline fracture. The doctors are almost done with his cast, so we won't be here much longer," she said.

"You mean he's being calm about letting them put the cast on?"

"Well, he's still crying, and it's tough on me, so I decided to sit out here with you for a bit." She paused. "Thanks for coming, Jay. It's damn near one o'clock in the morning, and I know you have to be at work in a few hours, so I appreciate you for being so caring."

"You don't have to thank me. That's my son. If you ask me to take a bullet for him, I will."

We both sat silent for a minute, and then Tracy scooted closer and placed her head on my shoulder. I had just begun to enjoy the tender moment when the doctor interrupted my brief enjoyment with news that Jason was all done. Tracy was excited.

"C'mon, Jay. Let's go see him," she said.

Tracy was ahead of me. We stepped into the room and saw Jason sitting on the bed with an orange cast, eating a red lollipop. "What? No tears?" Tracy asked.

"No. I'm a big boy. And look what they gave me, Mommy," he said, holding up his lollipop.

"Wow . . . I wish I knew how to be a big boy like you, Jason," I said.

He smiled. "I'll teach you."

We all laughed. Tracy sat on the bed with Jason and rubbed his back. "Jason, do you know who this handsome man is?"

Jason stared at me in silence for a moment. Then he spoke. "Yeah, that's Jay. The man we played with in the park that time."

"Mmm-hmm, that's right but he's also your daddy," she said as she continued to rub his back.

Jason stared at me for a few seconds. Then out of nowhere he said, "Is that why you always tell me I'm handsome like my daddy?"

Tracy and I busted out laughing as she turned to me and I wiped tears from my eyes. "Yes, honey, that's exactly why I tell you that."

I gave Jason a hug and stared at his mother, mouthing the words *thank you*.

Not long after that the doctor came in with Jason's prescription for pain medication, and we were out of there. It did my heart good to have Tracy formally introduce me to my son. And I felt even better knowing he could accept me despite the other man Tracy had in her life.

I was a little confused when Tracy had me drive her to her parents' place instead of her home, but I didn't ask her any questions. She probably just didn't want me to know where she lived or maybe her parents' house was closer to the hospital. Whatever. Besides, it was two o'clock in the morning, and I think everyone was tired. Heck, Jason was snoring in his mother's lap.

"There's no mistaking him as your son. He definitely gets his snoring from you," Tracy said.

"I don't snore," I disputed.

"Oh, so now you don't remember, huh?" she said, laughing. "Even if I never told you, I'm sure your current girlfriend must've told you."

"Believe it or not, no. But if you say I do, then I trust you're telling the truth. No woman has ever known me as well as you did."

She smiled and patted my hand with hers. "I know you say I don't have to, but I want to thank you again, Jay. I don't know what I would've done without you."

"You'd do what you're going to do on that *Pop Star* show. You'll survive."

"You know about the show?"

I could tell by her smile that she was elated. "Yeah, I saw your picture in the paper the other day. Congratulations."

"For what? I haven't won anything yet. They don't

even start the actual competition for about six. I just made it through the tryouts."

"Well, I have confidence in you."

"At least somebody does. My boyfriend's not speaking to me because of this, it's probably because he's not moved on to the next round."

"Sorry to hear that."

"No, you're not. You don't give a damn about that man." Tracy hesitated before she spoke again. "Your girlfriend's a lucky woman, Jay, I hope she knows that."

Out of nowhere, she planted a slow, loving kiss on my lips. She didn't use her tongue and I can't even say it was sexual, but it did send a message, a message that she still cared.

Her actions left me speechless as she opened the car door to get out. I jumped out and ran over to help her. Neither of us said anything as she cradled Jason, then headed up the stairs to her parents' place. I felt sad to see her walking away from me again. I felt an overwhelming urge to not let her get away again. But she had a man and I had Ashlee, at least for now.

CHAPTER 18

Ashlee

Why did Jay leave me hangin' on the other line, then end the call, forgetting about me? He must think I'm a fool. Well, I'm not that forgetful. Jason was his son, not his friend. Why do men always do that? Why do they always lie?

He knew damn well that wasn't no Jason or Jeffery, that was Jason's mother, Tracy Brown: five feet, five inches, short brown hair, large brown eyes, 120 pounds, a part-time receptionist at a family-owned real estate company, soon to be twenty-two years old, and a wannabe singer who'd recently made it to the TV round of *Pop Star*, currently residing at 32001 Georgia Avenue with a Melvin Langston, a thirty-five-year-old musician, and her three-year-old son, Jason, who attended Shining Star Day Care, Monday through Thursday from nine to one. I threw the information sheet Raymond Express-mailed me to the floor and popped in the DVD.

That bitch made me sick to my stomach. *Pop Star* was another one of those television shows where contestants had to compete, except *Pop Star* awarded multiple contracts in two areas—singing and acting, *better known as cheap commercials*—to one person.

"I'm sick and tired of watching this wannabe idol prance her behind up and down the stage slinging her hips, lips, and ass all over place." I reclined on my sofa and started thumbing through the pictures.

"Isn't Jason cute? Just like him mama and him daddy." Not that I needed to see any more after watching the DVD, but there was another batch of pictures of Tracy. "Holy shit!" I sat on the edge of the sofa in disbelief. "Raymond, you are the man!"

I wish Jay hadn't told me about Tracy, but then again I'm glad he did. Tracy was obviously using Jay's son as a way of holding on to him. Why else after three years all of a sudden this Tracy chick resurfaced? Unbeknownst to Tracy, she was in for a hell of a fight if she thought I was surrendering my man—the best man, the best dick, and my one and only friend—to her. I'd kick her ass and spank that snotty-nose kid of hers all the way to foster care before I'd stand by and let her take my man.

What is your problem? Get a grip! I thought, furiously pacing from my bedroom, to the living room, to the kitchen. I couldn't keep still. *Jay loves you, not Tracy. He told you so. Remember?* Well, Jay needed to tell me over, and over, and over, until I was convinced he was telling me the truth. 'Cause I'd just caught him in a lie.

Picking up my cell phone, I dialed Jay's number. He didn't answer. I waited five minutes, then dialed his number again, this time blocking my home phone number.

Lightly huffing, "Hello," he answered right away. That son of a bitch, he was avoiding me. The muscles in my stomach tightened. Why was he breathing so hard this early on a Saturday afternoon? Why didn't he answer when I called from my cell? "Jay, baby, this is Ashlee. Is everything all right? I was worried about you. I've been trying to call you."

Standing in the kitchen, I stared at the black-handled stainless steel knives I had contemplated slicing my wrist with after my breakup with Darius.

"Hey, baby, hey. Everything's cool. I just walked in from the gym. My cell phone was in my bag, so I missed your call and you beat me to calling you, but I'm glad you did. Thought about you the whole time I was pumping iron and working the hell out of my abs. I want to make you the envy of all women holding on to your firm and tight sexy chocolate man."

Oh no. Blood rushed to my head. My heart raced with anxiety. Jay started exercising? That meant double trouble. Now I'd have to fight off all those horny, desperate, undersexed, single women in skimpy clothes thrusting their breasts while prancing their asses in my man's face. I trusted Jay. Who I didn't trust were the women that wanted him. Based on how fine Jay was, that meant I had to keep my eyes on every bitch out there. Oh my God. What if . . . what if . . . Jay gave one of them my exclusive G-spot orgasm? I'd have to kill her.

"Did I do something wrong?" I asked, attempting to keep Jay on the phone.

"No, baby. You could never do anything wrong with me."

"Then why the sudden distance between us? And why haven't you told me you love me lately?" I said, circling the dining room table like I was playing musical chairs with eight empty seats.

"I told you 'I love you' several times last night when

we stayed on the phone till two this morning. Was your mom serious about you forgetting things? I'm beginning to get a little worried."

Clenching my teeth, I hissed, "Keep my mother out of your mouth. Literally. Besides, you didn't say 'I love you' like you meant it. It's Tracy, isn't it? Is she there with you? She's practicing for her next act, huh?"

Jay started laughing. "Ashlee, don't be ridiculous. What's gotten into you? If Tracy was here, why would I be on the phone with you . . . ? Sorry, baby, that didn't come out right, but trust me, you never have to worry about Tracy. Now, I am going to do right by my son. Yes, I am. I'm not messing that up for nobody."

"Who you callin' nobody?"

"Woman, please. Chill out. Look, I'm starting to get a headache. Let me call you back."

Ignoring him, I continued talking. "If I don't have to worry about Tracy, then who do I have to worry about? Huh, Jay? *And* if Jason is all that matters to you, then what about me?" I sat at the head of the table for three seconds before I was back on my feet making tracks lapping around the table again.

"Look, baby, I'm standing here dripping with sweat in these wet clothes that are starting to get cold. Let me call you back after I get out of the shower."

"I know what it is. I'm too far away. That's the problem. I don't like missing you either. If you'd like, I can come there for the weekend . . . a few weeks . . . or maybe a month . . . and we can work out together. Look, why don't I call the airline now?"

"Wait, wait, wait. Slow down. You're not making sense. Now, you know you can't come up here this weekend. My boy Kyle's supposed to be coming by for the weekend, remember? Now, if you like, why don't you come on Monday?"

The more Jay seemed patient with me, the more

impatient I'd become. I couldn't breathe. Gulping air, I wanted to keep him on the phone. I didn't want to hear that click in my ear. I needed him so badly. Why couldn't I let him go take a shower? Why did I make men, make him . . .

"Bye, baby," were the last words Jay spoke before I heard . . .

Click.

Every muscle in my body tensed as I screamed, "Noooooo!"

Anger raged through my body when the phone went silent. Slamming the phone on the base, I quickly snatched it back. I fell to my knees and redialed Jay's number. He didn't answer. *Oh, I forgot to block my number.* I called back again. Again. Again. Until hitting RE-DIAL no longer worked. Still no answer. My hands covered my face. My fingers dug deep into my scalp. Blood dripped into my palms. "I don't care! Bleed! Bleed! I don't care! Nobody cares about me!

"Why me? What did I do this time? All I want to do is be with Jay."

The knots in my stomach intensified. Churning. Burning. Stirring like a kitten mutilating a spool of yarn. There was no way I'd feel better as long as I was in Dallas and Jay was in D.C. I had to get to Jay. What was he hiding from me? The weakness in my legs, tremble in my arms, ache in my heart, I wanted to scream! But I didn't. The pain in my heart became a reality as my scalp stung from the sweat seeping into the open flesh.

I brushed my hair into a ponytail to cover the cuts. Entering my bedroom, I frantically packed my suit-case. I stuffed the DVDs, pictures, and papers into the FedEx envelope, then hid the package in my bot-tom drawer so Daddy wouldn't find out what I'd done. I was sure he'd be around snooping.

Zipping up my carry-on, I glanced at my wedding gown hanging so beautifully. I whispered, "I love you, Jay," before getting into my car and speeding 120 miles per hour. Jay had better not be lying to me, because at my wedding or at his funeral, one way or another, I was not wasting twenty grand. Make that twenty-one.

I was standing at the Dallas/Ft. Worth check-in counter purchasing a one-way ticket to D.C. Jay had no idea about my surprise. I'd packed a wig, lingerie, and a pair of the softest black lace gloves to stroke Jay into an unforgettable orgasm or wring his dick off, depending on what, I mean who, I found in his bed.

I sat in first class, my left leg shaking the entire flight as I thought about the trip I'd taken with my mother to D.C. My mom hadn't spoken to me since we last parted, and Darius hadn't called me since we'd spoken on the phone. That's okay. I didn't need them. I only needed Jay.

All the way to Reagan National Airport I couldn't relax. My eyelids twitched, my lips tightened, and my feet stomped all the way to the Hertz rental car counter. Bad visions crept into my mind as I gripped the steering wheel tight. I was thankful few cars were on the road. I started to swing by Tracy's house to see if Jay's car was parked outside but changed my mind.

By the time I arrived at Jay's house, midnight stars were clustered in the sky. My heart stopped, then damn near broke through my chest when I saw a car blocking Jay's car in his driveway, so I parked on the street, blocking both of them in.

Fumbling for my keys, I quietly tiptoed to the door, eased the key into the lock, entered the living room, then headed straight to Jay's bedroom.

"Uh-huh. Yes, Daddy. Give me this big-ass dick. Oh, yeah, that's my spot. Lick my spot right there, baby. Oh, you so nasty. I like that shit."

Aw, hell no! Racing to the kitchen, I grabbed the first thing I spotted. A butcher's knife. Kicking off my shoes—one in the kitchen, the other in the living room—en route to Jay's bedroom, I stormed to the door, then stopped. Grabbing my breasts, I couldn't breathe.

"Ahh, yesss! I'm coming so hard!"

That's it! I busted open the door. The room was black. All I heard was scrambling. "Don't move!" I yelled. "You're one dead bitch!"

"Aahhh!" the woman screamed.

"That's right! Scream!" I yelled. I heard a hand muzzle her mouth, drowning out her fear. I wanted to see her face, see their faces, before stabbing their hearts out. Holding the knife high above my head, I turned on the lights . . . then froze with the knife in the air.

"Who in hell are you?" I questioned, lowering my hand to my side.

A man who wasn't Jay, and a white woman who wasn't Tracy, were so close under the covers rattling, their bodies looked like one huge twisted anaconda.

"Who in the hell are you?" the man asked, shielding the woman's body.

Ain't that some shit? I bet if she was black he'd have her ass in front of him.

A familiar voice resonated from behind me. "I must be dreamin'. What's going on in here?"

As Jay entered the room, I quietly dropped the knife next to my foot, then kicked it under the dresser.

"Jay, baby, there you are."

Jay shook his head. "Ashlee? What are you doing here?"

"Man, you're not dreaming. This bitch is crazy. Is this the Ashlee you've been bragging about?"

I couldn't move. I felt so stupid. Why couldn't I trust Jay? *God, please don't let him see the knife,* I thought, kicking it farther underneath the dresser.

"Ashlee, come here. Sorry, Kyle, man. Y'all can go back to sleep or to whatever y'all freaky behinds were doing."

"I'm outta here," the woman said.

The man said, "It's cool, Lisa. Jay has everything under control."

Jay closed his bedroom door and led me into the guest bedroom. Silently I sat beside Jay on the twin bed with my hands in my lap.

"Ashlee, why? What are you doing here?"

Hanging my head, I said, "I don't know. I wanted to see you. Jay, I can't stand being away from you." Tears streamed down my face.

Drying my tears, Jay said, "I miss you too, but you can't come in here unannounced, scaring my friends. What did you tell them?"

"Nothing. I just opened the door 'cause I thought you were in there sleeping and I wanted to—"

"Baby, stop it." Ever so gentle, Jay cupped my face into his palms, then continued, "I love you. Only you. I gave you a key because I trust you. You have to trust me too. Okay?"

Softly his lips pressed against mine as he wiped away my tears.

"Okay. Baby, I'm sorry."

Jay's hands gently cupped my face again. This time his lips caressed my cheeks. He kissed my forehead, my nose, down to my lips and my neck. Patiently he undressed me, laid me on the bed, and gave me what I'd come for . . . my G-spot orgasm.

As I climbed on top of Jay, neither of us asked

about a condom. Secretly I hoped we'd get pregnant for sure this time and start our own family. "Come with me, baby," I whispered in Jay's ear, grinding my pussy into his pelvis.

Holding my ass in the palm of his hands, Jay moaned in my ear, "Tracy, I love you, baby."

No, he didn't!

"What the hell did you just say?" I demanded, slapping Jay in the chest.

"I said, 'Ashlee, I love you.' What the hell is your problem?"

"That's not what you said, Jay." I sat beside Jay, waiting for a response.

"Then tell me. What did I say?"

"You called me Tracy."

"Don't be crazy. I'd never call you Tracy."

"Well, you just did. You still love her, don't you?"

"Yes, but not like I love you. She's my baby's mother, for God's sake. I'll always love her. But you are the one I want to be with. What more do I have to do to prove my love for you?"

"You can start by not calling me Tracy, ever again."

That was a demand, not a request.

CHAPTER 19

Jay

It felt good to be back in the Big Apple again. New York City had almost everything near and dear to me—my two girls, my friends, and my parents. The only thing it didn't have was Ashlee, Jason, and Tracy. Over all, my frequent visits were mainly to spend time with my girls. It had been a month since the last time I'd seen them, but I made sure to make up for lost time. The girls and I took advantage of doing things they don't normally get to do, like seeing the *Lion King* play on Broadway, dinner at a fancy restaurant, and shopping. Boy, did my girls love shopping! I think they got that from their mother.

I'd promised Kyle I'd spend my last night in town over at his place with him and my boys Allen and Wil before Ashlee and I headed to the islands. When I got there we hung out in his billiard room drinking beer and talking shit. Kyle had ordered ribs and wings from the rib shack on Linden Boulevard. I was ready to kick Allen's and Wil's butts at a game of pool like

I'd always do when I visited. Kyle was a different story, though. He actually played pool pretty good.

Kyle greeted me at the door with a beer. "Man, if I didn't know any better, I would say you've lost weight since I seen you last," he said.

I slid my hands down my sides and rubbed my chest. "Huh? What're you talking about, Kyle? I just seen you like last week. I look that bad since then?"

"Not bad . . . just, just different. You sure everything is all right?" he asked, as he closed the door.

We headed toward the billiard room. "I'm cool. As a matter of fact, I couldn't be better. I just won a hundred dollars on a scratch-off, I'm about to kick Wil's and Allen's butts in some pool, so I can take their money, and tomorrow I'm taking my baby, Ashlee, on an exotic vacation to Jamaica. So yeah, I'm pretty good."

"I guess you really are okay then, huh?"

"Oh yeah. And I forgot to mention me and the girls had a great time, too. I really appreciate those tickets to the *Lion King*. They loved it. And I never thought they'd enjoy sightseeing and shopping so much."

"C'mon now. They're girls, aren't they? What female you know don't love to shop?" He laughed.

"You got a point there, bro."

Allen and Wil had already started a game. From the looks of things, Wil was winning. I guess I came in at the right time for Allen's benefit. He needed something to be a distraction and break Wil's concentration.

"Yo . . . whaddup, dawg?" I yelled.

Wil missed his shot. He and Allen turned around. "Man, you know the rules," Wil said, fussing. "I'm glad to see you and everything, but coming up in here all loud when a man is about to make his next shot is rude."

We all laughed. I went over to slap five with Wil. "My fault, big man. I forgot."

"Forgot my ass," he said. "My money is on the line. I'm glad it was you because somebody else would've gotten shot for that shit," he said, giving me five. "By the way, put your money up because it's on. I ain't losing to you this time."

"Let the man get 'em something to eat and a drink before he gets his ass whipped," Kyle said. "I think he could take his whipping like a man on a full stomach. That way he'll feel his trip wasn't a total waste."

My boys all laughed at me. "Ha . . . ha . . . ha. He who laughs last—"

"Which will be me," Allen said.

"Ah, whatever," the rest of us said simultaneously.

I fixed a plate and watched as Allen and Wil continued to sharpen their skills on the pool table. The room had been pretty quiet with the exception of the clacking of the balls, and then Kyle struck up a conversation.

"So, Jay, what's up with that crazy shit that went down at your house last week?" Kyle asked.

I could feel both Allen and Wil turn to me like I was being set up.

"What shit? What you talking about?" I was looking around in all their faces.

"Man, you know what I'm talking about. Why'd old girl bust up in the room like the Incredible Hulk's wife with a knife and shit? Yo, that was some crazy-ass shit. My wife thought she was going to kill us."

Allen and Wil looked shocked. I had no idea what Kyle was talking about. "Say what? Man, she didn't have a knife," I exclaimed.

Kyle turned to Wil and Allen as if I was lying. "Ask Lisa if you don't believe me. Jay, man, she was holding up a knife like she was about to kill us. If you hadn't popped up, somebody was gonna get hurt."

"Get the fuck outta here. I know you were pissed about her interrupting you getting your groove on, but Ashlee ain't like that. This was all just a big misunderstanding. I'll admit, Ashlee is a bit paranoid because of Tracy and all, but she wouldn't do no crazy shit like pull a knife."

"So where'd the knife come from? I know you saw it on the dresser when we left."

"Look, Kyle, it was just a big misunderstanding, all right?"

Kyle shook his head. "I know what I saw, Jay. That woman is crazy. You can see it in her eyes."

I was starting to get pissed. "Well, dawg, you saw wrong, aw'ight? This is the woman I love you're talking about and she ain't crazy."

"I hear you say this woman loves you, but I think it's the opposite of that. You might need to be careful. I think she's obsessed with you."

I was disappointed to hear how Kyle felt. I wanted my boys to be happy for me. Ashlee was scheduled to fly into La Guardia the next morning to join me on a flight out to Jamaica. Our six-month anniversary had rolled around pretty fast, and we had planned to celebrate. I had no doubt about the love between Ashlee and me, and after six months of bliss, I felt it was time to make things more official between us. I had bought her a two-carat, princess-cut diamond engagement ring. Unbeknownst to Ashlee, she was about to experience a perfect marriage proposal in Montego Bay. Despite all Kyle had said, I continued to defend Ashlee.

"Well, I love her, and I know she loves me. That's

why by this time tomorrow night, I plan to make her the happiest woman alive," I said, opening the ring box.

They gasped. "No . . . no . . . hell no. Jay, man, I think you're going too far," Allen said. "I get a bad vibe from that girl."

"What? C'mon now, Al. You know Ashlee." Now, this was a complete surprise because Allen and his wife lived in Virginia and visited with me and Ashlee several times. "So is anyone in my corner? Wil, what's up? What about you, big man? Can you at least be happy for me?" I asked almost pleadingly.

"I wish I could, Jay. You know you my boy, and all. And I want nothing but the best for you. Hell, I've never met the woman, but I can tell from the talks we've had about her that she ain't the one."

I was baffled. "Man, how can you say that? I've always told you how happy she makes me."

Wil put his pool stick down, then looked me in the eye. "Yeah, but you've got some things twisted. Some of the shit she does isn't love. Man, that girl is obsessed with you. You've told me the sex is banging, and it sounds like that's all you two really have to keep you going. That's not a healthy relationship."

"What about how I feel? Don't you all think I would know when I'm in love?" I asked, looking around at all three of them.

Wil stepped over and put his hand on my shoulder. "Not necessarily," he said, then pointed at Allen.

Kyle walked over and stood in front of me. "You know Al has been down this road before. Do you remember how you felt when he told us he was going to marry Rose? We all knew Rose wasn't the one for him, and I remember distinctly that you told Al he needed to listen to his boys. That's because we're on the outside looking in, and we can see some things you can't. And now I'm telling you: You need to listen to your boys."

I looked at Al. I never thought I'd be sitting in the same shoes he once wore when he planned to marry the woman he loved. As I sat looking into each of their faces, I could tell there was nothing I could say to persuade them otherwise toward Ashlee. Wil wasn't done with me yet.

"What about Tracy?" he asked.

"What about her?" I asked, shocked he'd bring her up.

"You still have feelings for her. Why not make things right with her and your son?"

"Wil, I guess you don't understand. Tracy is not an option for me. She has someone. She's moved on."

"Okay. I don't wanna sound like I'm not going to have your back. I think I speak for all of us when I say the decision is yours, and whatever you decide, we'll be here for you."

I nodded. I couldn't deny I still loved Tracy, but I loved Ashlee too. And besides, I had promised her father I would do right by her. *Once I put this ring on her finger, she knows she's the only one for me,* I thought. *All of her paranoia will be gone, and the fellas will see she truly loves me.* My thoughts were interrupted by my cell phone. Ashlee was calling me.

"Hey, sexy, what's up?" I said when I answered.

"You. Just calling to see whatcha up to," she said.

"Right now I'm at Kyle's house about to play some pool."

"Mmmm . . . I bet you are," she said, giving me attitude.

"No, baby. I really am over to Kyle's."

I could feel the fellas watching me. I turned my

back to avoid facing the embarrassment. Ashlee seriously doubted me, and it didn't feel good. "Who's over there?" she asked.

"Just Kyle, Allen, Wil, and me," I said, trying to remain calm.

"Mmmm. Whatever."

I became very annoyed. "Look, Ashlee, we're about to get this game going. Let me call you a little later, okay?"

She didn't bother to respond. She just hung up the phone in my face. I thought heavily about the things my boys had said to me. Ashlee's behavior had become aggravating, and I felt I didn't deserve to have to put up with such pettiness. I took the ring out of my pocket, then opened the box. When the salesman told me it would set me back a few grand, the money didn't matter because I felt Ashlee was worth it. After her phone call, I began to think like my boys. *Maybe she ain't the one.*

CHAPTER 20

Ashlee

I sing because I'm happy.
For the first time in my relationship with Jay, I relaxed. No meds. No stress. No Tracy or her brat. We were on day one of five event-filled days in Montego Bay, at an all-inclusive resort. Immediately upon check-in, the hostess briefed us on their rules prohibiting Jamaicans from entering their hotels unless the natives were employees of their establishment. She stood there with her curvaceous cocoa hips winding and grinding to a reggae beat resonating in the background.

How rude of her. Glancing from her hips to her lips, I nodded. *I got your number. Forget it, missy! It ain't happening.*

"Eliminating the competition, huh, ladies?" I said, kissing Jay. They weren't slick. I read straight through what they were trying to do. Steal my man.

Right away my blood pressure rose several degrees. Those hoochies at the front desk ignored the fact that I was pissed off and started dancing together. Close together. The Jamaican woman in the middle handed Jay his VISA, cheesing and eyeing my man like he really was chocolaty dickalicious and possibly her one-way ticket to America.

Aw, hell no! Not over here too. That meant the single women at our resort including the staff were ready to have a fuck-fest with my man? I'd hurt all of 'em before I let that happen.

"He's taken," I said so loud I didn't have to repeat myself for anyone *else* to hear.

"Baby," Jay pleaded, "stop it. We just got here. C'mon, let's hit the beach and have some fun."

At first I was apprehensive about us taking *all* of our clothes off in front of strangers, but after we'd lounged on the beach for an hour, having clothes on felt more uncomfortable than being nude. Besides, we had the best bodies out there.

Whenever I caught women sneaking a peek below my man's waist, I simply backed my ass into his dick, or dragged Jay into water above his waist, wrapped his arms around me, kissed him hard and long, then waited until those dick *head*-hunters lusted after somebody else.

"Baby, let's go shopping. I want to buy you something special to remember our six-month anniversary and our first vacation together," I suggested, already leading Jay toward the car I'd reserved to take us to the best jewelry store in MoBay.

This would be the only time I'd let Jay out of my sight. Since Jay had paid for everything, I wanted to buy him something nice so I bought him a brilliant eighteen-karat white gold tennis bracelet with diamonds, praying that he'd buy me an engagement ring. I didn't care what size the diamond was. That's

not exactly true, but more importantly I desperately
wanted to make plans to wear my wedding dress soon.
I was thinking ahead and packed my gown in a sepa-
rate suitcase. If things went the way I wanted I'd be
married on a Caribbean beach sometime this week.

I thought my prayers were answered when Jay went
to the restroom. Purposefully I stayed with our driver,
and when Jay entered the restroom, I frantically opened
his bag. My heart stopped. Covering my mouth, I stared
at the white box.

Hurry up and open it before he returns, I told myself.

Tears streamed down my cheeks as my trembling
hands slowly opened the box. Gasping for air, I
frowned. "Ruby earrings!" I snapped the box closed.
Mad as hell, I dropped the box into the bag when I
saw Jay walking toward us.

*Calm down. Act normal. Maybe it's a test of some sort.
Maybe he went to the restroom and put the ring in his
pocket.*

"Don't cha dare say any *ting,* mon," I said to the
driver, slipping him five hundred Jamaican dollars.

Quickly stuffing the money in his pocket, the driver
answered, "It's bad luck, ya know, not ta trust 'im."

No, that gigolo didn't just check me. What did he know
about us? He was merely our driver.

Sternly, I asked him, "What's your name?"

"Barker," he said with a friendly smile, looking like
he didn't have a care in the world.

I was sure Barker should've been the last person
speaking about trust. With his rich black licorice complexion, waist-length locks, perfect white teeth, bulging
biceps, flat abs, firm ass, and sexy Jamaican accent—
hypnotic enough to make a woman come instantly—
I was sure that wide smile was from getting more
than his share of *punanni.*

"Well, Barker. You don't know me, so stay out of

my business." Right before Jay got in the car, I hissed to Barker, "Keep your mouth shut."

His smile vanished. Barker did as I demanded, remaining quiet the entire time he zipped down the road, getting us back to our resort in half the time it took for him to get us to the jewelry store.

"Hey, mon, you awfully quiet," Jay said, touching Barker on the shoulder.

"Sometimes silence is golden, ya know?" Barker said. Turning up Bob Marley on his CD player, Barker started singing along, "No woman, no cry. No woman, no cry."

Thankful to be back at the resort, I couldn't wait to get out of Barker's car.

The water slide at the hotel was Jay's favorite and the swing was mine. Jay told me that zooming down the slippery slide gave him a rush, but splashing into the pool dick first felt like having an orgasm without coming. *I guess.*

My favorite thing to do was swing. Naked. Right before sunrise and sunset, the world seemed at peace. At first when I told Jay, "Let's swing," his eyes opened wide. Slapping his shoulder, I said, "Not that kind of swing." Jay had better not try any of that kinky stuff with me or nobody else.

Throwing my legs up in the air, I thrust myself into the salty sea breeze that engulfed my nostrils while blowing through my hair. Hoisting backward, gaining more momentum, I must've inhaled and exhaled a million times, each time releasing my lifelong frustrations into the wind. Having Jay all to myself made me feel worry-free. I could stay in MoBay with Jay forever. I swung every day, wondering why life couldn't be this way all the times . . . carefree as the wind. The wind could be gentle. The wind could be destructive. The one thing the wind could never be is predictable.

With each passing day, Jay too had become a little

unpredictable in a good kinda way, making love to me morning, noon, and night.

"Mmm," I moaned along with Jay.

His teeth nibbled, and then he wrapped his moist lips around my pinky toe. My leg contracted as Jay sucked my other toes like a harmonica, making his way to my big toe.

Gasping, I exhaled, "Oh my God."

"Relax," Jay whispered, opening his mouth wide.

Slowly his lips cupped my big toe. His teeth clamped ever so slowly, grazing my toe until he reached the tip of my nail. Trembling, I swear my eyeballs did a 360-degree rotation as I exhaled a long "Oooh."

Jay raised my leg higher. Pressing his lips into the socket behind my knee, he French-kissed my crevice while lightly dragging his fingernails up my leg, over my ass, and then he pinched my nipple.

"Mmm," we moaned in unison.

As I grabbed the sheets, my head, neck, and shoulders leaned forward.

He pushed me flat back onto the mattress. "Relax, baby. This is our last day here. I want us to remember every second, of every minute, of every hour."

I stared at the ceiling.

Jay's lips trailed up my leg to my pubic hair. Then he sniffed. "Mmm."

His wide flat tongue curled beneath my vagina. At a snail's pace, I swear, Jay's tongue approached my vaginal opening, continuing up, overlapping my outer lips, to my inner lips . . . I shut my eyes tight. Although he hadn't touched my clit yet, his tongue was so close I felt the heat rising from his taste buds.

Just lick it. Please, please, lick it! What! He missed it!

I couldn't believe Jay's tongue bypassed my clit, dipped below my vaginal opening, and started all over as if he'd messed up and needed to hit it right.

"Mmm, huh," I moaned, popping the fitted sheet off the corners of the mattress.

When Jay missed again, I tried to help him out by repositioning my hips.

"Ba-*bee*," I groaned.

Jay rose upon his knees, dragged my ass to his chest, placed my legs over his shoulders, then buried his face into my pussy. My neck shrank into my head like a turtle's. The only parts of me remaining on the mattress were my head and shoulders.

Jay repeated his tease, dragging his tongue over my vaginal opening, except this time he didn't miss my clit. Softly suctioning my clitoris, then delving his tongue into my pussy, Jay alternated his rhythm, focusing more attention on my clit.

"Oh, shit, Jay, baby. That feels sooo good."

I felt fluids streaming from my clit like a faucet when the minty tingle of a tiny Altoid unexpectedly pressed against my clit. Another Altoid crept toward my G-spot when Jay inserted his tongue inside me.

"Mmmmm," Jay hummed with passion, licking my come button while stretching my shaft upward.

When Jay lightly blew cool air all over my pussy, I screamed, "Oh my God! Jay," I panted. "Ba-*bee*. Please stop. I'm about to lose it. I can't take any more. What are you doing to me?"

Ignoring my plea, Jay sucked my clit while finger-fucking me, and I began to pee, except I wasn't urinating. I knew exactly what was happening this time. I was experiencing another one of those wet 'n wild G-spot orgasms.

"Oooh! Oh my God . . . oooh!" I opened my mouth wide but nothing came out. I couldn't breathe. I whispered, "Bay," then yelled, "beeeeeeeee!" so loud I could hear people cheering outside our window.

Part two of our lovemaking session was starting

right after a brief intermission and I was determined to make Jay yell just as loud or louder.

I sang, "I love you" to Jay all the way to the glass-bottom boat, praying this time one of his sperms would successfully penetrate one of my eggs. I was ovulating, so after Jay came deep inside me, I held my legs above the headboard, elevating them against the wall. When he asked what I was doing, I told the truth first, then lied, "You made me come so hard, I have to get the blood circulating back into my legs."

Sticking out his chest, Jay smiled, so I smiled too.

The shallow water required everyone to walk a few feet out into the ocean, then climb the white ladder in order to board the boat I floated on cloud nine, not remembering how I'd gotten the strength to shower and get dressed for what would be our last outing. For whatever reason, he insisted we were the first two to get on the boat. Leading the group of tourists, Jay tightly held his travel bag high in the air, and gently held my hand in his other.

"I love you, Jay."

"I love you too, baby."

"Aw, that's so sweet, the woman behind us said.

Ain't nobody talkin' to you, I thought, ignoring her.

Normally, I would've turned to check her out, but I was riding high on my big O.

I'd worn my sexiest canary-yellow two-piece with a multicolored wrap, which complemented my new even tan. I thought Jay couldn't possibly get any blacker, but I was wrong. Over the course of our vacation, thanks to the nude beach, his feet, legs, butt, and privates, were evenly colored.

"Baby, this vacation is the best! Whew, I love you so much and I'm happy as hell that my boys were wrong," Jay said, helping me reach the first step of the ladder, which was higher than I'd imagined.

Stepping aboard I asked, "Wrong about what, honey?"

"Oh, nothing," Jay said, smiling wide. "Let's sit below-decks. I don't want to miss a thing below the sea. You know what I mean."

I was pondering what Jay meant about his boys, so once we were sitting by the clear window surrounded by crystal-blue water, Jay hugging and kissing me, I figured I could drill him.

This was the best surprise! No other man had sprung an all-inclusive paid tropical vacation on me. I didn't need Jay to pay for any of my expenses, but the fact that he insisted I leave all my credit cards, traveler's checks, and cash in my purse was wild!

We'd done everything from hanging out on the beach, to making love in the sand, shopping at the market, partying at the nightclubs. The moment that female stripper at the Rated-X Club offered me and Jay a lap dance, I insisted we leave and demanded Jay never go back. On our way out the door of Rated-X, men and women were on the stage having sex. Real sex. But I'd bet money on the fact that none, I mean not one, of those Jamaicans was better than my Jay. I was sad our trip was coming to an end and this was our last night on the island.

"Jay, baby," I said, holding his hand as the boat rocked along the shore. "I've had the time of my life. Everything was perfect. Thank you, my love."

"C'mere." Jay paused, then said, "Closer . . . now kiss me."

"Aw, that's so sweet," the same woman said.

This time I shot her a quick look.

"I'm over here, honey," Jay said, redirecting my attention. "Ashlee, you complete me. You're my everything. I brought you to Jamaica not only to show you—"

Covering my mouth, I gasped.

Jay's cell phone rung. On the ocean? This technology shit was becoming too efficient.

Unzipping the black bag, Jay silenced his phone. We were now far out enough to see the most colorful combinations—red, blue, green, black, purple, white—tropical fish and a few baby sharks and hopefully too far for Jay to get service.

Probably his boys calling again. I wish Jay would've left his phone in D.C.

Jay looked at me and said, "Where was I—"

That woman seated next to us said, "I brought you to Jamaica not only to."

Smiling at the woman all friendly and shit, Jay said, "Hey, thanks. That's right."

I shot her an angrier look that said *Shut the hell up!*

"Baby, I'm over here. Look at me. I want to show you—"

Jay's phone rang again. This time I exhaled as he silenced it again. "Baby, I'm sorry. Let me—"

This was incredible. "Turn off the damn phone, Jay. You should've left it at home."

Giving me a *shut the hell up* look, Jay removed his cell phone from his bag, checked the ID, then said, "I have to take this. I'll be right back. Wait here."

No need for that. I followed Jay on deck, but he was in such a hurry he must've thought I was downstairs when he answered, "Hey, is everything all right? . . . Are you sure about this? You realize what you're asking me to do? Look, stay at my place. I have an extra key under the mat. We'll talk about this when I get home tomorrow."

Jay turned around, damned near tripping over my feet. "I thought I told you to stay downstairs."

"You can't tell me what to do. Who in the hell were you calling, baby?"

"Nobody. What are you talking about?"

"So nobody is staying at your house too, huh? And what do you have to talk to her about?"

"That was a friend who needs a place to stay for a few days."

"So when did you start calling her baby? And why is she staying at our house? Answer me, Jay!"

"I didn't! I didn't call her anything. What I said was hey. If you weren't so fuckin' suspicious, you could hear straight. And it's not our house, it's my damn house!"

"Uh-huh. Gotcha! So it was a woman. I know what I heard, Jay. And I do have my own key, you know."

"Well, I know what you won't hear. And if you keep acting crazy, I know what you won't get," Jay said, removing a different box than the one I'd seen earlier from his travel bag.

That was not the box with the earrings. That had to be . . . "Baby, please, I'm sorry," I pleaded, reaching for the box. I wanted that ring. I deserved that ring. I earned that ring.

Jay flipped opened the lid, but I couldn't see what was inside the box. All I saw were sparkles that almost blinded me.

"Yes, Jay," I said, anticipating his offer.

"No, Ashlee," he countered.

"Give me my ring!" I yelled, scratching Jay's arm, trying to reach the box hovering high above his head.

Jay backed away from me. I stumbled with the sway of the boat, falling into Jay. Slapping him repeatedly in his chest, I began to cry, "Jay, please," grabbing him around his knees.

"Ashlee, I love you. But I can't keep dealing with

your insecurities. It's over," Jay said, tossing the box into his travel bag.

"Don't you walk away from me, Jay Crawford! This isn't about marrying me, is it? It's about you getting back with that wannabe *Pop Star* bitch, Tracy."

I hadn't realized that nosy woman had come aboard too until she said to Jay, "The night is young and I'm lots of fun."

Grabbing her around the legs, I hurled her ass overboard.

Jay shook his head, diving in to help rescue the drowning woman. I knew her no-swimming ass wished she would've shut the hell up now.

"He was supposed to be my rescuer."

Opening Jay's travel bag, I flipped open the box. The most beautiful princess-cut solitaire blinded me. The first thing I was doing when we got back home was refilling my prescription. The second was planning our wedding.

CHAPTER 21

Jay

When I realized I loved Ashlee, I thought we'd be together always and forever. Now I'd realized forever isn't a very long time anymore. When I got back from Jamaica, I walked around the house with a little gloom in my heart because I just couldn't believe we really broke up. The signs were all there to warn me the ending was close, but I was in denial. I wanted things between us to work, and at first, I thought I could put up with her paranoia, but Ashlee was a bit too close to the insane side for me.

I was stunned to receive a call in Jamaica from Tracy. Her timing couldn't have been more perfect—just before I was about to ask Ashlee to marry me. When she asked me not to marry Ashlee, I wondered if I was hearing things. Tracy, the woman who once said she didn't need anything from me, actually called to stop my proposal to another woman. I was baffled to say the least.

It was nine o'clock at night, but the sky had been dark ever since I left work at five. According to the weather report, severe thunderstorms had consumed all areas from D.C. to Philadelphia. I took my candles out of the closet and set them in places where they could be easily reached in case of a blackout. I put the lighter on my nightstand and went to fix myself a drink.

I sipped on some Hennessey as I paced my bedroom, trying to calm my nerves about calling Tracy. I needed get to the bottom of her phone call. I took a deep breath and dialed the number. She answered the phone quickly, as if she was expecting me to call at that moment.

"Hello," she said.

"Tracy, it's Jay. What's up?" I asked.

She sounded relieved. "Jay, thank God. I didn't think you'd call."

"Why? Is anything wrong?"

Tracy's silence frightened me. She finally spoke up after I'd called her name several times. "I'm here, Jay. I just . . . I . . . I need to see you," she said, sounding sad.

It was late, but there was no way I was going to turn her down after hearing how pitiful she sounded. "Okay. Why don't you taxi over to my place? I'll pay the driver once you get here."

She agreed, and then I gave her the address. I began to tidy up my place a bit. I couldn't imagine what was going on with Tracy. First, she deliberately intervened with my marriage proposal, and then she asked to come see me. I became even more nervous than before, and every minute it took for her to get to my place seemed like hours. The thunder grew louder and the rain fell harder. I opened my door and there was practically no visibility. More than two hours had passed since I'd spoken to Tracy, and I felt she should've arrived within an hour of hanging up the phone with me. Once all the power blacked out, I lit the candles, then kept a lookout for Tracy. I began to worry about her being in that cab. I wondered if he was a cautious driver or a roadrunner like most I'd experienced. I repeatedly opened the door to see if she had been standing outside knocking, but I hadn't heard her due to the rain. On my fifth time opening the door, I noticed the cab pulling up.

I grabbed an umbrella and my wallet to pay the fare. Tracy stepped out of the car. She leaned in to hand the driver the money, and then we sprinted into the house. I shook the umbrella and set it next to the door. I turned to take Tracy's raincoat, but she walked over to the couch to take a seat.

"Sorry the place is so dimly lit. All the power went out," I said.

"That's okay," she responded, looking around. "The candles are nice."

"Would you like me to take your coat?"

"No . . . no . . . I'm fine." She pulled the hood off her head.

My eyes met hers in shock. "Oh my God. You . . . you cut your hair? And dyed it blond again."

She nodded, smiling, while I was speechless and having flashbacks of the old days when she first sported the Eve look.

"Well, what do you think?"

Tracy continued to smile. She looked like the goddess I'd met several years before. I liked her hair long, but I hadn't met a woman who could turn me on with a short haircut like Tracy could. There was no doubting she was sexy, but with a capital S. I sensed she knew how erotic she looked by the way she smiled and crossed her legs as she sat, revealing much of her bronze-colored thigh through the split in her raincoat.

"You look terrific, absolutely fantastic." I offered her a drink. "I've got some Hennessey. Would you like some? Or would you prefer wine?"

"A glass of wine would be nice." For the past few months we'd just been friends, but by the way she was looking at me I was starting to think I might have a chance. Only problem was, if I was wrong I could set back our friendship by years.

I poured her wine, then sat next to her. "Tracy, you must know you've got me blown away right now. Why did you call me to stop my engagement?"

She sipped her wine, then sat up. " 'Cause I still love you, Jay," she said. "I know I told you I'd moved on, but not long after you came back in Jason's and my life I decided to leave my boyfriend."

Although I was glad to hear her news, I felt perplexed. "Tracy, I don't understand. Weren't you happy? I mean . . . you told me he was a great guy. He took you and Jason on trips and treated him as his own son. What would make you decide to leave a man so loving?"

She shook her head. "Truth is, he was convenient. I needed to be away from my parents . . . out of their house, and he enabled me to do that. I cared for him, and I might've even thought I loved him, but I knew I was fooling myself when I ran into you."

"Trust me. I understand the difference. That's one of the reasons Kenya and I didn't stay together."

"Speaking of Kenya—I still can't believe the two of you are divorced."

"Yeah? Well, I tried to tell you. You didn't believe me. But that's all water under the bridge now. You didn't come here to talk about our past. Why are you really here?"

"Jay, ever since you've come back into the picture, I realized I've always loved you. I told you I'm thinking with my head and not my heart these days. I've come to grasp that you've got my mind and my soul." She slid closer. "So, did you do it? Did you give her the ring?"

"No. You asked me not to, remember?"

"And that was enough for you?"

"Yeah, guess when it really comes down to it, it was."

Tracy's smile widened. "Well, where is it? Can I see the ring?"

I didn't know what she was getting at, but I obliged. I went to the bedroom and came back out with the two-carat treasure that had almost belonged to Ashlee. Tracy sat with her mouth open as she stared at the ring in the box. She took it out and put it on her finger. It was a perfect fit.

"Damn, this is nice," she said, grinning.

"Yeah, I thought so, too. But, oh well, I've still got the receipt."

"Maybe I should wear it?" she asked, holding her hand out to get a better look at it.

I had a sudden revelation, and for a minute I didn't know how to answer. I didn't want my instinct to be wrong, so I sat silently for a moment. Tracy looked at me as if her feelings were hurt.

"What's wrong now?" I asked, rubbing my hand across her hair.

She had tears in her eyes. "I asked you if I could wear it. Do you not have a response for me?"

I could tell by her emotions that my instinct was right, so I acted on it. "Are you asking me to marry you?"

She smiled. "Why, are you accepting?"

We both smiled and then shared a bit of laughter before I could answer. "Tracy, I want to, but I just broke up with Ashlee. She's still calling me every fifteen minutes. Although I'm not answering. And I sense I'll have to cross her path a time or two before she gets the picture that it's really over between us. I wouldn't want you to think that I'm playing you."

"Jay, listen. I understand that after every relationship there's a cooling-down period. I know you and Ashlee will probably even screw a time or two before things are completely dissolved. But what I understand the most is a good relationship is not built on sex alone. It's about having each other's back. And one thing you should've learned about me is that I've got you. I'm not worried about Ashlee. You'll be right here . . . with me. The only thing I wanna know is, do you still love me?"

"Yeah, I love you. I never stopped loving you."

Tracy had definitely grown up since we last dated. We sat kissing while loud claps of thunder attempted to distract our intimate moment. Tracy wasn't giving in and neither was I. Once I'd tasted enough of her cherry lip gloss, I allowed her to breathe. She seized the opportunity to reask her question.

"So, Jay Crawford, you gonna marry me or what?"

I kissed her lips, then answered, "Yes. Yes, Tracy. I'll marry you."

She grabbed my face and sucked my lips some more. I didn't want her to stop, but she did. Then she stood over me as I sat on the couch. She opened her coat, causing me to have a sudden déjà vu. Tracy stood before me in her birthday suit, which still possessed the same sleek, tender frame that used to drive me crazy. She dropped her coat to the floor, and my dick sprang to attention.

"Remember this?" she asked, standing seductively.

"I sure do," I responded.

I stood, then picked her up. I proceeded to carry her to the love nest—my bed.

CHAPTER 22

Ashlee

If you do this, you know you're going to piss him off.
Why should I give a damn about making Jay upset?
We'd been back from Jamaica for ten days and he
hadn't so much as called me once. Pacing in my
newly furnished D.C. apartment, I cried, reminiscing
on the demise—the day we'd returned from Jamaica
to the States—of our relationship.

Spying from my apartment, I watched that bitch
Tracy stand there waiting for Jay to open the car door.
The hairs on the nape of my neck curled. "Whatever!
He doesn't love you the way he loves me!" Jay was
using Tracy to try and forget about me. Tracy was no
more than a doormat for Jay to wipe his feet on. Bet
she didn't have a key like me. Bet she didn't tell him
her little secrets.

I sat at the window wondering, how could Tracy
have known the exact moment Jay planned to propose
to me? Her timing couldn't have been that great.
That bitch had used roots or voodoo on him Now
the comment about his boys made sense. But why?

Why take me all the way to Jamaica to embarrass me, to use me, to sex me crazy, then emotionally abandon me?

I'd had no intention of going to Dallas when Jay and I returned from Jamaica, but Jay insisted we take a break from one another for a while. No time period like a week or two or three. Just a break. That seemed too permanent for me and I wasn't having it. Undeniably I was the best thing that'd happened to Jay. He just didn't know it.

The day our plane landed at La Guardia, Jay headed to the gate for his connecting flight to Reagan National Airport in D.C. Jay was so upset he didn't hug or kiss me good-bye. A wave from a distance was all I got while I watched Jay walk away with my engagement ring stuffed in his pocket. I deserved better treatment. I knew he was testing me to see if I would chill out. So far, so good, but my patience was thinning.

Peeping through the blinds, I watched Jay place Jason in the backseat, fasten Jason's seat belt, then get into his BMW and drive off.

I sat in a chair by the window, continuing my thoughts. After we'd parted at La Guardia, I pretended I was going to my gate to go home, then detoured to ticketing and purchased a one-way ticket to Baltimore Washington International Airport. The last thing I wanted was to run into Jay at Reagan National. I'd made arrangements to have my luggage rerouted back to BWI, and then I boarded my flight to Baltimore with my toiletries in my tote.

I picked up a rental car at BWI. With no destination in mind, no reservation for a place to spend the night, somehow I drove to Jay's house. Why I couldn't control my obsession to be with Jay, I don't know. Next thing I knew, that day, I was standing in front of Jay's doorbell.

I convinced myself, *Give him a day or two, then come back.*

Returning to the car, I sat staring at Jay's house. Looking across the street, I noticed a FOR RENT sign in the window. The lower unit of the fourplex had a phone number listed. Immediately I dialed the number, started up my engine, then parked on the opposite side of the street. The manager, who lived upstairs, greeted me at the vacant unit.

"Yes, hello," I said, flashing my best smile. "I'm new to this area, and well, this seems like a good quiet neighborhood."

"Quiet it is. Nothing ever happens around here. The postman leaves packages on your doorstep. Occasionally kids rip and run in the street, so you have to keep an eye out for 'em. Other than that, no worries."

"You mind if I see the apartment?"

"Not at all," he said, opening the door. "Everything was done up nicely. New drapes, carpet, refrig, stove. Just put the sign in the window today."

Peeping through the horizontal blinds, I saw I had a perfect view of Jay's place. "I'll take it."

"Well, I'll need you to fill out an application, and make a deposit," he said, sniffing the air around him.

Yeah, you smell like weed, Mr. Manager, I thought. This was going to be easy. Since I hadn't spent much money in Jamaica, I pulled out two grand in cash. "How much?" One thing Darius taught me was that anything and everyone had a price.

The manager's eyes lit up. "Um, five hundred deposit and one thousand for the first month's rent."

I handed him the whole two thousand. "When can I move in?"

Handing me the keys, he said, "Welcome to the neighborhood. Your parking garage is number two right below your unit. I'll slide the application under your door."

I'd been living across the street from Jay ever since.

Waiting for Jay and Tracy to leave, I dashed across the street, used my key, and entered Jay's apartment. The aroma of cinnamon candles and warm vanilla lingered in the air. I walked into Jay's bedroom. The bed was neatly made. Everything was neat and clean.

Bitch. She couldn't wait to take my place. *That's all right, I've got something for her ass.* Glancing on the nightstand, I noticed the ring box.

"That's my damn ring," I said, opening the box. *What the hell?* The box was empty.

Oh, I wanted to call Jay and curse his ass out. Instead I left, went home, and waited for them to return.

Sooner than I thought, Jay parked in front of his house. Quickly I dressed into my baggy jeans and long T-shirt, hid my hair underneath my baseball cap, slid on my glasses, and followed them all the way to the D.C. zoo.

I parked about eight spaces from Jay, waited for him to get out of his car, then trailed them at a distance.

Unexpectedly my cell phone rang. It was Darius. I debated taking his call, fearing I'd lose track of Jay.

Walking over to the monkeys, I answered, "What?"

"What? What do you mean, what?"

"I'm busy. What is it?"

"Your son, that's what. We're going to be in Dallas tomorrow."

"And?" I said, moving toward the pandas. "I'm in D.C."

"You are truly a piece of work. We'll be in D.C. next week to play the Wizards. I'll have my agent send you two courtside tickets. If we see ya we see ya. Bye."

Damn! Darius made me lose track of Jay. That was okay. I returned to the parking lot, removed an ice pick from my trunk, and knelt beside Jay's car. In between people passing by, I punctured all four of Jay's tires on the sides multiple times. I guess I got carried away and started stabbing Jay's doors, his hood, his windshield.

"I hate you, Jay! I hate you!" I yelled with each strike.

"Hey, man! What the fuck are you doing!" Jay yelled, running toward me.

Dropping the pick, I raced to my rental car, fired up the engine, and ripped out of the parking lot. I'd have at least two hours to go back to Jay's house and plot my next move while going through all his shit.

That'll teach you to fuck with me.

CHAPTER 23

Jay

There should be a rule written somewhere that prohibits exes from pestering each other after a breakup because Ashlee was about to drive me crazy. I'd never in my wildest dreams ever thought this woman could be so obsessed, but I was wrong. I hated to admit it but Kyle was right. She wasn't obsessed, that girl was nuts. One day she'd literally sent six dozen roses to the job, with the sweetest notes I'd ever read. I almost felt bad about how things had ended until the next day when she sent me a set of Ginsu knives with a note that read *pick one of these so I can cut your balls off.* After reading that I was starting to think she might have been the one who messed up my car. Thank God I got rid of her before a wedding occurred, or even worse, she got pregnant. Oh, and the crazy gifts were just the tip of the iceberg.

It was the constant phone calls that really drove me crazy. That girl was blowing up my phones twenty-four-seven. I swear to God, she would call my phone a minimum of a hundred times a day. As it was I'd changed her ring tone on my cell phone to the robot's voice from *Lost in Space*. So now whenever she called, my phone would chime, "Warning! Warning! Will Robinson!" over and over again. My son Jason thought it was funny, while Tracy and I thought it was scary shit.

Monday morning began with even more aggravation from Ashlee before I could make it to work. She'd called my cell phone at least fifty times before I left the house. She was probably mad because I called the phone company and changed my home number. My home phone rang so many times last night I had to switch it to SILENCE in order to get any sleep. When I saw her number on the caller ID at work, I asked Steve Jamison, a coworker, to take the call and tell her I was out of the office for the day. As far as I was concerned, Ashlee and I were through . . . finished . . . a done deal. The only problem was she just couldn't get it through that thick skull of hers. She ended up cursing Steve out and calling him a liar.

On the drive home, I thought about Tracy and Jason a lot. They'd left to go out of town on Friday, something to do with *Pop Star*, and they weren't due back until sometime late tonight. We were all supposed to hook up in the morning at Jason's day care. They were having some type of program. I couldn't wait, I really missed them.

I had a few errands to make, including getting a new cell phone number. Maybe now that she couldn't get in touch with me Ashlee would get the big picture. When I got out the rental car, I made a mental note to call the auto body place about my car. There was almost ten thousand dollars' worth of damage and a promise from my insurance company that my rates were going to go up. Man, if I ever found out who messed up my car, there was going to be a funeral.

My immediate thoughts went to Ashlee, but then I dismissed it because she was in Dallas. She wouldn't do that. Would she?

The second I walked up to my door, my nose was met with a tantalizing aroma. I could hear water running in the kitchen sink and dishes clacking. Somebody was in my house, and Tracy was halfway across the country in California. *Oh, hell no. Please, God, no,* I thought as I opened the door. I put my keys and jacket on the couch and headed into the kitchen. When I turned the corner and saw Ashlee, my temples started throbbing. I wanted to run up and choke the life out of her. What the fuck was she doing here? She had no right to enter my home without my permission. I was pissed, and she was about to find out just how much.

"What the fuck are you doing here?" I yelled. I could tell I had startled her because she jumped and nearly dropped a plate when she turned around.

"Oh, Jay. There you are, baby. I've been trying to reach you all day. Did you know your number was disconnected? And then I called your job and they said you weren't at work. Did you play hooky today? Because if you did, well, I jumped on the first plane. I've been worried sick about you," she stated with concern. Believe it or not, she had tears in her eyes as she walked toward me with her arms wide. "I've missed you."

I knocked the first arm coming toward me down to her side, causing the plate she'd been holding to crash on the floor. "Look what you've done," she screamed, pointing at the broken pieces. "That was real china. I purchased it earlier today. It was part of your surprise with dinner tonight."

"Surprise?" I questioned angrily. "Don't you mean more like a disturbance? I broke up with you, Ashlee.

Now why the fuck are you in my home, and how did you get in here?"

At first she looked stunned at my reaction, but then she took a deep breath and smiled. "We didn't break up. You said we needed some time apart. Well, we've had time apart, Jay. I don't wanna be apart anymore."

Suddenly I could feel a migraine coming on. "How the hell did you get into my house?" I couldn't control my voice.

"I used my key, sweetheart. How else would I have gotten in?" she responded, then walked away.

I had forgotten about the spare I'd given her. I could've shot my own self at that moment for not remembering to take back my key. Ashlee opened the oven to check on the food. I couldn't see around her to tell what it was, but the smell was heavenly. I desperately wanted to throw her ass out, then eat up her food in solitude. She pranced about the kitchen and began repeatedly singing a line from one of Diana Ross's ole school songs.

"It's my house, and I live here . . . It's my house, and I live here . . . It's my house and I live here," she sang.

"Ashlee," I yelled. "Do you not see me standing here?"

She smiled again. "Of course I do, dear. I'm sorry. I was just making sure the lasagna was ready," she said, pulling the pan out of the oven. She took a long sniff. "Mmm. I can tell this is going to be sooo goood." She placed the pan on top of the stove, picked up a serving spoon, and then turned to look at me. "Sweetheart, you shouldn't be just standing there. You should go get out of those clothes and tidy up for dinner because everything is almost done."

I blew a fuse. "I'm standing here because I want

you to get the fuck out," I screamed. "Get out . . . get out . . . O-U-T . . . get your ass out!"

She dropped the crooked smile she'd worn since I walked in, then set the serving spoon on the stove. "You really want me to leave?" she asked, trying to sound pitiful.

"If I could say it in another language to help you better understand it I would, but I don't speak anything except English."

She folded her arms across her chest and leaned against the counter. "Hmph. Well, that's too bad because I'm not going anywhere. And you're going to behave yourself and sit down for dinner."

Enough was enough. I darted toward her, then tussled to grab her around her waist. I tried unsuccessfully to pull her out of the kitchen. She put up a good struggle and won after I became tired trying to restrain her without physically hurting her. I backed against the refrigerator, panting and ogling her. She held herself up on the counter, trying to catch her breath while staring back and apparently awaiting my next move. I was too disgusted to fight any longer.

"Ashlee, if I have to call the police, I will," I stated.

She didn't say a word. She slowly staggered toward me, then kissed me. Her lips were soft and moist. Her breath was sweet. I wanted to kiss her back, but I knew I'd be sending mixed signals. I stood with my eyes open and watched as she continued to place slow kisses on my face and neck. By the time she made it back to my lips she was crying.

"I still love you, Jay," she cried. "Please kiss me back."

"Ashlee, you need to lea—" I started.

"I'm sorry I fucked up. I still love you, Jay," she whispered.

She began stroking my dick. I tried to grab her

hand to stop her, but she put up resistance. Ashlee knew the right things to say and do to me. She knew it would be tough to refuse her sex.

"I need you, Jay," she said, caressing me through my pants. "Just let me taste him. I promise you'll like it." She slid to her knees. I wanted to pull my dick out and feed it to her, but I stayed strong. I knew I couldn't have sex with her. If I did, I'd mess up everything with Tracy.

"Ashlee, get up," I said, helping her off the floor. "We're just not right for each other."

"Yes, we are," she said. She tried to kiss me and this time I resisted.

"No, we're not." I pushed her away.

"Jay, don't do this. Please, I need you." She grabbed me, pulling me in close. "I was going to wait until our wedding night for this, but I want you to make love to me anally. I want you to fuck me in the ass like those guys do in the pornos we used to watch together. Come on, baby, don't you wanna fuck me in the ass?"

I raised both eyebrows, a little surprised by her offer. Anal sex was the only thing Ashlee and I hadn't done. It wasn't high on my agenda of things to do, and we never even talked about it when we were together, but the freakish way she offered it to me somehow managed to excite me and get me hard— Ashlee's cue to keep up her attempt of seducing me.

"Come on, baby, fuck me in my ass. Please, baby, you know you want to." She kept repeating those words as she continued to play with me through my pants. I'm ashamed to admit it but a few seconds later my fly was down and my dick was fully erect, standing at attention. Ashlee stood up, pulled down her skirt and panties, then turned her ass toward me. Beyonce didn't have shit on her. Her ass was just as plump and as inviting as could be. She slapped one cheek, then the other, leaving two red handprints on her ass. My dick jumped a half inch longer.

"You want some of this, baby? You wanna fuck me in my ass?" she purred in the most erotic voice I'd ever heard.

Lord forgive me but I nodded my head yes.

"Okay, baby, Mama's gonna give you some." She walked seductively over to the kitchen counter where she'd been cooking and grabbed a bottle of olive oil. She laughed as she opened the bottle. "Guess what, baby. Extra virgin, just like me."

She turned around again and poured the entire bottle onto her ass, making it shine like a bright yellow lightbulb.

"What you waiting for, baby? Don't you wanna take my virginity?" She grabbed hold of the kitchen table, stuck out her ass, and started to make her booty clap like the video dancers do. "Come on, baby, she's calling you."

I'm sorry but at that point I was done. I swallowed hard, letting my pants fall to the floor, as I rubbed the five o'clock shadow of my beard. There was an awkward silence in the room and both of us knew I was about to do what I didn't want to do.

That is, until the answering machine clicked on. I had forgotten that I'd turned the ringers off on my phones, so Tracy's voice was a shock to both me and Ashlee.

"Hey, baby, this is Tracy. I got the new number. I'm glad you did it," she said. "I just wanted to remind you that Jason's program's at his preschool begins at eight o'clock tomorrow morning. I know you wouldn't miss it for anything, so I don't know why I'm so worried. I guess I'm just nervous. I figured I should've heard from you by now, so I was just touching base. I'll probably call your cell phone, but if you get this message before I talk to you, give me a shout. Thanks. Love you."

I don't know what came over me, but I couldn't move during her message. Ashlee and I both froze when we heard Tracy speak. "Forget her, Jay. Come on over here and get some of this virgin stuff. Come're, baby, and make it hurt so good."

"Oh my God what the hell is wrong with me?" I glanced at Ashlee, then the phone. My dick immediately went limp and I reached down for my pants. "Ashlee, put your clothes on 'cause you got to go."

"You mothafucker," she yelled. "You're shooing me away for that bitch! And after all I did for . . . all I was about to do for you?"

"Save it, Ashlee. You wasn't about to anything but get me in trouble. Now where's my key?" I spotted it on the counter, then snatched it before she could.

"Mothafucker, I don't believe—"

I interrupted her. "Ashlee, like I said before: I don't have time to fight. I've got things to do, so I need you to leave."

"You can't treat me like this!" Ashlee screamed like a madwoman. "You're not going to get away with this! I promise you, Jay. I'm gonna get you for this."

"Yeah . . . yeah . . . I hear you. Now get the fuck out."

She began putting her clothes on. She cussed me between sticking each leg into her pants and pulling her top over her head. "You motha . . . fucking . . . son . . . of . . . a . . . bitch! You won't get away with this, and I mean it, or my name isn't Ashlee Anderson."

CHAPTER 24

Ashlee

Some men don't recognize a good woman until she slaps him in the face.

I sat by my window all night waiting for Tracy to show up. Lucky for her she didn't, 'cause I probably would've burned down Jay's apartment with both of them in it. Barely keeping my eyes open, I paced the floor still in shock about what had happened last night.

Jay was standing there all big and bad with his chest stuck out telling me to get the fuck out. I tried being nice to Jay, but after that bastard threw me out of his house—greasy ass and all—he left me no choice except to get real ugly. What man in his right or wrong mind would turn down a home-cooked meal, a blow job, and a butterball virgin booty oiled up for him to hit all night long? Jay would pay for that one because what he didn't know was I had the power to destroy his life within minutes. I knew all about Jason's little program.

Tracy had left several messages on the answering

machine earlier, interrupting me in the middle of preparing my fiancé's dinner. How rude of her. I deleted them all. When a woman suspects another woman is fucking her man, she's usually right, and I could tell from the tone in Tracy's voice that she had had some of my dick. That and the "I love you" and she had his new home and cell numbers and I didn't. That was not okay, but I wasn't focusing my energies on Tracy. Not yet anyway.

The only way Tracy deserved more attention than Jay was if she had my wedding ring on her finger. If that was the case, all of America would see her hold a microphone with three fingers and a thumb! Tracy would publicly become my enemy, and I didn't give a damn if *Newsweek* had us on the cover every week. Oh, if she had my ring on, she'd best believe I was fuckin' her up. I'd battle with her ass until she coughed up a lung, gave up my man, and handed over my precious jewel. If Tracy valued her three-year-old crumb snatcher, she'd readily concede. Jay would too if he had sense.

Didn't Jay know I'd made a triplicate of his house key? I didn't have to go past the living room to borrow the key to his rental car that he'd left on the coffee table. Grabbing a plastic bag from his kitchen, I stuffed it with oregano. I unlocked Jay's car, hid the seasoning in Jay's glove box, returned his car key, then snuck back to my apartment and made a phone call to my father's investigator.

"Hey, Raymond. I need a really big favor."

After a few huge lies, Raymond agreed to help me out. I was becoming pretty good at lying to people.

Easing into my bed, I had to think this plan all the way through or else my conniving ways were going to backfire in my face. Jay would explode if he ever found out the truth. Let's see, I couldn't kill Jason like I'd . . . I got it!

The only way I'd serve time for kidnapping was if I got caught. But I wouldn't. I could sell Jason on the black market. *Hell, I thought, I'ma give his spoiled butt away for free.* There's lots of families looking to adopt a cute, adorable, well-mannered toddler.

According to Raymond, Jay's BMW would be delivered to his job today fully repaired. That was good because the next and only woman riding in that car would be me. That is, after Jay was set free.

Raymond had agreed to have a police officer stationed outside Shining Star Day Care. Since rookies were underpaid, they were relatively easy to bribe. The officer would stop Jay, illegally search his car, and find the bag of oregano that resembled weed. In an attempt to defend her baby's daddy, Tracy would leave Jason's little program to go argue with the cop in Jay's defense. As instructed, the cop would arrest both of them. Then I'd make my move.

Hurrying across the street back to my apartment, I ran into my landlord. What was he doing up at six in the morning?

"Hey, I'm gonna need that app and you need to remove that 'for rent' sign from the window," the manager said, greeting me at my front door. "People keep calling me."

"I'll get that to you today," I lied, unlocking my door.

"You could get me in trouble with the owner if he finds out I moved you in without a lease."

"Aw, you look so sexy when you're begging."

"I do?" he said, looking down, trying to see what I saw.

"Yes, real sexy. Why don't you . . ." I puckered my

lips, then continued, "Come by later and get whatever you need?" Easing in sideways, I closed the door.

Sucker. Did he honestly believe I'd give him anything, including an application? By the time I left his apartment, no one would ever know I was there.

What was it going to take for me to get through to Jay? That's what I wanted to know.

Quickly I showered, changed clothes, then headed to Jason's preschool. "I hope I'm not too late."

Shining Star Day Care had four rows of six chairs. I divided my time between watching the play and glancing at the faces in the audience. They had the same worried expressions. After the preschool play was over, observers weren't so observant. No one noticed I'd walked behind the stage into the kid's dressing room.

A woman who appeared to be in her late teens to early twenties asked, "Can I help you, miss?"

I pulled her aside, then whispered, "I know everyone doesn't know that Jason's father and mother were arrested. It's best if we keep this quiet as possible and that you cooperate fully."

"Did I do something wrong?"

"No, you're going to do something right. I'm from Child Protective Services and I'm here to pick up Jason Brown."

"What do you want me to do?" she asked.

"Go get Jason and his things, bring him to me, and escort us out of the back door. I don't want to cause a disturbance. Hurry."

Quickly I ushered Jason into my car. I stopped at the grocery store, toy store, video store, and bought enough to keep Jason happy for a few days. I parked in my garage, then sat by the window all evening watching Jay's apartment.

"I'm hungry, An-tee," Jason said, addressing me as I'd told him.

"What would my favorite nephew like? Huh? Let's see, we have chicken."

Jason shook his head.

"You can have an apple."

Jason continued shaking his head.

"Or you can have milk and cookies."

A big smile accompanied several nods.

"And ice cream," he added.

"It's your world, kid. Whatever keeps you happy."

I sat to the side of the window so no one would notice me. I started to nod until right around midnight I noticed Jay opening his door, escorting Tracy inside. I couldn't breathe. We hadn't been apart for two weeks since Jamaica and he already had her staying at his place.

Jason started crying. That kid shocked the hell out of me when he screamed, "I want my mommy."

I yelled back, "Well, I want your daddy, so that makes us even. Now shut up." Not knowing what to do with Jason, I handed him a toy, popped in a *Barney* DVD, and gave him some more milk and cookies.

That lasted all of twenty minutes until Jason screamed a piercing howl into my face. With his snotty nose and teary eyes, I coaxed Jason into the bathroom and slammed the door. I grabbed the scissors, cut the bottom of my shirt, and wrapped his mouth to muzzle his screaming.

"Jason, your mommy will be here shortly," I lied. "You need to calm down."

He screamed again.

Not being a good mother to my own child, I grabbed Jason by his biceps, rattled him, and said, "Shut up before you make me hurt you."

Jason screamed again. Tying the cloth tighter, I barely heard him muffle, "I want my mommy," as tears streamed down his cheeks.

"That's better. An-tee tried to ask you nicely to be quiet. See what you made me do? Now if you promise not to yell, I'll take this off."

Jason nodded, sniffling, trying to behave. Slowly I untied his mouth.

What had I gotten myself into? The last thing I wanted was kidnapping charges pressed against me for detaining some snotty-nose kid. Laying Jason across my sofa, I comforted him as best I could until we dozed off.

We awakened to loud sirens outside my door. Peeping through the window, I thought, *Oh, shit!* The kid was barely missing a day, and six police cars were swarming in the middle of the street. I knew after calling Shining Star Day Care and CPS that Jay and Tracy would discover CPS hadn't taken Jason, but my gosh, the cops were responding this soon?

What were they telling the police? Tracy had on one of Jay's T-shirts, and a pair of jeans.

The police were going door to door. I started to get nervous but I was glad I'd never taken the FOR RENT sign out of my window when the police didn't knock on my door for questioning. This random nonsense lasted over an hour. I stood back from the window peeping until all except one police car left. I kept a watchful eye on Jason as he dozed back off.

"What am I going to do with this kid?"

Dialing 411, I said, "Yes, may I have the number to Child Protective Services?"

Since they'd taken away my kid, hopefully I could convince CPS that Jason was abandoned by his parents. All I had to do was give them copies of the nude photos of Tracy, and CSP would place Jason with a foster family. If they needed more convincing, I'd tell them about the verifiable arrests. Once Jason was out of the picture, Jay would have no need to keep Tracy around.

When the last police car left, I sat by the window for hours. I don't know what came over me, but I picked up Jason and whispered, "I'm taking you to your mommy, sweetheart," praying he wouldn't start screaming. "Lay your head on my shoulder like a good little good boy."

Right before sunrise, I crept across the street with Jason. "When you can't see An-tee anymore, ring the doorbell."

"Okay," he said, immediately pressing the lighted doorbell.

I didn't have time to argue with a toddler. Quickly I ran back to my apartment and shut the door.

Through the curtains, I watched Jay scoop up Jason. Tracy smothered his face with kisses, and then that bitch kissed my man. I never should've given her back her damn kid. That was okay. I knew where to find Tracy and I also had a few more tricks up my sleeve. This wasn't over by a long shot.

CHAPTER 25

Jay

Two weeks after the whole Jason going missing thing, I opened the door, expecting Tracy to welcome me home with open arms. I was in a good mood and was having a pretty good day, which meant no calls at work from Ashlee's crazy ass. I thought it was going to be even better when I saw the lights from the house were dim. I smiled. Tracy probably had something romantic planned.

Oh, how wrong I was! She had something planned all right, but it damn sure wasn't romantic.

Crash!

Just as I closed the door, a still full coffee cup went flying by my head. The cup missed me, but severely attacked the door. *What the fuck!* I thought, shaking my shirt, trying to keep hot tea from sticking to me. I looked up, and Tracy stood less than three feet away with her hands on her hips. She looked a hot mess, with bloodshot red eyes and mascara running down her face. The first thing that came to mind was *What the hell has Ashlee done this time?* The next thing that came to mind was Jason. Little man usually met me at the door, but he was nowhere to be found.

"Baby, what's wrong? And where's Jason?" My heart started beating fast and my stomach started to do flips. After his little disappearance the other day, I was more than a little paranoid.

Lord, please don't let nothing have happened to my boy.

"Where's Jason, Tracy?" I asked again.

"I asked my mother to pick him up."

I let out a long sigh of relief. "Okay, so then what's the matter with you? Why you acting nasty?"

Her face was sorely angry, and she sounded like a demon when she spoke. "I know you ain't talking about nasty! With that shit you carrying?"

"Carrying? What the hell are you talking about?" I walked toward her and tried to touch her, but she flinched. I reached for her again. This time she didn't flinch, she began beating my chest with both hands repeatedly. At first she was swinging with all her might. Then a few seconds later, she stopped. I pulled her into me close. She resisted, then finally collapsed in my arms. I could feel her tears on my chest.

"Tracy, baby, what's going on? What's the matter?" I looked at her, hoping she'd explain, but she just kept crying. "Tracy, what's going on?"

"Don't act like you don't know. That bitch! Your bitch! She came by to see me today at my job." She continued to sob as she spoke. "At my fucking job, Jay. How does she know where I work? How the fuck does Ashlee know where I work?"

"I don't know, Tracy. I really don't know." I was so mad I could spit fire. "If it's any comfort, she's stalking me too."

"I don't wanna hear that shit, Jay. You're not rich and you're no celebrity. What other bitches have you been fucking?"

The evil way she was looking at me gave me goose bumps.

"I hate you."

"Tracy, please. Baby, just tell me what's wrong. What did Ashlee do?"

Tracy let out a loud scream, something she obviously needed to get off her chest. She took a few deep breaths before answering. "I trusted you, Jay. I was just beginning to think I'd gotten myself on the right track. I began to feel good about being with the man I love and raising my son with you. My music and acting career is starting to shape up, and I figure I could actually win the *Pop Star* contest. Now it's all going right down the fucking drain, and it's all because I trusted you." She cried some more. "God, I hate you."

I tried to touch her again, but she jumped back. "Tracy, I love you. I would never do anything to hurt you. What could Ashlee possibly have said to tear you apart like this? She's crazy, and you know she'll do anything to get back with me."

Tracy frowned. "Well, as far as I'm concerned, she can have you."

She handed me a piece of paper. I unfolded it and discovered a letter from the District of Columbia Health Department, stating that Ashlee was HIV positive. My knees almost gave out from under me. "No . . . no . . . no, this can't be. Ashlee and I took an HIV test together when we went down to give blood. The results she showed me were negative. This isn't right. It can't be." I grabbed one of the kitchen chairs and sat down. I was confused and suddenly scared. Beads of sweat were pouring down my forehead.

"Damn right it isn't right. You were fucking that bitch raw, Jay. And don't try to lie because she already told me."

Our eyes met, and I didn't know what to say. I'd already lied and told her we hadn't had unprotected sex.

"You bastard. You fuck me without a condom. You knew, didn't you? You fuckin' knew and still exposed me to this shit, didn't you?"

I lowered my eyes and noticed her ring finger was bare. "Tracy, where's your ring?"

With a smirk on her face, she hissed, "I threw your fuckin' ring down the toilet, Jay."

I felt so bad. I could buy another ring, but I couldn't find another Tracy.

"Tracy, you gotta believe me—"

She cut me off. "You really must hate me to do this to me. I just wanna know, why would you do this to me?" Tracy screamed, barely able to keep her eyes open as she cried.

Putting myself in her shoes, I would feel angry and betrayed, too, but I knew there had to be another explanation for the paper. Ashlee and I took our tests at the same time, and both of us got clean reports.

"Tracy, you got to trust I didn't know."

"Well, you know now. There it is in front of you in black and white, you bastard." She continued to cry like the world had just come to an end, and in some way, maybe it had, for both of us.

I held the paper and stared at it for a while as Tracy sobbed. When my eyes traveled to the date on the paper, something dawned on me.

I grabbed Tracy's hand. "C'mere, baby," I said, leading her to my home office. I went into the file cabinet and pulled out my original paperwork from the Health Department, comparing it to the paper Ashlee had left with Tracy. The dates were the same, but there was no denying Ashlee's paper was a photocopy. I pointed it out to Tracy.

"Look here, boo," I said, holding the paper down for her to see it. "Can you tell the word 'positive' has been added? If you look closely, you can still see part of the 'n' from the word negative. She didn't white it out all the way. Besides, her paper isn't even the same stock the Health Department used. This shit isn't real." I let out a long sigh, hoping this information would calm Tracy.

Tracy snatched the papers out of my hand. She began to study them, then she said, "Same date . . . Wait a minute. Oh my gosh, Jay, you're right." A small smile crept up on her face. It became bigger as she continued to read. "I don't believe this. That bitch is crazy."

"Yeah, she really is."

She sat down on my lap. "I wanna kill that bitch."

"Yeah, well, you're going to have to stand in line behind me."

"I'm sorry, Jay." She looked down at her ringless finger as she apologized.

"No, boo, I'm sorry. But you don't have to worry because I'll never let Ashlee or anyone else hurt you or Jason." I felt like crying myself as I held her tight. She kissed me, and somehow that kiss led to us making love on the couch. Once again, Ashlee had tried to rip apart the love that Tracy and I had, and once again she did nothing but make it stronger. I knew she was going to be up to something again real soon, and next time we'd be ready.

CHAPTER 26

Ashlee

I arrived a half hour early at the Verizon Center and sat in somebody else's seat. I was close enough to see Jay, but didn't want him to realize I was the one who'd sent him the ticket to the game. The arena was sparsely populated with fans stuffing their faces with hot dogs, popcorn, beer, and other concessions. I downed two antidepressants as I sat sipping on my diet cola, waiting for the moment to see my honey's face up close and personal. God, did I love that man! He looked so good in his blue turtleneck and gray slacks when he walked in. What I would do to take him back to my hotel room and make love to him. I closed my eyes for a brief second, then smiled. What was I thinking? I was going do that anyway. I opened my bag and glanced at the white envelope inside. My smile widened. *Damn, I love having power!*

"Do I look okay?" I asked the well-dressed, actually overdressed, gentleman seated next to me.

This man had a tailored suit, expensive cologne, a fresh shave, spotless shoes, a Rolex watch, and a diamond ring on his pinky finger. He could fit in well with the NBA players' new dress code. Maybe he was a former player, I thought. Nah, he'd have a better seat. Unless he was cheap, and God knows there's nothing worse than a man who looks like a million dollars when he only has a few in his pocket.

I wasn't looking too bad myself. I'd gotten an M.A.C. makeover at the Pentagon Mall. What I'd worn to the mall was sexy, but I saw this dress that was guaranteed to make Jay's eyes stay on me, not the game. It was a simple red halter-top minidress that showed off my freshly waxed arms, underarms, legs, and, well, with the overlapping layer in the front, Jay would actually see my Brazilian bikini wax when I sat next to him.

Ripping every strand of hair from my pussy hurt like hell, but my God, I felt so liberated and excited afterward. When Jay's chocolate lips kissed this smooth pussy, he would swear it felt just like my mouth.

I'd pinned up my hair in the front and let the back hang wild and long enough for me to sling it with the sway of my hips. A light spritz of cinnamon in my hair and a dab of pussy juice behind my ears got more attention from the women than from the men.

"Are you kidding? You look better than okay. You look good enough to . . ." He paused, nodded, smiled, seductively then continued, "To . . . whew! Be warming up with those dance girls down there on the floor. Maybe I can take you out sometime."

If I weren't already taken, he might've been the one for me. Sharing his smile, I politely shook my head, pleased with his response, then wrapped the pink shawl over my shoulders.

"If you change your mind, let me know. Here's my card."

I didn't want to be rude, so I tucked his card in my purse, then moved two rows back, reminiscing on the first day Jay and I had met.

"What!" I screamed uncontrollably. My heart almost broke out of my chest. Lowering my voice, I said, "Oh no, he didn't." I eyed the center court section three rows behind the media. I hadn't planned on this shit happening. She wasn't supposed to be with him!

With all the fans in the crowded arena, there was no denying that the persons seated next to Jay were a woman and little boy—Fancy and my son. My red lace-up stilettos marched out the exit, accompanied by my bouncing titties, which practically popped out of my dress. Covering my head with the shawl, I slipped on my dark sunglasses. I stomped, knowing I should've tiptoed ladylike down the aisle, but I was too pissed. Stopping a few rows back, I sat directly behind them, contemplating my next move.

Darius's stride commanded my attention as he ran onto the floor fourth in the starting lineup. My focused changed. Tears welled in my eyes as all the old feelings resurfaced. My emotions went from hatred to love, back to hatred for both Darius and Jay. The only male I didn't hate at the moment was my son, who was seated with Fancy, and they were sitting next to Jay. A lump the size of a golf ball sat in my throat. I couldn't breathe, couldn't swallow. Darius did this on purpose.

Fancy tapped Jay on the arm and asked, "So, how'd you get this seat?"

I had to do something quick, but what?

I got it!

I left. Not the arena, but the seat I was sitting in. I went to the lobby, scribbled a note, and charmed the security guard into delivering the paper to Fancy. Moments later, Fancy and my son were gone on a wild-goose chase to find me in the crowded arena's private lounge. As Darius's wife, she'd have no problem getting in, but I doubted she'd get out any time soon.

Easing into my ticketed seat, I said, "Hi, baby."

"What the fuck are you doing here?" Jay yelled, leaping from his seat like I was some kind of leper.

"Jay, please sit," I said, touching his hand. "We don't want make a scene, do we?"

He snatched it back. "Don't touch me. Don't fucking touch me, you psycho!"

"Be careful what you say about me, love, 'cause I might take it out on that bitch of yours." His eyes were burning mad, and I actually thought he might slap me until he realized we were in public. "Now, sit down and stop making a scene. I got something to show you, and believe me, you might learn something about Tracy that you never knew."

"You mean like that fake HIV test?"

I smirked and he shook his head.

"You know what? I'm out." He started to walk away and I grabbed his arm.

"Can I come? I have a room at the Hyatt. We could start up what we were so rudely interrupted doing last week. I'm still saving it for you." I was hoping to get a reaction out of him, which I did. Just not the one I was expecting. He jerked his arm away and gave me the finger.

"You're one sick woman. You know that?"

"Sick?" I did not like his choice of words. "I'll show you sick." Reaching into my purse, I removed a photo from the envelope and handed it to him. "No, this here is some sick shit."

Jay stared at the picture of Tracy posing naked with another woman, then nonchalantly tore the photo into eight pieces. "We don't have any secrets,

Ashlee. I know about the pictures. Matter of fact, we
have the negatives."

I have to admit I was surprised but not discour-
aged. My plan to get Jay in bed was going to work. It
had to work. "Maybe you do, but as long as I have these
six prints, little miss wannabe is going to be a falling
star, not a pop star. I could ruin her career in a snap
of my finger."

"You wouldn't."

"Trust me, I would." I reached in my handbag
again and handed him a list of tabloids. "I'll be root-
ing for her, at least for the first few weeks." Suddenly,
he didn't look so confident.

"There's a lot more where that one came from.
Unless you do exactly as I say, Tracy's dream of becoming a pop star will turn into a nightmare of becoming a porn star. You do know how these shows
feel about scandal, don't you? I bet the *National En-
quirer* will give me six figures. What you think?"

Jay's lips tightened. "What do you want, Ashlee?"

I smiled at Jay's frustrated dimples. Knowing I had
him by the balls felt great. "Sit down and I'll tell you."

Jay did what he was told and took my hand. I wanted
him so badly. Spreading my shawl over my lap, I
guided his hand to my pussy. I felt a twinge of excitement and surprise when he touched my wetness.

"You want to know what I want? I can show you
better than I can tell you." I ran my hand across his
dick. "I want my dick, Jay. I want my dick one last
time before I go back to Dallas. You give me that, and
I'll give you the pictures. Plus I'll never bother you
again."

He stared at me, contemplating my offer, but it
didn't take him long to decide. "Aw'ight, I'll do it.
But I swear to God, if you don't give me those pictures and leave my family alone, I'll kill you."

"Temper, temper, baby. Remember your blood pressure. Now, meet me in front of the stadium in fifteen minutes." Reluctantly, he got up, but before he could leave, I grabbed his ass with my hand, giving it a squeeze in front of the entire stadium crowd. "Mmmm, now, that's what I call an ass."

CHAPTER 27

Jay

I pulled in front of the Hyatt Hotel and sighed heavily as the valet approached the car and opened my door. His counterpart, a short Latino doorman, opened the passenger-side door, and Ashlee stepped out of my car, grinning. I wanted to smack that damn grin right off her face. I kept asking myself if I really wanted to go through with this shit. Then Tracy and Jason came to mind, and I realized I had to give Ashlee what she wanted. I had to protect Tracy and her dream of winning *Pop Star* because if it wasn't for me, Ashlee would never have come into her life.

There was no doubt in my mind that Ashlee was crazy. The fact that I actually thought I was in love with her once was making my stomach churn.

"Welcome to the Hyatt, sir. Are you checking in?" the valet asked.

"No, I'll be out of here in less than thirty minutes," I said angrily. I handed the valet a twenty-dollar bill. "So, keep my car close. Understand?"

He nodded and I followed Ashlee into the lobby.

She sang as she strutted to the elevator, pushing the button. When the doors opened, she turned around with the biggest smirk I'd ever seen.

"You ready, sweetheart?" she asked, stepping into the elevator. "'Cause I can't wait. It's been so long since I felt you inside me."

I rolled my eyes, tempted to let the elevator doors close and run back to my car. "Yeah, just remember your promise. You said you'd leave us alone after this."

"Yeah, yeah . . . blah, blah, blah. I know what I said. If you take care of me tonight, I'll give you the pictures and stay away from you, your wench, and that brat," she said as I stepped inside the elevator.

My eyes threw daggers at her. "Hey, watch your damn mouth. I'm gon' give you what you want, but I swear I'll leave if you bad-mouth my girl and son."

"Your girl, huh?" She put on an evil grin, then laughed. "Don't worry, I'll be good. I'll be damn good. I promise."

I wanted to strangle her ass, but I knew I couldn't. Once the elevator started moving, Ashlee went on and on about what she wanted to do in bed. It's a good thing she did because the only words I had for her were four-letter or started with the letter *b*. Once we got to the room, I hesitated at the door.

This would all be over in a half hour, I reminded myself. *Just keep your cool, man. It's for Jason and Tracy.*

Ashlee set her purse on the table, then came toward me, taking hold of my hand. The thought of running into the room, grabbing her purse, and getting the pictures came to mind just before she pulled me inside.

"Remember this, Jay?" she asked, rubbing on my chest. "Honey, this is the same room we spent our first night together in. I didn't even give you any that night, because we didn't have a condom, remember?"

"Yeah, I remember now," I forced myself to say.

She kissed my lips. I didn't reciprocate. "Remember what you did to me?" she asked. I kept silent. "You caressed me in all the right places," she said, taking my hand and rubbing it between her legs. "You made me come all over your fingers, remember? Can you do that again, Jay? Make me cream in your hand?"

I didn't care much for the talk. I just wanted to fuck her ass so I could leave. I reminded her of why we were there. "Is that what you want? You want me to finger you rather than screw you?"

"Jay, don't be ridiculous. I want it all. I want a G-spot orgasm, baby. I want to squirt in your face. Then I want you to slide that big black snake of yours into me as hard as you can." She began unbuttoning my shirt with her teeth and I wanted to spit on her.

You're doing this for Tracy and Jason, Jay. You're doing this for your family, I kept repeating in my mind.

"Then why are we talking about it? Let's just get it over with so I can get out of here," I said, prying her hands from my waist.

I went to sit on the bed. I took my shoes off, then pulled off my pants. Ashlee stood, watching as if I were doing a striptease. When I was fully undressed, I looked at my deflated dick. It had no life to it whatsoever. It wasn't until Ashlee began taking off her clothes that I got a bit of a rise. As much as I hated to be there, I still couldn't deny how erotic she could be, especially when she ripped open her shirt and started to stick her fingers in her kitty, licking them like a lollipop as she walked toward me. Once she got over to the bed, she sat next to me and began kissing my neck.

"What the hell is wrong with you?" she complained when she stroked my dick and it wouldn't get fully erect.

I instructed her to take care of business. "Ah, Ashlee, this isn't gonna work. I'm going to need a little more help."

She barely stopped kissing me as she spoke. "Tell me what you need, baby. You know I'll take care of you."

I put my hand on her head to push her south. She didn't ask any questions before damn near swallowing me whole. I hated to admit it to myself, but it felt good. I was a man, after all, a very weak man, and she was a woman, and very good at being a woman. Her wet, warm tongue made my shit stand straight up like a baseball bat. I got harder by the second. I could hear her gag every time I pushed her head down, forcing her to deep-throat me. She was doing me so good I was about ready to bust, so I pulled her up or else our business would have been all over. I managed to get excited for her once, but with my mind frame, there was no guarantee she'd get another rise out of me.

Ashlee pushed me back on the bed and climbed on top of me. I closed my eyes for a second. I don't know how she managed to get up there so fast, but when I opened my eyes, Ashlee's moist pussy was in my face. She squatted and awaited the visitation of my tongue.

I cannot believe I'm doing this. Tracy would kill me if she could see me.

I knew there was no way around returning the oral favor, so I obliged. I began to suck and lick her clit, and when she started to moan, I slipped my finger inside her, gently rubbing her G-spot. It must have felt good to her because she was making hard circular motions as she grinded into my face. She left me very little space for breathing, but I continued until she began to lift away from me and scream at the top of her lungs. A half second later, she began to spray, and her body went into convulsions as she collapsed on top of me.

Once she'd rested enough, she took hold of my dick and slid down on it. My mind told me to protest, but my body wouldn't listen. I'd be lying if I didn't admit she felt good.

"Look at me, baby. I can take all of you," she said with glee, rocking back and forth. "Remember when I couldn't? That was then and this is now. God, I love my dick."

In spite of everything, she looked sexy as hell sitting on top of me with her titties bouncing. Then, if I didn't know any better, I would've sworn she read my thoughts. She took my hands off her waist and placed them on her breasts, continuing to rock me as she helped squeeze and massage her tits. They were plump but soft. I had the opportunity to feel just how soft when she leaned over to place one of them in my mouth.

"Aahh, yeah, baby," she moaned. "Suck it. Now bite it. Harder! Harder!"

I did what I was told, and she moaned even louder, although I'm sure I drew blood. I actually enjoyed hearing her moan, so I began to thrust my hips into her. She gasped and moaned some more. Her language became more and more erotic. She started kissing me, making sure to lick all of her moisture from my face. I could feel her pussy getting hotter. I knew it wouldn't be long before she came, and I'd be right behind her.

"Wait, baby," she said, stopping. "I want you to give it to me from the back hard."

Ashlee got off me, bent down to slurp my dick a few times, and then assumed the doggy position. And like a dog in heat, I proceeded to fuck the shit outtta her with short, rapid strokes. I held her waist and helped her throw it back on me.

"Oh yes, baby! Give it to me. Fuck me harder," she pleaded. She was extremely loud. "That's it, Jay! Harder! Harder! Please, I need it harder!"

My dick felt like a rock it had gotten so hard. I spanked her ass a few times, and then she asked for more, begging me to slap it even harder. I felt like I was giving her all I had, but she kept screaming for more. I'm not going to lie; the whole damn thing was intoxicating.

"Harder! Harder, Jay! I need you to beat this pussy up. C'mon. Is that all you got? Just imagine I'm that bitch of yours. I bet she won't let you fuck her like this."

I was pissed, but extremely turned on. The more shit she talked, the harder I'd fuck her. I pushed her face into the mattress, then banged the shit out of her. She met me for every stroke, and we continued to fuck like we were both possessed for at least a half hour. Finally, she began jerking and trembling as her pussy tightened up around my dick, releasing warm, soothing female come all over my dick. Before I knew it, I'd come too.

Ashlee's legs had given out on her. She lay on her stomach, and I collapsed onto her back. We were both sweating and panting. "Was that what you were looking for?" I asked, still breathing heavily.

She turned over to look at me. "Yes, and thank you. God, that felt good."

After several minutes, Tracy ran across my mind. I began to feel guilty about being there with Ashlee because I had truly enjoyed it. I wanted to jump up and go home, but I was too weak. After catching my breath, I rolled off her.

I got up and walked over to her purse. "So, you're gonna leave us alone now, right?"

She sat up slowly with attitude. "Excuse me?"

"You promised. You said you'd leave my family alone after this." From the look she gave me, you might have thought I'd told her to go fuck herself.

She grabbed a pillow, then popped me in the face. "I know you aren't saying this is it, are you? Not after the way I just fucked you."

"It was good, but it doesn't change anything. I want you to leave us alone." I opened the purse and took out the envelope.

"Get the fuck out of my bag, and get you ass over here. You ain't going nowhere. We need to discuss our future."

"Don't play games, Ashlee. We already had this discussion. We weren't here to rekindle anything, and you know it."

"So, even after the sex we just had, you can just drop me?"

"Ashlee, you knew. You said just one more time. I don't know what the fuck is going on with you, but I'm telling you, you better stick to your word. I'm not going to tolerate you messing with my family."

I started to put on my clothes, quickly tucking the envelope in my pocket. Ashlee sat on the bed, looking possessed. Her hair was a mess, and her eyeliner was smeared like black tears down the sides of her face. I tried to ignore her, but she started laughing.

"What the fuck are you laughing at?" I asked.

"You and your pitiful ass," she said. "You love that heifer, don't you? Or you're with her because of the kid, right? Yeah. I should've known. It's the kid. I knew I shouldn't have brought him back."

I did a double take, then stopped buttoning my shirt. "What did you say?"

"You heard me," she said, laughing. "You were scared shitless, weren't you? I took your kid, but after I realized how pathetic you were looking for him, I returned him. If I had known you were still gonna walk out on me, I would've duct-taped his mouth and his entire body, then thrown him in the Dumpster."

"You're fucking crazy!" Before I had time to really think about it, I ran over to Ashlee and grabbed her neck. I pushed her back on the bed and mashed my knee into her stomach. "Leave us alone, Ashlee," I said, watching her turn shades of blue and purple. "You hear me? Stay the fuck out of our lives."

I released her. She sat on the bed, coughing, trying to take in some air as I put on my shoes. I heard her manage to laugh a few more times in between gasps for air, but I tried to ignore it. All I could think about was getting the fuck out of there.

I had started toward the door when she called out to me. I acted as if I didn't hear her, but she caught me at the door and slammed it shut and blocked my exit.

"I'm sorry," she said, reaching to touch my face.

I slapped her hand down. "Move, Ashlee, before I hurt you."

"Jay, I said I'm sorry. Why are you treating me this way? Is it because of that brat—I mean, surely you know I'd love your son too."

"I'm only gonna say this one time. If I think you've come anywhere close to me and my family, I'll kill you."

"We'll see," she said, smirking. "Now, I'm getting a little tired of you. I'm going to give you one more chance to get back in bed. After that, I'm going to ruin your life and that bitch's for good."

"No, you're not." I drew back my fist, but then caught myself. "Ashlee, I swear to God." My fist was inches from her face.

"Go ahead. Hit me. Do it! If that's what you want to do, then do it." She laughed and taunted me. "You've already raped me."

"Huh?" My hand dropped to my side. "I didn't rape you."

"Yes, you did."

I opened the door, but was stopped when she slammed into it, headfirst. She was on the floor, startled and holding her head.

What the fuck?

She shook her head rapidly a few times, then got up. What started as laughter turned into a piercing scream for help.

"Shut up! What the fuck is wrong with you?" I asked.

She made sounds like a growling wolf, then ran face first into the wall. Pictures fell off the wall, and she bounced onto the floor. I couldn't believe what I was seeing. Ashlee got up and went into the bathroom. I couldn't help but follow to see what she would do next. She had to be having a nervous breakdown. Her entire face was bloody, but that didn't stop her from crashing her forehead into the mirror. Her face was covered with flowing, bloody stripes, but she continued to laugh. Before I could get out of the way, she latched on to me. She buried her face into my shirt and held on to my waist as she continued to scream.

"Why?" she cried. "I know I said I didn't want you anymore, but you didn't have to rape me like this!"

I couldn't believe my ears. "Look, Ashlee, this isn't funny. I know what you're up to, and it's not going to work. No one is going to believe that I raped you."

"They'll believe me now." She reached out, scratching her fingernails across my face. "If I can't have you, she sure as hell isn't going to have you."

"Don't do this, Ashlee. This isn't funny. My life is not a game."

"Do I look like I'm laughing?" She took a deep breath, then screamed, "Rape! Somebody please help me! He raped me!"

For the first time since I'd gotten there, I was truly scared. I ran out of the bathroom and headed right for the door. When I reached the hallway, I could still hear Ashlee screaming. What the fuck had I just gotten myself into?

CHAPTER 28

Ashlee

So it's been said, so I am living proof, women are smarter than men. What made Jay Crawford think he could give my dick and my engagement ring to another bitch, and I'd disappear at his command? *So you're gonna leave us alone, right?*

Looking back, I saw that Tracy was the reason Jay had asked me that night at Zanzibar, "Do you think a man can be friends with his ex?" His ass knew before he screwed me that he wanted to get back with her. I wasn't some fuckin' dog on a leash waiting for Master Jay's instructions. My life wasn't a game he could play at his leisure.

Sit, Ashlee. Stand, Ashlee. Roll over, Ashlee. Fetch, Ashlee. Lie down and lick your wound, Ashlee. I was fed up to my blocked, manure-stuffed nostrils with whorish men rubbing my face in their bullshit.

I didn't give a damn if Webster's dictionary defined a female dog as a bitch. From now on, I would be that female that sits only when she gets good and ready, I'd stand when I fuckin' well pleased, and I wasn't rolling over for no man or begging him to love me or validate me!

Never again would I be the victim. From now on, any man who used me, I'd serve him justice, branding his ass with my infrared pussy for life. Jay Crawford would never forget the third-degree burns of Ashlee Anderson. In about two minutes, he'd have zero doubt as to who wore the pants in our relationship.

Ha! I marveled over my own performance in the bedroom. *And the winner for best leading actress is . . . Ashlee Anderson. Yeah! Bravo! Great job!* I actually heard voices cheering in my ears. All Jay could do once I started riding his dick was hold on and take his pussy-whippin' like a man. After my baby finished making love to me, why'd he have to go and bring up his family? He wasn't thinking about his family when he was busting a nut inside me.

There was no way in the world Jay could resist my tight, juicy pussy. I realized a nice booty and a cute face were worth more than any man could afford. All men, no matter how rich, how broke, how famous, how confident, how insecure, how straight, how gay, how smart, how dumb; there was one thing they shared in common—a weakness for sex. Many men would lie, others would kill, some would die, and several men, like Jay, would serve time behind bars.

Which price was greater? Murder? Suicide? Depended upon what the man valued most. In Jay's case, obviously he valued his son and Tracy, maybe. Or perhaps he claimed them more, using them as his way to get rid of me. Jay didn't love me, Tracy, his son, or himself. That snotty-nose kid yelled, "I want my mommy," the entire time I had him, not once asking for his daddy. Whatever.

If I was lucky, Jay would get the same sentence as

Eddie Murphy and Martin Lawrence in the movie *Life*. Solitary confinement, sodomy, tossing salads, and knowing firsthand what it was like to be somebody's bitch would give Jay's ass plenty of time to wish he'd done right by me.

A cheating man could make the nicest, sweetest, most innocent woman an honorary top-notch forensic scientist who could stage any crime scene, making him the culprit and the victim at the same time. I didn't solicit Raymond's assistance for my plot against Jay. I'd done my homework, and of what I found in reference to D.C.'s first degree sexual assault laws, I made sure I had all bases covered.

Worst-case scenario, whatever happened to the woman who cried rape? Not a goddamn thing. That's why I kept laughing in Jay's face . . . ha, ha, ha, ha, ha . . . sucker! Rape was the only charge where a woman could lie under oath and never perjure herself. All I had to do was create doubt in the minds of the jury, and it didn't have to be reasonable. I'd already established a convincing case, and Jay wasn't even fingerprinted yet. A woman's balls were always bigger than a man's. Most women just didn't know it. Thanks to Darius and Jay, I did.

I knew when Jay stepped through my hotel door that he was doomed. I recalled thinking, *This is going to be easier than I thought*. I didn't need a fishing rod. I reeled Jay in like a guppy on a string. That softie didn't even put up a fight. He didn't have to. His dick did all the talking I wanted to hear. Once a man's dick got hard, a woman could stroke both heads to her advantage. Sure hope Jay didn't drop the soap that night because he was being booked with every charge I'd read in the law books.

My fifteen minutes of fame lasted about thirty seconds; long enough for me to run out of my hotel suite behind Jay, screaming at the top of my lungs. With blood pouring from multiple gashes in my once beautiful face, my ripped shirt barely hanging on to my mutilated body, and my most important asset—womanhood—in ruins, who wouldn't believe me? I made sure my tittie, the one Jay had bitten, was completely exposed. Red-skin girls bruise easily. I smiled at the purple-and-black ring around my nipple. And being hit from the back hard, well, that would cause enough vaginal bruising to convince any doctor.

I started screaming hysterically, "Heeeeeelp! He raped me! He beat me! He raped me! Look at my face! Oh, Jesus! I'm gonna die!" I cried louder, forcing tears, gasping, while pleading, "Somebody help me!"

An elderly white man shouted, "Holy mackerel! Mildred, quick! Get yourself back inside and call the police!"

Everyone started echoing, "Call the police!"

If Jay were in my position, all of the twenty witnesses trying to help me would've run back into their rooms and locked the doors. And instead of calling the police to help Jay, they would've tied up the house lines calling the front desk. Good or bad. Right or wrong. Not many citizens would come to the defense of a black man, even if he was the victim. Good for me. Unfortunate for Jay. When a man knows better, he should do better. Breaking a woman's heart is a serious offense. Jay knew I loved him. He just didn't care about me no more.

The hotel security guard raced to my aid while others stared in disbelief. My new rescuer wrapped his jacket around my partially naked body.

"My God, lady, who did this to you?" the security officer asked as he dialed his phone.

"His name is Jay Crawford. He's my ex-boyfriend, and he wouldn't take no for an answer."

I swear I didn't move a muscle the entire time. I think I missed my calling. I should've been an actress. Halle Barry didn't have shit on me. I could hardly wait for Act Two in the courtroom.

CHAPTER 29

Jay

When the bailiff escorted me into the court-room, all eyes were on me. It had been six months to the day since Ashlee falsely accused me of rape. Today I would finally learn my fate. I wondered what most of the people in the courtroom were thinking. Probably that I was a dead man walking, because that's how I felt. My fate was in the hands of twelve people, five sistas, three brothers, two white women, and two white men who didn't know shit about me other than what the judge would allow into evidence, and half of that was bull. This was a so-called jury of my peers. How comforting could that be?

My attorney pleaded a hell of a case, despite the mountain of false evidence against me, and like he said, it would only take one vote to hang a jury. That all sounded good during the trial, but the jury was coming back with a verdict, which meant there would be no hung jury today. I was going either home or back to my jail cell for good.

I sat next to my attorney, Michael Brown. He patted me on the back. Michael was the best attorney that my boy Kyle's money could buy. But in all honesty, I was not sure if he was good enough to defeat Ashlee's lies.

"How you doin', Jay?"

I took a deep breath. "I'll be doing a whole lot better when this is all over."

"Well, the jury will be out in a minute. They've been deliberating for five days. I think that's a good sign. Hang in there."

"I'm trying. Believe me, I'm trying," I said, turning to look at the faces of my loved ones. I'm not going to lie. I felt like crying. Seems like I'd been doing a lot of that lately, especially late at night in my cell.

My boys, Wil, Kyle, and Allen, were all there, with their wives, too. They looked like they were at my funeral rather than my trial, but I nodded and gave them a confident smile—one that truly took some acting to pull off. I loved those guys. They'd been there for me when no one else had. Each one of them offered to put up his house for my bail. Unfortunately for me, Ashlee's politically connected parents put a stop to that by somehow forcing the judge to hold me for the past six months with no bail. Some justice system, huh?

I remembered the day my boys tried to warn me about Ashlee. I wish I had been smart enough to listen. Wil's voice kept repeating in my head. *And I'm telling you now, you need to listen to your boys.* God, if I could just do it all over again . . .

Sitting just behind my boys was my ex-wife, Kenya, and our girls. Kenya hadn't been to any of the trial, so it was a surprise to see her there now. I don't think she'll ever know how much I appreciated it. Our girls were our glue, but I couldn't take away anything from her as a mother, nor could she say negative things about me as a father.

If only she'd been called as a character witness. She would've made the jury understand I'm no rapist, I thought. Not that it mattered. My attorney had at least fifteen of my friends, relatives, and coworkers on the stand as character witnesses. They all made me sound like Mother Teresa up there on the stand. But I didn't know how they stacked up against all the doctors that testified on behalf of the prosecution, or the DNA evidence inside her, the vaginal bruises from our rough sex, the blood on my shirt, and the hotel's security tape of me leaving that hotel like a bat out of hell.

My girls waved at me while Kenya nodded and gave me a thumbs-up. As I returned her kind gesture, my eyes slid one row up to Tracy and Jason.

Tracy had Jason sitting on her lap. She looked as if she'd been crying. I winked and blew her a kiss. She blew one back, but she didn't flash a smile. I wished there was something I could do or say to fix the way she was feeling. I could see pain in her eyes, but my girl, Tracy, knew how to hold up despite the fact that she was going through a lot of guilt and self-blame.

During the first two months I was in jail, Tracy wouldn't even come see because she thought I was guilty of raping Ashlee. I couldn't blame her after the way the news reporters and press were portraying me. Not until Kyle, Wil, and Allen sat her down and explained what really went down, including the fact that I slept with Ashlee to save her career, did she finally understand. She had already seen Ashlee's lies in action with the false HIV test, so it wasn't much of a stretch to believe Ashlee could be lying about this. It took another month before Tracy came up to the jail, because she was so embarrassed. Ashlee had taken everything from her, including her shot at winning *Pop Star*, and I'll always hate her for it.

You see, when I got back to my house that night, the cops were waiting for me. They found the envelope in my pocket, and with Tracy being my girl, and about to go on *Pop Star*, the whole thing became tabloid news. What really pissed me off was that Ashlee's name was left out of the news because she was supposed to be the victim. Something about the rape shield law. To be truthful, it was bullshit. Tracy had been practically seconds away from fame, and we were minutes away from being happy together for the rest of our lives.

She picked up Jason's hand and told him to wave at me. He did, and he seemed very excited to see me. I had to fight back tears at the thought that I might not be able to see him or the girls grow up.

The jury marched in and took their seats. I smiled at my mom, and then my eyes wandered over to the prosecution's side of the courtroom. I looked over at Ashlee. She winked at me, but I imagined if anyone saw her, it wouldn't have made a difference at that point. For five days, Ashlee came into the courtroom wearing an innocent schoolgirl look. She wore long skirts and blouses that buttoned at the neck. She wore very little makeup, and she kept her hair pulled back with the exception of some Chinese-cut bangs across her forehead. She even wore a pair of black-rimmed glasses to each hearing. I doubt if they were prescription glasses, but if they were, she picked a fine time not to wear her contacts. I couldn't stand that bitch, and I wanted to jump across the railing and strangle the shit out of her.

As the jurors walked in, I tried to read their faces, but none of them would even look at me. I turned to my lawyer for some reassurance. "What do you think? Do they look like they voted me innocent?"

"We'll know in a minute," he replied. I couldn't read anything in his tone.

I glanced at Ashlee, and every muscle in my body tightened. "I hope they don't believe that bitch, 'cause she's a fucking liar."

"Jay, you need to settle down. You've already been removed from the courtroom once for being out of control."

"This is my life on the line," I said angrily. "When this is all over, you get to go home regardless. Maybe if you had caught her up in some of those lies she was telling when she was on the stand, I'd be able to calm down."

The door opened from the judge's chamber. Then the bailiff spoke. "All rise," he said. "Court is about to begin. Please remain standing until the Honorable Judge Henry Mitchell takes his seat." The judge came into the room and took his seat. "You may all be seated," the bailiff stated.

The judge asked the jury if they'd reached a verdict. The foreman stood and answered, "Yes, we have, Your Honor."

A folder was taken to the judge. He opened it and looked at a piece of paper inside. I waited for his eyes to meet mine, but they never did. He spoke to the jury spokesperson. "Are you satisfied with your verdict?"

"Yes, Your Honor," the man said.

The judge turned to me. "Mr. Crawford, will you please stand?"

My heart felt like it was going to jump out of my chest. We stood, then waited as the bailiff took the paper back over to the spokesperson. He began reading from the paper, and his words echoed in my ear.

"We, the people of the District of Columbia, in the case of Jay Richard Crawford, find the defendant . . ." I felt my knees turn to jelly as he paused. "Guilty of first degree sexual assault."

He continued with the other two charges, but I didn't hear another word. I just kept mumbling, "But I'm innocent, I'm innocent . . . I didn't do this."

The courtroom was in an uproar. I couldn't believe it, and neither could my family and friends. I heard Tracy screaming like she'd just been shot. I turned to look at her, and to my surprise, Kenya was holding her. Kyle, Wil, and Allen were crying like babies, and my poor mom looked like she'd fainted. The judge pounded his gavel, trying to regain order.

"Order . . . order in the courtroom!" he yelled. "I need order or I'll clear this courtroom" The room quieted, but I could still hear Tracy's cries muffled by Kenya's shoulder. The judge continued. "Here is my ruling: Jay Crawford, you have been found guilty of first degree sexual assault. Before I pass judgment on you, would you like to say anything in your behalf?"

Do I wanna say anything on my behalf? Of course I wanna say something in my behalf, I thought. *This bitch is the biggest liar in the world and she set me up. And I'm about to tell everyone I can.*

Just as I was about to speak, my lawyer tapped me on the shoulder and whispered,

"Don't, Jay. You're just going to make it worse. Let me talk to him. You have to trust me."

I did what he said, but I didn't trust him.

"Your Honor, due to the fact that Mr. Crawford is a first time offender, I respectfully ask that he be given the minimum sentence of three years."

"I'm sorry, Mr. Brown, but this is a horrible crime that your client has committed against Ms. Anderson.

He was offered a five-year plea agreement before trial, which he turned down. And I'm still concerned that he has no remorse." The judge turned to me directly. "Jay Crawford, you have been found guilty of first degree sexual assault I'm sentencing you to serve ten years in a maximum-security prison. Bailiff, take him into custody."

Again, the entire courtroom was in an uproar. When the bailiff came to handcuff me, Tracy screamed even louder. "No! No, please, no!" she cried, pushing people out of her way as she ran toward me.

I shook the bailiff off me, then grabbed Tracy. I held her so tightly, I could've broken her into pieces. "I love you, Tracy."

"I love you too. It's not fair, Jay."

"Life's not fair, sweetheart. Life's not fair."

Tears formed in my eyes as I held Tracy and rocked her. She never answered. She just pressed herself against me and cried. The bailiff forced our moment to end. Tracy and I exchanged repeated I-love-you's as I was handcuffed. As the bailiff led me out, Ashlee slithered up behind the prosecutor's table to watch me go through the door.

I looked at her and she smiled.

"Hey, Jay," she hissed. "Don't drop the soap."

EPILOGUE

One year later

I was excited as I walked the long, cold corridors of the prison to the visiting area. It was Thursday, the first of this week's visiting days, and I couldn't wait to see Tracy and Jason. Even though we could only speak through a phone and see each other through the thick glass, just having them around gave me comfort and the will to survive. Doing time had been hard at first. Not because I was weak, but because I knew I shouldn't be there. I honestly felt like someone was going to realize they'd made a mistake and let me go at any minute. It took six months before reality finally settled in that innocent or not, I needed to make some friends because I wasn't getting out anytime soon.

Despite it all, I never gave up. I still had a couple of appeals left, and my boys Kyle, Wil, and Allen had promised they'd find a way to get my sentence overturned. I probably should've just given up hope, but my boys had never let me down. In the meantime, I still had Tracy. During the year I'd been locked up, she hadn't missed one visiting day. She'd sworn to me that she would do my time with me, and in many ways, I think me being locked up was harder on her than it was on me. For the first time in my life, I truly understood the meaning of unconditional love.

I signed the visiting log and anxiously awaited my turn, until one of the corrections officers called out my name. "Crawford, booth number six."

Right before I walked into the visiting area, I wrapped my light blue jail-issued shirt around my waist. Like most of my fellow inmates, I'd been working out, and I liked to impress Tracy by wearing a wife beater.

I was surprised when I didn't see Tracy at cubicle number six. Thirty seconds later, my surprise became horror when Ashlee sat down in the cubicle. I could feel my temples start to throb as I balled my hand into a fist.

What the fuck is she doing here? I wondered. She smiled at me then reached for the phone on her side. I hesitated before picking up my receiver.

"Hi, Jay," she whispered. I guess she was trying to sound sexy, but the only emotion she brought out of me was anger, and I wanted to jump through the glass to choke her.

"What the fuck are you doing here?"

"Now, Jay, you should calm down. You wouldn't want them to put you in solitary or anything, would you?" She smirked. "By the way, is it true? Do they rape rapists here? You must be scared to death."

She was so fucking smug. I was having a very hard time containing my anger. "I asked you a question. What the fuck are you doing here?"

"Oh, I was in the neighborhood and thought I'd stop by since Tracy wasn't going make it over here."

I thought my heart was going to stop. "What have you done to Tracy? If you've hurt her, I swear I'll—" She raised her hand to cut me off.

"You'll what? What the fuck are you going to do

behind these bars?" She angrily ridiculed me. "Besides, I don't know why you're getting all upset. You know I like Tracy. It's you I can't fucking stand."

"Well, bitch, believe me, the feeling is mutual. Now, what the hell did you do to Tracy, and why isn't she here?"

Ashlee scratched her head as if she was thinking. "You know, I think she has four flat tires. Matter of fact, I'm sure of it. It's amazing how that keeps happening to her."

The scowl on my face told my emotions. "You're not going to get away with this shit, bitch. You're not going to get away with none of it."

She laughed into the phone. "Guess what, Jay? I already have."

I glared at her as I slammed the phone down. Before I could stand up, she was knocking on the glass. I couldn't hear her clearly, but I could make out some of what she was saying when I read her lips.

"Don't you wanna know why I'm here?"

I took a deep breath then picked up the phone again. "Yeah, I wanna know why you're here."

"Sit down and let me tell you."

I reluctantly did what she asked. The woman looked so elated, I thought she might have come on herself. "Gosh, I don't even know where to start . . . it's all so exciting. Well, first of all, I just wanna let you know that I'm completely over you."

I sat back in my chair. "Well, thank God for small favors. Now if you could just drop dead, all my prayers would be answered."

"You know what, Jay? I am not going to let you block my blessings. Especially since I've finally found the perfect man."

I laughed. "So what, is he blind, deaf, and dumb?"

"Cute, Jay. But you and Darius are the only dumb men I've dated."

"Will you just get to the point? I know you didn't come down here just to tell me you're dating some stupid ass nigga."

"No, Jay. I came down here to let you know that while you're rotting in this jail, I'm going to get married." She stuck out her right hand and flashed a rock the size of a jelly bean.

"Oh my God. Who was stupid enough to give you a ring?"

"His name is Trent Duncan, and he's the man of my dreams."

"Well, next time you see Trent, you give him a message for me."

"And what's that, Jay?"

"Tell him I said he's marrying one crazy-ass bitch." I started to laugh.

"I am not crazy," she said angrily. I could see the fire in her eyes.

"Sure you are," I told her as I continued to laugh.

A string of curses came out of her mouth, and I laughed even harder, hanging up the phone. I sat back in my chair with folded arms, laughing.

She began to pound on the glass. "I am not crazy . . . I am not crazy . . ."

It didn't take long for the corrections officers to remove her from in front of me. I'd been in jail for 368 days, and for the first time, I truly felt like Ashlee was finally gonna get hers. What she didn't know was that I knew exactly who this guy Trent Duncan was. He was Wil's brother, and probably the biggest con man I'd ever met. And believe me, if Wil and Kyle got him involved Ashlee had no idea what she'd gotten herself involved with, because believe me, *He Ain't The One!*

She Ain't the One

Insecurity was the key
That opened my third eye
I wish I would've overlooked
The good pussy between her thighs
The squeeze of her vaginal muscles
The taste of her chocolate truffle

I wish I would've overlooked
The curve of her lips when she smiled
The sweet scent lingering on her neck
The booty wiggling in her jeans
With her hard nipples pointing at me

But the way her hips slung the letter X
Translated in my heads
. . . sex . . . sex . . . sex

I regret I didn't overlook
All of those superficial things

Bypassed her ass in them jeans
Listened to her heart
And heeded the warnings
When shit fell apart

But I didn't

Guess it's true
Men really aren't that smart
I kept fooling myself
Nobody else
Can hit her pussy like me
Make her come and scream
Scream and come
The ass was so good
I really couldn't see
She truly was not
The one for me

Instantly
She became my girl
I became her world
She wanted to be my wife
I didn't realize she didn't have a life
Outside of me
I'd become her everything
So I kept on fooling myself

Why is it that everyone else
Knew her ass was crazy
Demanding
Insecure
Trying to have my baby

Deep down inside
I was crazy too
Gave up the best woman I had
To try something new
In exchange for someone blue

I couldn't save this miserable woman
She couldn't save herself
The one thing we shared in common
We could write a book
The sex was truly off
The mothafuckin' hook!
I'd crisscross that ass
Like a pair of scissors
Slinging my dick side to side

I'd spread her sweet cheeks
Nice and wide
Hittin' it from behind

I'd lick her pussy
Oh so good
Until I made her cry

So I kept on patting
Myself on the back
No other man
Could hit it like that

I kept on believing
I was the man
And my dick was golden
Until all of a sudden
My freedom was stolen
She started planning my days
Imposing upon my nights
Questioning my whereabouts
Starting fights

I promised my mother
I'd never hit a woman
But I'm telling you, man

This woman was so evil
I could have easily laid hands

But I didn't

She scratched me
And kicked me
And hid my car keys
Threw herself to the floor
Grabbed me round my knees
And pleaded for me not to leave
All so she wouldn't be alone
All so her dick wouldn't leave home

You ain't goin' nowhere tonight
So to avoid a fight
I'd say aw'ight
But I was mad as hell
And one step away from going to jail

Now that I look back
That shit was hella funny
I had to give myself props
For making that girl lose her mind
Sure wish I could hit that pussy
Just one more time

I remember when
We used to laugh
Hold hands
Just chill
Kickin' it in the park
till way after dark

I remember when
We used to wrestle

Make love
Stay on the phone all night
Take walks
Go on trips
Now we don't even talk

I had one mother
Didn't want two
I'm a grown-ass man
I'll be damned
If any woman
Can
Or will
Tell me what to do

If I have to prove
I love her
And she doesn't believe
I'm telling her the truth
I'm done

She Ain't the One

If I had paid attention
To the signs
Not answered so many questions
At a time

If had listened to my boys
To my inner voice
I would've made the right choice

Insecurity was the key
That opened my third eye
I wish I would've overlooked
The good pussy between her thighs

The squeeze of her vaginal muscles
The taste of her chocolate truffle

I wish I would've overlooked
The curve of her lips when she smiled
The sweet scent lingering on her neck
The booty wiggling in her jeans
With her hard nipples pointing at me

But the way her hips slung the letter X
Translated in my heads
. . . sex . . . sex . . . sex

I regret I didn't overlook
All of those superficial things

Bypassed her ass in them jeans
Listened to her heart
And heeded the warnings
When shit fell apart

But I didn't

Don't miss the exciting follow-up to Carl Weber's
Something on the Side

Big Girls Do Cry

Coming in February 2010 from Dafina Books!

Prologue

The taxi pulled into the circular driveway, rolling to a stop in front of the expensive double oak doors of the large brick colonial. Roscoe, the driver, a forty-something-year-old dark-skinned man, placed the car in park and turned toward the woman in the backseat.

He liked the way she looked. She was just his type of woman, thick and pretty like a chocolate bar, with large, melon-sized breasts. Yes sir, Roscoe loved a woman with some meat on her bones. He had even thought about asking for her number or perhaps offering to show her around the ATL when she first entered his cab at the airport. Over the years, Roscoe had bedded many a lonely female passenger after picking them up at Atlanta's airport. All it usually took was some small talk and an invitation to one of ATL's bars for a drink. But this sister spent most of the ride on her cell phone, probably talking to some insecure boyfriend or husband back home who was afraid her fine ass would wind up with a Southern charmer like him. Now that they had reached her final destination, he would have to make his move quick.

"That'll be forty dollars, ma'am." He smiled, revealing a mouth full of gold teeth.

Tammy, a woman in her late thirties, didn't notice his unattractive smile or his country accent, things that would have surely caught her attention if she weren't already preoccupied with looking at the house they'd just pulled in front of. She would never admit it to anyone back home, but a twinge of jealousy swept through her body as she stared at the house. The large colonial was at least twice the size of her Jamaica Estates home back in New York, and compared to her tiny yard, this house appeared to be on an acre of land, maybe two.

This has to be the wrong address.

"Are you sure we're at the right house?" she asked without moving her head. She was still trying to process what she saw before her.

"Yes, ma'am, you said four Peach Pie Lane in Stone Mountain, didn't you?"

Tammy glanced at the paper in her hand, then looked at the large number four on the house. "Yes, that's what I said."

"Then this is where you want to be. Do you want some help with your bags?"

She reached in her purse. "How much do I owe you?"

"Forty dollars. I usually charge fifty, but havin' a pretty woman such as yourself in my cab, I feel like I owe you. Maybe I could show you around town before you leave. My name's Roscoe."

Tammy rolled her eyes and shook her head, preparing to put this homely country fool in his place. But before she could reply, she saw someone come out of the house. A big, shapely, light-skinned woman, not quite as large as Tammy, came running toward the taxi. That's when Tammy knew there was definitely no mistake; she was at the right address. But how the hell did her best friend Egypt get a house like this?

Tammy handed the driver a fifty-dollar bill, then stepped out of the car without asking for change.

Egypt threw her arms around Tammy's neck and pulled her in closely. "Tammy, girl, I missed you something awful." Egypt placed a huge red-lipstick kiss on her cheek.

Tammy smiled at Egypt when she let her go. She'd missed her friend too. "Girl, you moving on up, aren't you?" They turned their gazes toward the house.

"You think? Come on in and let me show you inside." Egypt was grinning from ear to ear. "You can leave her bags by the front door," she instructed a disappointed Roscoe.

Tammy nodded and followed her friend. Yes, she wanted to see her house. She wanted to see if the inside looked anything like the outside, and even more importantly, she wanted to know how Egypt and her soon-to-be husband Rashid could afford such a nice house when they earned far less than Tammy and her husband did. Did someone hit the lottery and not tell her?

Tammy and Egypt had known each other for almost thirty years and had been best friends since they met back in elementary school. But even best friends could have rivalries. As close as they were, the two of them had played a one-upsmanship game when it came to material things, like clothes, men, houses and such since they were teenagers. Tammy had been winning this competition handily for the past ten years, thanks to her marriage to her successful husband, Tim, but as she walked into the flawlessly decorated foyer of Egypt's house, for the first time she was afraid that the tides had changed.

As she followed behind her friend from room to room, she was so amazed that she barely noticed the people sitting in the large family room until Egypt shouted out, "B.G.B.C. in the house!" and the people in the room all stood in unison and echoed, "B.G.B.C. in the house!"

Tammy couldn't help but blush. She smiled at Egypt, who gave her a thumbs-up. Tammy could feel tears welling up in her eyes, and she experienced a sudden rush of pride. One of her dreams had actually become a reality: She was witnessing the first meeting of the new Atlanta chapter of the Big Girls Book Club, a group Tammy had founded in New York five years ago. Now that Egypt had moved to Atlanta, she was starting her own branch of the book club. Looking around the room at those in attendance, Tammy was happy to see that the requirements for membership in the group seemed to be the same; not one person in the room was smaller than a size fourteen.

Enjoy the following excerpts from
Carl Weber's previous novels,
Up to No Good and
Something on the Side

Available now wherever books are sold!

CHAPTER 1

James

"So, are you going to take me back to your place, or are we going to make Benny rich by running up a ridiculous bar tab?" Crystal whispered seductively.

Her eyes traveled over my body, stopping a little below my belt as she took a sip of her drink. This was her way of letting me know that she was ready. The next move was mine, and her body language was begging me to make it. She lifted her head, her eyes meeting mine as she put her drink on the bar. I smiled, giving her my own once-over. I couldn't help but respond with a devilish grin as I placed my hand on the small of her back, high enough to be respectable but low enough to have an effect. She shuddered slightly under my touch, even though her face failed to give anything away.

We hadn't seen each other in almost a year, and probably wouldn't see each other for another one, unless our son Darnel's wife-to-be Keisha became pregnant in the next few months. Crystal had traveled back to New York from Richmond, Virginia, for Darnel's wedding, which was tomorrow night. We'd met at Benny's bar, one of our old neighborhood haunts, to catch up on old times after the rehearsal dinner.

"So?" she asked again, this time with a little more desperation in her voice. She wanted me. She wanted me bad. She wanted me to do what only I could do for her—satisfy that sexual itch that nobody else seemed able to reach. I know it sounds rather arrogant, but I'd been sleeping with this woman off and on for the better part of twenty-eight years, so I knew what she needed in the bedroom, just like she knew what I needed.

I glanced at her again. Even in a conservative pantsuit, she had a way of enticing me. Her face was a beautiful bronze color, highlighted by a beauty mark right above the left side of her lip. She'd gained a few pounds over the years, and her hair showed a hint of gray around the edges, but hell, whose didn't? Besides, truth be told, I liked a woman with some meat on her bones and some mileage on her engine. Experience meant a lot in life, especially in the bedroom.

She turned her head slightly, exposing a small tattoo with the letters *DB*, our son's initials, on the lower side of her neck. A memory of the way she cooed when I kissed her neck came to mind. Then I looked down at her chest, and the thought of her neck was quickly replaced with an image of her large, plump breasts and the silver-dollar nipples that rested atop them. My heart rate increased, and my breathing became heavier. It never mattered where I touched her; Crystal's body was so sexually in tune with mine that I didn't even have to take off my clothes to give her an orgasm. Oh, but when I did get undressed, she would return the favor like very few women I'd ever known. Having a child together bonded us, but it was the sex that kept us hungering for each other year after year.

She licked her lips, and my manhood sprang to life. I flicked my wrist so I could see the time on my watch. I was wondering if Crystal was planning on a quickie or one of our all-night marathons. I'd already canceled a date to meet with her, so an all-nighter with someone of her sexual prowess was fine by me. That, of course, left only one question.

"Where's your husband?" I asked, getting straight to the point.

Crystal looked annoyed by my question. Yes, she was married, going on five years now, and she definitely preferred that I didn't mention her husband when we were getting ready to get busy. We both knew that her marital status really wasn't a factor in all this anyway. We'd played this game before, Crystal and I, through countless boyfriends and two husbands. She didn't make any excuses for the fact that she was a woman who needed a man in her life. She always said that she would prefer it if that man were me, but after a while, she stopped holding her breath and moved on.

One thing was for sure, though: It didn't matter who she was with. If we saw each other or had the chance to talk on the phone, it was never a question of *if* we were going to get together, but rather when and where it would happen.

"He had to work third shift. He'll be here sometime early tomorrow morning." Crystal slid off her bar stool and folded her arms as if to say, "So, come on. We got time, but we ain't got all night." I knew her well, and she was not about to take no for an answer. And as good as she was looking, I wasn't about to give her an argument.

"Okay, but only if you're going to respect me in the morning," I teased.

She didn't laugh. Instead, she came back with, "Please. You my baby daddy. I ain't got to respect you."

Unfortunately, I knew she wasn't joking, and her words stung like hell.

"You don't?"

"Hell no. Everybody knows you ain't shit, James. As much as I love our son, I should have never had a baby with you." She'd been using this same line on me since Darnel was a baby, and now here he was, a grown man getting ready to get married and have babies of his own. Jesus, I was getting old.

"Then why do you want me to take you home? Why do you keep sleeping with me after all these years? You tryin' to say you ain't got no love for me?"

"Please, James. You broke my heart more times than I care to remember and in more ways than I will ever forget. I'd be a fool if I still had love for you."

"If you ain't got love for me, then why are you trying to sleep with me?"

"Good dick is hard to come by," she said, like it was a simple fact of life that everyone understood. "And you've got some really good dick. Now, are you going to sit here and debate it, or are you gonna take me home and remind me why I rented a car and drove seven hours up here instead of waiting for my husband so we could drive together?"

I reached in my pocket and pulled out a twenty-dollar bill. I slapped it down on the bar, nodding my head.

"You know me. Last thing I want is for anyone to make a seven-hour trip in vain," I said with a laugh. The truth of her words could have deflated my desire for her, but I knew this was not an opportunity to waste on being overly sensitive or sentimental. Besides, I'd known this woman my entire adult life, and there wasn't a thing she could say that I hadn't heard at least a dozen times before. We were too far past that naïve stage to believe we'd ever be anything more than what we were today.

Crystal leaned in and kissed my full lips, then smiled as if I had just given her a large sum of money. The way she stared at me made my manhood grow, making it clear that I was the one about to hit the jackpot. In less than twenty minutes, we'd both be in my bed, as naked as the day we were born, making love like there was no tomorrow. And as it had always been between the two of us, there would be no tomorrow—only a here and now.

Five hours later, Crystal was snoring with a purpose, her back to my chest and her round hips and ass securely resting against my groin. I'd wake her up in about ten minutes for another round. She would have to leave after that in order to make it back to her hotel before her husband showed up. Part of me didn't want her to leave, because I was having such a good time. I always had a good time when Crystal and I got together.

I stared at her face as I stroked her sweaty hair. We'd gone at it for the better part of an hour—twice. The way she called out my name and told me that this would always be her dick was definitely good for the ego. It also told me that after all these years, no matter what she said, she was still in love with me.

Crystal had sacrificed most of her adult years chasing after me. We'd met right after high school. I was far from being faithful, but she was as close to a steady girlfriend as I had during those days.

She looked out for me when no one else would, sometimes even when it wasn't in her best interest. There wasn't anything Crystal Jackson wouldn't do for me. I knew that better than anyone on this earth, and the thing that haunted me the most was that she wanted only one thing in return: my love. But as much as I tried, I just couldn't give it to her the way she wanted it.

Like most women, she wanted to be a wife much more than a girlfriend. Don't get me wrong; I liked her, but I wasn't having no part of getting married. I was having too much fun with all the other women in my life. Crystal, on the other hand, wouldn't take no for an answer. As far as she was concerned, she was in love with me, and all I needed was a little coaxing to understand that I loved her too. She was so convinced of this that she got pregnant, hoping it would settle me down enough for us to get married. It didn't. All it really made me do was act the fool even more. It was something I wished could have been changed, but I still had no regrets. I'd had a good life, a fun life. Why would I mess it up by getting married?

"I'm sorry," I whispered.

"Huh?" She lifted her head. "What did you say?"

"Ah, nothing." I leaned over and kissed her cheek. She rolled over to face me. "If you're gonna kiss me, kiss me right."

I smiled as I studied her face through the dim light that peeked between the curtains. She really was beautiful, and I'd never seen a woman age so well.

I pressed my lips against hers, and our kiss became passionate. My hands roamed her body hungrily. Just as she mounted me for another round, my bedroom door flew open and blinding light flooded the room.

Crystal dove under the covers to hide her nakedness.

"What the—" I shouted, squinting my eyes to adjust to the bright light as I saw what looked like a woman standing in my doorway. In that brief moment, my mind went into overdrive, trying to understand who had just broken into my house. It could have been one of any number of women I'd been seeing over the past few months—but most likely the one I had broken a date with to meet Crystal. But how the hell had she gotten into my house?

The woman yelled, "I knew you was here with her!" and suddenly I knew who the intruder was. This wasn't just any woman standing in my doorway. This was a woman I loved with all my heart, but when it came to me pursuing my love life, she could be described with only one word: *trouble*.

CHAPTER 1

Tammy

I love my life.
I love my life. I love my marriage. I love my husband. I love my kids. I love my BMW, and I love my house. Oh, did I say I love my life? Well, if I didn't, I love my life. I really love my life.

I stepped out of my BMW X3, then opened the back driver-side door and picked up four trays of food lying on a towel on the backseat. I had only about twenty minutes before the girls would be over for our book club meeting, but I'd already dropped off my two kids, Michael and Lisa, at the sitter, so they weren't going to be a problem. Now all I had to do was to arrange the food and get my husband out of the house. The food was easy, thanks to Poor Freddy's Rib Shack over on Linden Boulevard in South Jamaica. I merely had to remove the tops of the trays from the ribs, collard greens, candied yams, and macaroni and cheese, pull out a couple bottles of wine from the fridge, and voilà, dinner is served. My husband was another thing entirely. He was going to need my personal attention before he left the house.

I entered my house and placed the food on the island in the kitchen, then looked around the room with admiration. We'd been living in our Jamaica Estates home for more than a year now, and I still couldn't believe how beautiful it was. My kitchen had black granite countertops, stainless-steel appliances, and hand-crafted cherrywood cabinets. It looked like something out of a home-remodeling magazine, and so did the rest of our house. By the way, did I say I love my life? God, do I love my life and the man who provides it for me.

Speaking of the man who provides for me, I headed down the hall to the room we called our den. This room was my husband's sanctuary—mainly because of the fifty-two-inch plasma television hanging on the wall and the nine hundred and some odd channels DIRECTV provided. I walked into the den, and there he was, the love of my life, my husband, Tim. By most women's standards, Tim wasn't all that on the outside. He was short and skinny, only five-eight, one hundred and forty pounds, with a dark brown complexion. Don't get me wrong—my husband wasn't a bad-looking man at all. He just wasn't the type of man who would stop a sister dead in her tracks when he walked by. To truly see Tim's beauty, you have to look within him, because his beauty was his intellect, his courteousness, and his uncanny ability to make people feel good about themselves. Tim was just a very special man, with a magnetic personality, and it only took a few minutes in his presence for everyone who'd ever met him to see it.

Tim smiled as he stood up to greet me. "Hey, sexy," he whispered, staring at me as if I were a celebrity and he were a star-struck fan. "Damn, baby, your hair looks great."

I blushed, swaying my head from side to side to show off my new three-hundred-fifty-dollar weave. I walked farther into the room. When I was close enough, Tim wrapped his thin arms around my full-figured waist. Our lips met, and he squeezed me tightly. A warm feeling flooded my body as his tongue entered my mouth. Just like the first time we'd ever kissed, my body felt like it was melting in his arms. I loved the way Tim kissed me. His kisses always made me feel wanted. When Tim kissed me, I felt like I was the sexiest woman on the planet.

When we broke our kiss, Tim glanced at his watch. "Baby, I could kiss you all night, but if I'm not mistaken, your book club meeting is getting ready to start, isn't it?"

I sighed to show my annoyance, then nodded my head. "Yeah, they'll be here in about ten, fifteen minutes."

"Well, I better get outta here, then. You girls don't need me around here getting in your hair. My virgin ears might overhear something they're not supposed to, and the next thing you know, I'll be traumatized for the rest of my life. You wouldn't want that on your conscience, would you?" He chuckled.

"Hell no, not if you put it that way. 'Cause, honey, I am not going to raise two kids by myself, so you need to make yourself a plate and get the heck outta here." He laughed at me, then kissed me gently on the lips.

"Aw-ight, you don't have to get indignant. I'm going," he teased.

"Where're you headed anyway?" I asked. A smart wife always knew where her man was.

"Well, I was thinking about going down to Benny's Bar to watch the game, but my boy Willie Martin called and said they were looking for a fourth person to play spades over at his house, so I decided to head over there. You know how I love playing Spades," Tim said with a big grin. "Besides, like I said before, I know you girls need your privacy."

Tim was considerate like that. Whenever we'd have our girls' night, he'd always go bowling or go to a bar with his friends until I'd call him to let him know that our little gathering was over. He always took my feelings into account and gave me space. I loved him for that, especially after hearing so many horror stories from my friends about the jealous way other men acted.

Tim was a good man, probably a better man than I deserved, which is why I loved him more than I loved myself. And believe it or not, that was a tall order for a smart and sexy egomaniac like myself. But at the same time, my momma didn't raise no fool. Although I loved and even trusted Tim, I didn't love or trust his whorish friends or those hoochies who hung around the bars and bowling alleys he frequented. So, before I let him leave the house, I always made sure I took care of my business in one way or another. And that was just what I was about to do when I reached for his fly—take care of my business.

"What're you doing?" He glanced at my hand but showed no sign of protest. "Your friends are gonna be here any minute, you know."

"Well, my friends are gonna have to wait. I got something to do," I said matter-of-factly. "Besides, this ain't gonna take but a minute. Momma got skills . . . or have you forgotten since last night?"

He shrugged his shoulders and said with a smirk, "Hey, I'm from Missouri, the Show Me State, so I don't remember shit. You got to show me, baby."

I cocked my head to the right, looking up at him. "Is that right? You don't remember shit, huh? Well, don't worry, 'cause I'm about to show you, and trust me, this time you're not going to forget a damn thing." I pulled down his pants and then his boxers. Out sprang Momma's love handle. Mmm, mmm, mmm, I've got to say, for a short, skinny man, my husband sure was packing. I looked down at it, then smiled. "Mmm, chocolate. I love chocolate." And on that note, I fell to my knees, let my bag slide off my shoulder, and got to work trying to find out how many licks it took to get to the center of my husband's Tootsie Pop.

About five minutes later, my mission was accomplished. I'd revived my husband's memory of exactly who I was and what I could do. Tim was grinning from ear to ear as he pulled up his pants—and not a minute too soon, because just as I reached for my bag to reapply my lipstick, the doorbell rang. The first thought that came to my mind was that it was probably my mother. She was always on time, while the other members of my book club were usually fashionably late. I don't know who came up with the phrase "CP time," but whoever it was sure knew what the hell they were talking about. You couldn't get six black people to all show up on time if you were handing out hundred-dollar bills.

Tim finished buckling his pants, then went up front to answer the door. I finished reapplying my makeup, then followed him. Just as I suspected, it was my mother ringing the bell. My mother wasn't an official member of our book club, but she never missed a meeting or a chance to take home a week's worth of leftovers for my brother and stepdad after the meeting was over. Truth is, the only reason she wasn't an official member of our book club was because she was too cheap to pay the twenty-dollar-a-month dues for the food and wine we served at each meeting. I loved my mom, but she was one cheap-ass woman.

My mother hadn't even gotten comfortable on the sofa when, surprisingly, the doorbell rang again. Once again, Tim answered the door while I fixed four plates of food for him and his card-playing friends. Walking through the door were the Conner sisters—my best friend Egypt and her older sister Isis. Egypt and I had been best friends since the third grade. She was probably the only woman I trusted in the world. That's why sometime before she left, I needed to ask her a very personal favor, probably the biggest favor I'd ever asked anyone.

Egypt and Isis were followed five minutes later by the two ladies I considered to be the life of any book club meeting, my very spirited and passionate Delta Sigma Theta line sister Nikki and her crazy-ass roommate, Tiny. My husband let them in on his way out to his spades game. As soon as the door was closed and Tim was out of sight, Tiny started yelling, "BGBC in the house," then cupped her ear, waiting for our reply.

We didn't disappoint her, as a chorus of "BGBC in the house!" was shouted back at her. BGBC were the initials of our book club and stood for *Big Girls Book Club*. We had one rule and one rule only: If you're not at least a size 14, you can't be a member. You could be an honorary member, but not a member. It wasn't personal; it was just something we big girls needed to do for us. Anyway, we'd never really had to exclude anyone from our club. I didn't know too many sisters over thirty-five who were under a size 14. And the ones who I did know were usually so stuck-up I wouldn't have wanted them in my house anyway.

About fifteen minutes later, my cousin and our final member, hot-to-trot Coco Brown, showed up wearing an all-white, formfitting outfit I wouldn't have been caught dead in. I know I sound like I'm hatin', but that's only because I am. I couldn't stand the tight shit

Coco wore. And the thing I hated the most about her outfits was that she actually looked cute in them. Coco was a big girl just like the rest of us, but her overly attractive face and curvy figure made her look like Toccara, the plus-size model from that show *America's Next Top Model*. Not that I looked bad. Hell, you couldn't tell me I wasn't cute. And I could dress my ass off too. It's just that the way I carried my weight made me look more like my girl MóNique from *The Parkers*. I was a more sophisticated big girl.

Taking all that into account, some of my dislike for Coco had nothing to do with her clothes or her looks. It had to do with the fact that she was a whore. That's right, I said it. She was a whore—an admitted ho, at that. Coco had been screwing brothers for money and gifts since we were teenagers. And to make matters worse, she especially liked to mess around with married men. Oh, and trust me, she didn't really care whose husband she messed with as long as she got what she wanted. Now, if it was up to me, she wouldn't even be in the book club, but the girls all seemed to like her phony behind, and she met our size requirement, so I was SOL on that. I will say this, though: If I ever catch that woman trying to put the moves on my husband, cousin or not, she is gonna have some problems. And the first problem she was gonna have was getting my size 14 shoe out of the crack of her fat ass.

As soon as Coco entered the room, she seemed to be trying to take over the meeting before it even got started. She was stirring everybody up, talking about the book and asking a whole bunch of questions before I could even start the meeting. And when she and Isis started talking about the sex scenes in the book, I put an abrupt end to their conversation.

"Hold up. Y'all know we don't start no meeting this way." I wasn't yelling, but I had definitely raised my voice. "Coco, you need to sit your tail down so we can start this meeting properly."

Coco rolled her eyes at me and frowned, waving her hand at Nikki, who had already made herself a plate, asking her to slide over. Once Nikki moved, Coco sat down. Now all eyes were on me like they should be. I was the book club president, and this was my show, not Coco's—or anybody else's, for that matter. But she still had something to say.

"Please, Tammy, you should've got this meeting started the minute I walked in the door, because this book was off the damn chain." Coco high-fived Nikki.

"I know the book was good, Coco. I chose it, didn't I?" I know I probably sounded a little arrogant, but I couldn't help it. Ever since we were kids, Coco was always trying to take over shit and get all the attention. "Well, once again, here we are. Before I ask my momma to open the meeting with a prayer, I just hope everyone enjoyed this month's selection as much as my husband and I did."

Egypt raised her eyebrows, then said, "Wait a minute. Tim read this book?"

"No, but he got a lot of pleasure out of the fact that I did. Can you say chapter twenty-three?" I had to turn away from them I was blushing so bad.

"You go, girl," Isis said with a laugh. "I ain't mad at you."

"Let me find out you an undercover freak," Coco added.

"What can I tell you? The story did things to me. It was an extremely erotic read." Everybody was smiling and nodding their heads.

"It's about to be a helluva lot more erotic in here if you get to the point and start the meeting," Coco interjected, then turned to my mom. "I don't mean no disrespect, Mrs. Turner, but we're about to get our sex talk on."

"Well, then let's bow our heads, 'cause this prayer is about the only Christian thing we're going to talk about tonight. Forget chapter twenty-three. Can you say chapters four and seven?" my mother said devilishly, right before she bowed her head to begin our prayer. From that point on, I knew it was gonna be one hell of a meeting, and Tim would appreciate it later when he came home and found me more than ready for round number two.

Mary B. Morrison's captivating Soul Mates Dissipate
series continues with
Darius Jones

Coming in August 2010 from Dafina Books

CHAPTER 1

Darius

For once in my life, I was happy. I mean, genuinely happy.

My mother, wife and son were my world. My mother was my rock. My wife was my rib. My son kept me focused on what was important in life . . . family.

Some thought me to be arrogant, cocky, a shit-talker, an asshole. Others thought of me as *the shit*. Fans begged for my autograph and photo ops, or lingered near the arena exit to touch my jersey or shake my hand. Groupies stalked me, followed me from city to city. Some even knocked on my hotel door, praying for a chance to suck or ride my dick.

I considered myself the best. I was the best in the professional basketball league. I worked out and practiced every day. Shot around on game day. I lived and breathed basketball. I could easily get into a zone and block out people and the things happening around me.

My wife taught me to make time for her and my son—who, by the way, wasn't her son. I slipped up and got my stepsister pregnant. At first, that was the worst mistake of my life. But having my son in my life was no mistake. Couldn't have created him with any other woman.

My mother showed me that people are more important than things and that things happen. Not beyond our control, but sometimes because we lost control. Letting ourselves go with the flow, we occasionally chased the people and things we felt were good for us, but not important to us. Moms said, "Sometimes we're right. Sometimes we're wrong. Darius, what's more important than making mistakes is learning from your mistakes."

I was happy my wife hadn't given up on me. Fancy was the only woman who could satisfy me. In my heart, my head, and the bedroom, that woman drove me fucking nuts. My nuts were hers and hers alone. I wasn't tripping off of no groupie chick tryna suck or ride my dick. I'd had enough head to know no woman sucked my dick better than my wife. And Lord, no woman had fucked me senseless until I'd met LadyCat.

MaDear, my grandmother, probably rolled over in her grave whenever she heard me say or even think of using the Lord's name in vain. But I was sure the Lord didn't mind my using his name to express how excited my wife made me.

I didn't ask my wife to sign no prenuptial agreement. I came from a self-made millionaire mom. Made my own millions. Although my wife had earned her own millions selling real estate, my money was my wife's money. Money didn't make Darius Jones. Took me awhile to realize that shit.

I looked at my wife and smiled. "Baby, I love you so much, I want to marry you again."

Her hand was at the top of the steering wheel. She slid her hand down and around, turning onto Wilshire Boulevard, then letting the wheel slide between her fingers as the tires realigned with our SUV. Damn, she had the sexiest mannerisms. Her hair flowed over her bare shoulders. Her titties were perched high under her summer dress.

"I'd marry you again in a heartbeat, too," she said, smiling back at me.

"Daddy, I want you to marry my mommy. Can you marry her too?" my son asked.

Kids said the darnest things, but my son was brainwashed by his mother, Ashlee. No telling what would come out his mouth. Ashlee had planted so many seeds in his head about our being a family one day and how he shouldn't call my wife "Mother" or "Mommy" but to call her by her first name, Fancy.

Fancy chuckled at DJ. I turned to my son, who was strapped in his car seat and said, "My man, marrying two women would send your daddy to jail. You don't want me to go to jail, do you?"

"Nope, but Mommy does."

I shook my head, then dialed my mom. She answered, "Hey, baby."

"Ma, what's wrong?" I asked right away. The tone of her voice indicated she was disturbed about something.

Fancy looked at my face. She frowned too. I held up my hand to my wife, letting her know I'd handle whatever was bothering my mom.

"Nothing for you to worry about, sweetheart."

"You still joining us for dinner tonight?" I asked her. "We're almost at Wolfgang's Steakhouse."

"I'll call you back and let you know. I'm not sure," she said somberly.

"Is that Grant Hill guy pressuring you? Is he tripping again? I told you I can make him disappear
from your life permanently."

"He wants me to go to a movie premiere with him
tonight. I wouldn't mind if his ex wasn't going to be
there. Just not sure I'm feeling up to any drama,
that's all."

"I'm sending a car for you, Ma. Come have dinner
with us. It's not often we're both back in our home-
town of LA at the same time."

"I'm okay, sweetheart. I'll call you in a few and let
you know what I decide. Give my lil' man a kiss for
me."

"That I can do too, Ma. I love you. Thanks for always being there for me. Let me be there for you."

Mom sniffled, then said, "I love you too, sweetheart.
Bye."

DJ was too far away for me to kiss his cheek, so I
kissed my hand, touched my son's hand, then said,
"That's from your grandma."

I had no problem showing my son love and affec-
tion. Had no problem keeping him in line either.
Didn't want him to become the spoiled brat I was. I'd
had so many women, I'd lost count by the time I'd met
Fancy. I was glad I hadn't married Maxine, my first fiancée. She'd contracted HIV. Sometimes I wondered
if that was my fault. Wasn't sure Maxine would've
cheated on me had I not cheated on her. With my
promiscuous ways, one would think I would've contracted the disease, not her. Maxine had two lovers. Me
and the dude that infected her. I was the male whore,
so to speak, and not ashamed of my past, mind you.
My whoring around before settling down made me a
better man.

The women I'd fucked, including my son's mother
Ashlee, had come to me with their pussies on silver

platters. Well, that wasn't exactly true about Ashlee. I pursued her. There was something pure and innocent about her. Ashlee was beautiful, friendly, and naïve. She believed in me, like my mom. And perhaps at one time, I was in love with Ashlee. Until she fucked my brother. I would've cut her off, dismissed her, gotten rid of her, all of that if she'd fucked any man.

But for her to have fucked my scheming, scandalous, trifling, conniving brother Kevin, the only brother I had alive since my brother Darryl died, was too much. I tried to bring Kevin's ass up, and he tried to bury me by stealing over a million dollars of my money and fucking Ashlee. Talk about ashes to ashes, that dude was dirt. Scum. Blood didn't make him worthy of my respect. Kevin deserved to die in that fire he'd set to my office building. He'd thought I was inside. Instead, Ashlee was the one burned. Her face, like her heart, was permanently scarred.

Fancy's hand slid from the top of the steering wheel to the bottom. "Baby, is your mother okay? We can cancel dinner if you'd like."

That was what I loved about my wife. She always considered my feelings. "Nah, I'll call her from the restaurant."

My wife looked at me and smiled. The steering wheel slid between her fingers.

I pointed at the car speeding in our direction. "Baby! Watch—"

Crash!

"Oh my god." In seconds, my airbag inflated, jamming my body against my seat. My face bent sideways against the headrest. My wife's airbag hadn't deployed. Her forehead was split from her hairline to her nose.

"Daddy!" my son screamed.

Fighting my way from underneath the airbag, I reached into the back seat and unbuckled my son. I pulled him into my arms and held his body close to mine, shielding his face from Fancy. My wife wasn't moving. All I saw was blood gushing from her head. I don't know how much time passed before a paramedic opened Fancy's door. All I could do was cry, "Please save my wife."

I got out the SUV with my son and ran to the ambulance to be close to my wife.

"Sir, we've got to go," the paramedic said, slamming the door in my face.

Anger consumed me. I stormed to the driver of the other car. "What the fuck have you done!"

His eyes were bloodred but he wasn't bleeding. His face was distorted. His apology was slurred: "Look, I'm sorry man. Hope your wife is okay."

I wanted to punch him in his drunken face. "For your sake, you'd better pray she's all right." Another paramedic and a police officer approached me, so I knew I couldn't leave the scene. So I did the best thing—dialed my mom.

My son locked his arms around my neck. "Daddy, I'm scared," he cried.

"Me too, son. Me too."

CHAPTER 2

Bambi

The way to a man's heart was through his mother. I had every news article on Darius Jones since he'd played basketball in high school. I also had a video of all his games and his wedding. I was at Madison Square Garden when he was drafted, went to all of his home games in Atlanta, traveled to all the away games. I had photos of his son, his son's mother, his wife, his mother, his biological father, and his stepfathers. Some of the pictures I'd printed from the internet, others I'd taken. I slept in his jersey each night, made life-size six-nine body-length pillows with images of him. I even picked up a dreadlock that fell from his head when he was sitting on the sidelines during a timeout. I was Darius Jones's number one fan. He just didn't know it . . . yet.

Being a private investigator by trade made me a professional groupie. It was no accident that I'd discovered Darius's mom Jada was attending the movie premiere for *Something on the Side*. Savvy groupies befriended celebrities all the time. Velvet Waters, the star of the movie, had become this overnight Holly-wood sensation. I added her to my list of people to know because Velvet used to live in Atlanta. She'd stripped as Red Velvet at Stilettos Night Club in Atlanta before landing the lead in *Something on the Side.* She was paid by Trevor to fuck Grant Hill before Grant started dating Darius's mother, Jada. Anyone attached to Darius, directly or indirectly, was also attached to me.

I'd been sitting at the bar one day inside of LA's most popular five-star hotel, passing time in between games when I met Velvet. While waiting to head to LAX for my flight back to Atlanta to see my Darius play for our home team, I noticed Velvet stroll in. Hair flowing. Makeup immaculate. Money had done her good.

She'd sat next to me, and I overheard Velvet confirm Grant Hill would be at her premiere. There was such a thing as luck in the PI world. I was at the right place, right time.

I hadn't been in pursuit of Velvet at that moment. I'd flown to Atlanta to temporarily distance myself from Darius. I was in Los Angeles to avoid having Darius's paparazzi get a snapshot of me in their photos. I was careful because I didn't want to be identified as a maniac stalker like the chick who was pursuing Fisher.

After Velvet ended her call, I'd said, "Hi, Velvet. Congratulations. You are my she-ro. And you're so beautiful."

She'd answered with a flat, "Thanks."

I'd leaned closer to her and said, "Girl, you went from stripping at Stilettos to Hollywood." Then I lied, "I use to make it rain on you but you're big time now. Probably don't remember little ole me."

Velvet had stared at me as if trying to recall my face. How could she remember me? I hadn't sprinkled her with dollar bills. How could anyone remember me even if they'd seen me? I was a chameleon. I changed my makeup, hair, and wardrobe every other day.

As she continued studying my face, I said, "Carl Weber is my favorite author. Is he going to be at the premiere? I'd love to meet him." I smiled at her. Shook my head. "My apology. Who am I to think I could ever go to a premiere? Good luck, girl."

Velvet eased from her barstool. Took five steps. I'd counted each one before she'd turned around and took five more in my direction.

"Give me your address. I'll mail you a ticket but I can only give you one."

"Are you serious?" I said, handing her my card with my Atlanta post office box.

She glanced at my card, nodded, then walked away. No "goodbye" or "nice meeting you." A few weeks later I was back in LA to attend the premiere.

Preparing to walk the red carpet, I sat at the vanity in my hotel room. I braided my natural jet-black curly hair into eleven cornrows, then covered my hair with a mesh net stocking cap. I applied a small amount of eyebrow glue to the back of my one-hundred-percent human hair eyebrows, then layered each blond-colored brow perfectly over my jet-black brows. Then I glued and attached my light-brown eyelashes. I trailed a thin line of glue along the edge of my hairline, then attached my full lace twenty-two-inch strawberry blond wig. I stood, held my head upside down, brushed, then fluffed my hair. Instantly, I went from being a fair-complexioned African-American woman to looking like a Caucasian woman with the perfect tan.

I applied my concealer, foundation, and brown eyeliner. I stroked on various hues of sparkling blue eye-shadow, toned it down with a hint of magenta, and brushed a soft pink lipstick on my mouth. I inserted my light bluish-grey contacts. After easing into padded butt-booster panties that would make Serena Williams jealous, I stuffed silicone breast pads into the sides of my bra to sandwich my D cups into a facade of DDs that gave me amazing cleavage. I stepped into iridescent stilettos, picked up my purse, and double-checked to make sure I had my ticket. I kissed the plastic covering on my photo of Darius, then placed it back in my purse. His picture was my good luck charm. With Darius by my side, all things were possible.

Slipping my room key into my handbag, I left my suite and made my way to the lobby. The bellman smiled at me. "You are one gorgeous woman. Can I, make that, *may* I assist you?"

"Thanks, but no thanks. My driver is outside," I politely declined, exiting the hotel.

I eased into the backseat of my white stretch limousine and gazed out the window, lost in thought about how I'd befriend Darius's mother tonight. Was my seat even close to hers? I had the advantage, since I knew what she looked like and she had no clue who I was.

A long line of limos led to the theater. My driver opened my door. I swooped my hair to one side, thrust my breasts forward, arched my back, and smiled as though I was Mrs. Darius Jones. The usher escorted me to my seat. I sat one row directly behind my future mother-in-law. By the end of the night, I'd become Jada's newest best friend or her worst enemy.

A very pregnant woman being escorted by a tall, thin man with a long ponytail stepped sideways in front of Grant and Jada. When the pregnant woman sat next to Jada, Jada turned to Grant and stared into his eyes. Squinted. Frowned. I noticed Jada's right jaw tighten.

Halfway through the movie, the pregnant woman moaned and held her stomach, but continued watching the movie. The screening was nice but I was in PI mode. Things moved quickly. After the credits rolled, the director proposed to Velvet, the pregnant lady's water broke, Velvet accepted the marriage proposal, then Grant asked, "Honey, is that my baby?"

My jaw dropped. I thought I was on top of everything but this was new and valuable information. Jada's cellphone rang, temporarily interrupting the flow of things. Honey answered Grant, "It's not your child but these babies are your twin boys."

Jada stopped speaking into her phone long enough to call Honey a liar. Jada walked off, then cried, "Fancy was hit by a drunk driver. We've got to go to the hospital."

Bingo! I said to myself.

Jada yelled, "Grant! Did you hear me? Darius's wife was hit by a drunk driver! Let's go!"

I guess people had the right to be consumed with their issues. Jada was worried about Fancy. Grant was worried about Honey. And I was concerned with Darius and finding out what hospital Fancy was in.

My intention to get Darius was no fly-by-night suck-his-dick groupie trick. Oh, no. I was determined to either marry him or massacre him. If I couldn't have Darius Jones, no woman would, especially Fancy. I'd make sure Fancy's hospital stay was permanent.

I stood in the aisle, waiting to follow Jada to the hospital.

Enjoy the following excerpts from
Mary B. Morrison's previous novels,

Unconditionally Single
Who's Loving You, and
Maneater

Available now wherever books are sold!

Prologue

Honey

Sometimes a woman had to kill herself to survive. My mother hated me. My father disowned me. Stepfather molested me. Johns used me. My ex-husbands abused me. I had scars on my heart. Blood on my thirty-year-old hands. Despite my hardships, I held my head high. I'd learned that bad things happened to good people. My life was bad. My heart was good.

I hadn't overcome countless trials and tribulations to exhale my last breath without dignity. The one man who truly loved me for me, I'd pushed away. If I died, right here, right now, I'd regret not telling Grant, "Baby, I love you. Forgive me." Determined to get my man back, stand at the altar, repeat after the minister, "I, Honey Thomas, take you, Grant Hill, to be my lawfully wedded husband . . ." and give birth to our children, I had to escape.

As I stared down the barrel of his .22-caliber pistol, my ex-man Benito pointed at the one place I was sure he would like to blast all of his bullets—my mouth. Eradicate his troubles, his jealousy, his insecurities, his love, his hate, his pain by shutting my—scintillating, candid, sharp, sarcastic, independent—ass up for good.

I stared into Benito's eyes. Women living in fear died at the hands of heartless men who were never worthy of their love. Good pussy made men do strange things. Isolate women. Stalk women. Kill women. Benito didn't want me; his ego didn't want another man to have me.

"What are you waiting for?" I asked Benito, pointing my gun at him. "Shoot me or let me go."

Too many women who were emotionally buried alive suffered in silence. Compromising their children, bartering their bodies, sacrificing their souls, surrendering their sanity in exchange for having a man, in many cases a man who didn't love, appreciate, respect, or deserve them.

Benito pleaded, "Lace, please don't make me do this. Put the gun down."

No way in hell was I going to die, not like this. Held hostage in a parking lot, a deserted guard shack in the distance. Abandoned brick buildings with broken windows created an eerie backdrop. The wind howled like a pack of hungry wolves preparing to feast on me. If my kidnappers killed me, then tossed my body inside one of those buildings, who'd think to search there for my remains?

I panic. They panic. Didn't want to die from freaking them out.

Valentino said to me, "I never imagined you'd cross me. Bitch, I am the one who got you off your back and you fucking steal my money." Then he spoke into his cell phone. "Onyx, if you want to see Lace alive, the ransom is non-negotiable—fifty million dollars."

The muscle in my calf cramped—horrible timing for the onset of a charley horse. I flexed my toes, inched toward the edge of the SUV. There was enough space between the two men for me to get out of the trunk. Benito stood to my left, Valentino to my right.

The chain-link metal fence surrounding the lot stood ten feet high. If I got a good running start, I could climb the fence, but the rusted barbed wire at the top made me change my mind. A bent STOP sign partially blocked the lot's exit, its pole rested horizontal to the ground. I could hurdle it praying my heels didn't get caught on the hem of my pants. Didn't want to be the chick in the scary movie who'd escape, run, trip, fall, and be killed.

Flexing my toes far back as I could, I kept quiet while Valentino barked out his demands to Onyx. Onyx had become my number-one escort after my favorite escort, Sunny, was killed. The one year I worked as Valentino's madam was my worst year in the business. Sunny Day was a gorgeous twenty-year-old girl who should've never started prostituting. Her parents loved her. Her twin sister adored her. The day I'd planned to send Sunny home to her family, Valentino refused to let her go. He'd shot Sunny in the head. A part of my spirit died that day. The six hundred thousand dollars Valentino paid me for those twelve months wasn't worth Sunny dying.

I tried calming myself with *there's nothing to fear but fear itself.* The words sounded great but with a gun a few feet from my face, I felt only one emotion: fear. Terror. They didn't know that was my truth. My reality was fear. Perspiration slicked my palms, making it difficult to hold my gun. Toes curled back, I alternated wiping my hands on my pants.

Valentino frowned, told Benito, "Nigga, don't watch me. Keep your eyes on that bitch." He bit his bottom lip, then said, "Onyx, you used to work for me. I know how you think. Don't fucking insult my intelligence. Make it happen today or else I'm coming after you."

Less than a block from us a few cars traveled east and west on University Avenue. Hotlanta commuters were too far away to notice the SUV I was trapped inside. Were they preoccupied with the declining economy, saving their homes from foreclosure, or worried about how the 11.1 million unemployed would impact them? Maybe they were en route to a Waffle House for breakfast. I had no idea where those people were going. What I did know was that none of them noticed me.

Summer visited winter. Sweat covered my breasts, arms, stomach, and back, causing my silk shirt to stick to my skin, irritating me more. Thoughts of not seeing Grant again motivated me to do whatever it took to get out of this situation. Dying was not an option.

Silently I prayed, *Dear God, please don't let me become a statistic.* I tried bartering with God. *God, do not, please hear me, do not let me die without fulfilling my purpose to help save the women who've given up on getting out of unhealthy relationships. Don't I get some credit for using Valentino's money to retire the remaining eleven girls? Answer my prayer and I promise You I'll help a victim every day of my life.* If that wasn't what He wanted to hear, I said, *God, You gave me a brain, courage, and a heart. Tell me which one to use first before I kill both of these fools.*

Benito stood there tilting his head side to side. "V, can you make arrangements for us to meet with Onyx? You're burning up my minutes, man."

During the time we dated, Benito accepted, though he seldom acknowledged, women were smarter than men. I was smarter than him. He hated my constant reminders that I was the one who'd paid the bills the three years he lived in my house. Didn't need him for much outside of sex. Proved it to him often. The day I'd tied him up, shoved a gun up his ass, left him in my bed in Las Vegas, I'd hoped was—the same as with my first and second husbands—the last time I'd see him.

I saw Benito again on Thanksgiving Day when I arrived at Grant's parents' place in Washington, D.C. He was seated at the dinner table. Benito was worse than a bad penny, making my world smaller than I desired in a bad luck kind of way. One step away from him, two back.

I kept staring at Benito. I should've remained his number-one fan instead of dating him. His wide shoulders aligned with his waist. His thick body, solid not fat, was the same as when I'd met him. Flat abs. Full lips. Muscular thighs. He'd gained a few pounds. Though his career was over, his football physique was intact. Benito was an excellent lover. His face had changed, though not his warm brown eyes or smooth toffee skin. It was the wild hairy beard I hadn't seen before.

I prayed silently again, *Lord, please don't let this man be my destiny.*

Our breakup made me realize I barely knew Benito. When we were together, Benito seldom talked about his family. Gave me no indication he had a half brother. Whenever he mentioned his childhood, he blamed his adoptive white mother for screwing up his life. College scholarships, multiple multimillion-dollar football contracts, and Benito was the same as O. J.—broke. No one took Benito's money; he'd given it away before we met. Pretended he still had it going on. Lied his way into my heart and my house. Communication between us had gotten so bad, I didn't bother putting him out. I left. According to him, nothing was ever his fault.

I asked Benito, "Haven't I given you enough?"

Valentino answered, "I don't give a fuck what you gave him. Bitch, you stole my money, not his."

"Why do you think I have fifty million?"

"Bitch, I've got eyes in the back of my head. I can tell you every time you take a piss."

Here we go. I was tired of men trying to scare women into submission. Who'd betrayed me? Who'd told Valentino where I live? It had to be one of the girls.

Valentino could charm or intimidate other women, not me. His hair was slicked into a luxurious ponytail that hung between his shoulder blades. His black hair was as long as mine. My black hair was dyed blond to match my golden complexion and highlight my natural green eyes. His blemish-free cocoa face was chiseled, strong, defined, and hairless with the exception of his full brows, long lashes, and trimmed mustache. His voice was seductive when soft, harsh when deepened. The two both stood about six feet two inches. Difference was Valentino was slim, not thick like Benito.

"I just want alimony," Benito said, shuffling his feet.

What? I never married that fool. His nervous energy bothered me. Was he imitating a boxer or preparing to swing at me? I wished he would. Put down his gun and I'd bust him in his head with mine.

Valentino told Benito, "Nigga, you mean palimony. That's not a bad idea."

I became enraged at them, more at Benito's pathetic behind. Wanted to shove my gun up his ass again. Tired, frustrated, angry, I found courage to pull the trigger. "Take this," I said, firing my .45, not knowing, not giving a fuck whose head I'd put a bullet in first.

CHAPTER 1

Honey

L ove sucks! I swore on my sister's grave, I wished
I'd never met him. His voice had lingered in my
mind with crisp clarity every damn day, like he was
standing behind me, leaning over my shoulder, whispering in my ear. But he wasn't. Not anymore.

"Baby," he used to say to me, and I would answer,
barely above a whisper, "Yes?" Seductively, he'd say it
again, "Baby," in a tone that quieted me. "Yes?" I'd say
softly. We'd go back and forth: then his long fingers
and strong hands would gently caress the side of my
face and massage my ears.

I'd quiver whenever he'd moan, "Ummmm, you're
fucking incredible. You know that? And I'm not talking about your bedroom skills. Baby, you are an amazing woman."

His eargasms would make cool waterfall secretions
flow from my pussy, wetting my lips, before he'd ease
his hand between my thighs, pressing his middle finger
against my clit. He was left-handed. I'd heard Dr. Oz
say on *Oprah* that left-handed people were smarter,

more balanced, and better capable of processing information than those of us who were right-handed. His index and ring fingers would straddle my shaft, nestling in the crevices of my lips, as he strummed my black pearl with his middle finger. That was my favorite finger.

Gasping at the sound of his voice in my head, I knew . . . I was incredible. But no other man had told me that. No other man had said to me, "I love you." Grant was my first. I let the tears fall, then closed my eyes, visualizing our moments together, lifting my lids to see only me, surrounded by olive painted walls, bright lime cabinets, dark forest granite countertops, and a kitchen floor covered with new hundred-dollar bills that had been permanently laminated into clear ceramic tiles.

Green was my favorite color. I loved walking on men and money. I'd admit I was a little extravagant. A grand total of one million dollars—in hundred-dollar bills—was embedded in every floor of my home, including the bathrooms. Some preferred to walk on sunshine. Money was my visual reminder of where I'd come from. I wasn't proud of how I'd stepped on and over a countless number of people to get where I was. *Live and Let Die* was my favorite James Bond movie and my motto. Standing in front of the kitchen counter, I slid an already sharp knife along the steel sharpener.

Grant had been my joy. We'd loved sharing Cherry Garcia ice cream while watching *The Boondocks* DVD series, and making love. In between orgasms, we'd laugh at Huey, Riley, and their granddad. One time we stayed in bed all day, eating, sleeping, and fucking until we wobbled like ducks when we made our way to the bathroom for a much-needed piss.

"Quack, quack," I'd teased him.

"Quack, quack, quack," he'd tease me back.

Then, suddenly, our relationship had faded to dark. He was out of my life, as if I had frantically awakened from the best dream of my life. Shutting my eyes, I fought to go back to him, to go back to sleep and pick up where we had left off, before he left me. I tossed and wrestled with my empty bed. I opened my legs, easing the memory foam pillow between my thighs, then pulled my red satin sheet around my erect nipples, trying to forget he was no longer mine. Opening my eyes, I found myself standing in the kitchen, staring at a blue crystal bowl filled with red potatoes.

How could my past ruin my future? I had tried my damnedest to give that man my best, and he had slammed the door to his heart in my face, as though I was a Jehovah's Witness trying to save his spiritual behind so he would become the one-hundred forty-four thousandth person to make it . . . Where? To Heaven? Wherever that was. Who'd been there? What did they do to get in? Mistreat others?

From hot to cold, within seconds he had swatted me away like I was a fly landing on his food, regurgitating shit. I'd meant nothing to him. It was as though he'd truly awakened to a stranger.

Words were powerful beyond measure, but his silence hurt me more. He'd made me make myself go crazy. Wow. Love or the lack thereof could do that. Make one go crazy.

"Answer your damn phone. You wrong for this shit, Grant! Dead wrong!" I yelled. I grunted loud enough to release my frustrations, but not so loud that someone in the house would come running to my aid with a straightjacket. My house had thirteen bedrooms. Twelve upstairs. Mine was the only one downstairs.

"I should kill him. Goddammit, son of a bitch!" I

screamed. Sucking the stream of blood oozing from my finger, I threw the knife, the potatoes, and the crystal bowl in the damn trash can. "Fuck this shit!"

Love hadn't hurt me. I was clear that I'd hurt the one I loved. Now I was the one suffering. Every time I got angry, so angry that I could harm Grant, something bad happened to my ass. Unzipping the first-aid kit, I pulled out a bandage.

"He probably has some other bitch in his bed, sucking his dick right now, while I'm over here trippin' on unresolved issues that I can't control." *Not by myself.*

As I wrapped the Band-Aid tightly around my middle finger, thoughts of the way we had constantly been together replayed in my mind, reminding me of the irreplaceable love I'd lost. Where was I going to find another six-foot-five, 235-pound, twenty-eight-year-old, successful black man with a body sexier than any Chippendales dancer I'd ever seen? Grant was my man, and I'd be damned if I was gonna let him leave me. I just knew some ex-chick or someone hoping to be the next chick had been waiting for me to fuck up so she could move in on him, with him.

"Not on my watch, bitch! Get your own man!" I grunted.

Each morning I reached out my hand to touch him; rolled over, expecting to kiss him; opened my eyes, longing to see him. I called out his name, but he wasn't there to answer, "Yes, Honey?" as he had so affectionately done. Had he been sincere when he'd said, "You're the best thing that ever happened to me"? I wanted another chance. Hell, I deserved the opportunity to explain why I'd lied. Not everything I'd told him was a lie. Actually, most of what I'd shared about my past was the truth.

"Grant, listen to me," I said. "Are you seriously going

to take someone else's word over mine? So what if Benito is your brother! Hell, your own mama don't like his ass. I can't believe you're upset with me about something that happened before we met. You're not making any sense. Okay. Answer this one question. 'Do you still love me? Yes or no?'"

I wasn't getting the answer I wanted; he wasn't here to respond. All of this vacillating in the kitchen, talking to myself, had to stop. One minute I loved him; the same minute I hated his ass to death. I stood topless and barefoot in the middle of the kitchen, text messaging him: *Baby, it's not what you think. Please call me.* I was trying to give him the impression I was being patient with him, but my patience had run out a long fucking time ago.

CHAPTER 1

Seven

"Lose the weight, or the wedding is off."
What the hell did he just say to me? The air in my lungs caught in my throat, struggling to escape. Where did his unwarranted demand come from? His words echoed like ping-pong balls, slamming against my temples fast and furious. I took a deep breath, restraining from screaming in his face. *Forget that.* Why should I be the sensible one?

"You didn't say that last night, when I was sucking your dick!"

Casually, he said, "Timing would've been off. Agree?"

I was in shock, a quiescent mime unable to respond. *Ping-pong!* Round after round. *Somebody please stop the ricochets!*

Sitting in silence, I prayed, *Give me a sign that this is an April Fool's joke in the middle of October. Someone please drop a coin in the invisible metal bucket perched at my feet, triggering him to say, "Baby, I was kidding. I love you just the way you are."* Motionless, breath trapped inside my throat, I waited and waited and waited. He didn't speak a word.

Mama used to tell me, "Don't be an angry woman. Be a thinking woman. If you feel pressured, silence yourself, take a few deep breaths, and think about what is best for you."

As silence filled the air, we emotionally drifted apart.

Swallowing the despair clawing at me, I mustered myself and said, "I can't breathe." Claustrophobia overwhelmed me, causing me to lose my composure and slump into the sofa beside my callous fiancé.

All I'd done since he'd proposed was joyfully plan our perfect wedding. Two years living together, the last year engaged, and this was his way of calling off the wedding? Sweat seeped between and underneath my thighs, soaking my black Chicago Bears panties. I'd understand his behavior if we'd argued, fought.

Was his love a façade?

I loved this man with all my heart, my being, my soul. But that's my fault, not his.

"Who?" I dreaded asking what I had to know. "Is she prettier? Smaller? Smarter? Is she better than me in bed? I can please you more. Do some other things if you'd like. Anything. I'll do anything to make this . . . work." The words strangled me with desperation. Fear of losing the man I loved to another woman consumed me. "Who is she? Please tell me."

No woman was a bigger freak than me. My big, delicious caramel titties with bubble-gum-sized nipples had easily sandwiched many dicks when I was in high school and in college. I'd done things to make grown men cry like babies. A few women, too. I could prove it to him. Right here. Right now. I called myself being safe. Careful not to scare him away, I'd reserved my best bedroom skills to blow his mind on our honeymoon in St. Barts.

He remained stoic, gazing out of the living-room window, beyond Highway 41, to the blue waters of Lake Michigan. Flatly, Maverick said, "There is no she. All you need to know is you mean the world to me."

I scratched the brow above my twitching left eye. Maverick hadn't witnessed the best or worst of what I could offer him. *Think, Seven. Think.* "You can't be serious," I said faintly, lightly strumming my numb jaw. "Something or someone changed you overnight. You don't love me like you used to. Last night, the sex, my updating you on our wedding plans, then our watching the presidential debate, I had no idea. No clue you felt this way. What's wrong with my body?"

I sat up straight, rubbed my stomach, swallowed air while forcing back tears. I nervously tugged a fistful of my long, curly hair. "I thought you liked my body. You've never complained before. There has to be someone else. Is she younger? Older? Or are you tripping off of your father again? He's dead, honey. Stop letting him ruin your life from his grave."

His parents and mine were deceased. I couldn't imagine any parent being as cruel as Maverick said his dad was to him. We were both only children. I had one best friend, Zena, and he had two close friends from high school. At times Maverick acted more like a child than a grown man. Nothing was ever his fault. I had to think my way out of what was bothering him.

Last night, Obama made me believe change was good and that all things were possible. McCain made me fear four more years of a Republican administration, declining property values, vanishing stocks, bank failures, homes foreclosing, more major companies and small businesses filing for bankruptcy, and diminishing 401Ks forcing retirees back to work.

At this moment, Maverick made me think I'd slept in the same bed for two years with a complete stranger.

While the economy was unpredictable, my relationship was supposed to be recession-proof. So I'd thought. *Foolish me.* I wasn't giving up on him.

"Ouch." I touched my bottom lip, glanced at my finger, and rubbed the speck of blood on my white Devin Hester jersey. Disappointment layered my sadness with disgust. The slits of my lids narrowed, shrinking his six-foot frame to the three inches he made me feel. Scooting to the opposite end of the apricot-tinted Italian leather sofa, I stared at my fiancé. My palms ached to slap him upside his shiny bald head.

His rejection overwhelmed me. For the first time in my life, I felt fat. Miserable. Dirty. Sticky.

Don't slap his selfish ass. Calm down. You are not a violent person. You're just upset. Maybe this is some sort of last-minute pass or fail test from him. The kind that reassures him he's not about to marry a woman who is violent or vindictive.

Finally, he answered, "I'm dead serious." He pulled from his pocket a pair of my yellow Lycra boy-cut underwear with SWEETER THAN HONEY embroidered in gold across the pubic area.

Sideswiped by premeditated premarital sabotage, I tried my best not to look at him. I might go off.

Why'd he have to pick the yellow ones? Any other color would've appeared smaller. Black. Red. Snatching the drawers from him, I threw them in his beautiful brown-sugar face, then watched them fall to his lap. A well-trimmed shadow beard trailed a thin line from his ears to his chin, framing his succulent lips with a perfectly aligned goatee, a replica of G. Garvin's. I shouldn't have prepared so many of Gerry's mouthwatering recipes. Too late to regurgitate any of the carbs from my hips. Fat cells had already doubled, tripled, inviting cellulite to the sides and backs of my thighs.

Maverick's stern demeanor hadn't wavered.

A bottle of tequila would help me through a lipo-suction procedure, a few hCG injections, laser cel-lulite treatments, and a series of body wraps. A quick fix might salvage our relationship or keep me from . . .

Quietly I stood, went upstairs to his library, removed the shoe box from the top shelf. I held Maverick's prized possession in my hand. Cold, heavy like my heart. I placed the gun in my laptop bag, closed and locked the safe, then returned to the living room. Here I was, not married yet, already fighting to hang on to my man. I sat beside him. He was not leaving me. Not alive.

I hate you . . . Kiss me. Hold me. Please tell me you're not serious. I love you so much. It hurts.

Magnificent crystal gray eyes, dilated black coal pupils sparkled like carbonado diamonds. Maverick was perfection personified. A self-made multimillion-aire. The wealthiest, most eligible bachelor in Illi-nois, according to the tabloids. He'd given me more than any of those housewives of Atlanta and Orange County had combined.

"That's cool," he said, twirling my drawers on one finger. "But getting upset isn't going to help your case. I spent a half mil on an engagement ring, which is in the jewelry box because it doesn't fit!" Calmly, he continued, "That means the wedding band won't fit, either. You need to get real about your fat ass or get up out of my house. It's just that simple."

Ooh wee, Seven, don't go back upstairs for the gun. Tears streamed down my cheeks. Breathing heavily, I thought, *Mama, what should I say to this man?*

"I'm not a damn Barbie doll! I'm a woman. I have feelings. For God's sake, can't you see how much I love you?" I didn't know what to do or say next. I struggled to rationalize his behavior but couldn't.

Maverick replied, "True. Barbie is white," adding no comment about his love for me.

I sat there on the verge of a nervous breakdown. This man was my everything. My friend. My lover. My fiancé. I had to marry him.